# THE DEVIL'S BRIDE

**THE DEVIL'S BRIDE**

Seabury Quinn

ISBN 978-1-902197-52-4

A Scorpionic Book

Published 2012 by Creation Oneiros

Copyright © Creation Publishing

All world rights reserved

**THE DEVIL'S BRIDE** (1932)

| | |
|---|---:|
| 1. "ALICE WHERE ARE YOU?" | 5 |
| 2. "BULALA-GWAI" | 12 |
| 3. "DAVID HUME HYS. JOURNAL" | 17 |
| 4. BY WHOSE HAND? | 26 |
| 5. THE MISSING CHILD | 32 |
| 6. THE VEILED LADY AGAIN | 38 |
| 7. THE MUTTER OF A DISTANT DRUM | 43 |
| 8. "IN HOC SIGNO–" | 50 |
| 9. THOUGHTS IN THE DARK | 57 |
| 10. WORDLESS ANSWERS | 61 |
| 11. THE STRAYED SHEEP | 69 |
| 12. THE TRAIL OF THE SERPENT | 76 |
| 13. INSIDE THE LINES | 82 |
| 14. THE SERPENT'S LAIR | 89 |
| 15. THE MASS OF ST. SECAIRE | 95 |
| 16. FRAMED | 101 |
| 17. "HIJI" | 106 |
| 18. REUNION | 116 |
| 19. THE LIGHTNING-BOLTS OF JUSTICE | 121 |
| 20. THE WOLF-MASTER | 126 |
| 21. WHITE HORROR | 132 |
| 22. THE CRIMSON CLUE | 137 |
| 23. PURSUIT | 142 |
| 24. THE DEVIL'S BRIDE | 150 |
| 25. THE SUMMING UP | 163 |

**THE HOUSE OF GOLDEN MASKS** (1929)     169

# THE DEVIL'S BRIDE

## I. "ALICE WHERE ARE YOU?"

Five of us sat on the twin divans flanking the fireplace where the eucalyptus logs burned brightly on their polished-brass andirons, throwing kaleidoscopic patterns of highlights and shadows on the ivory-enameled woodwork and the rug-strewn floor of the "Ancestors' Room" at Twelvetrees.

Old David Hume, who dug Twelvetrees' foundations three centuries ago, had planned that room as shrine and temple to his *lar familiaris*, and to it each succeeding generation of the house had added some memento of itself. The wide bay window at the east was fashioned from the carved poop of a Spanish galleon captured by a buccaneering member of the family and brought home to the quiet Jersey village where he rested while he planned new forays on the Antilles. The tiles about the fireplace, which told the story of the fall of man in blue-and-white Dutch delft, were a record of successful trading by another long dead Hume who flourished in the days when Nieuw Amsterdam claimed all the land between the Hudson and the Delaware, and held it from the Swedes till Britain with her lust for empire took it for herself and from it shaped the none too loyal colony of New Jersey. The carpets on the floor, the books and bric-a-brac on the shelves, each object of *vertu* within the glass-doored cabinets, had something to relate of Hume adventures on sea or land whether as pirates, patriots, traders or explorers, sworn enemies of law or duly constituted bailiffs of authority.

Adventure ran like ichor in the Hume veins, from David, founder of the family, who came none knew whence with his strange, dark bride and, settled on the rising ground beside the Jersey meadows to Ronald, last male of the line, who went down to flames and glory when his plane was cut out from its squadron and fell blazing like a meteor to the shell-scarred earth at Neuve Chapelle. His croix de guerre posthumously awarded, lay in the cabinet beside the sword the Continental Congress had presented to his great-great-grandsire in lieu of long arrearage of salary.

Across the fire from us, between her mother and her fiance, sat Alice, final remnant of the line, her half-humorous, half-troubled glance straying to each of us in turn as she finished speaking. She was a slender wisp of girlhood, with a mass of chestnut hair with deep, shadow-laden waves which clustered in curling tendrils at the nape of her neck, a pale, clear complexion, the ivory tones of which were enhanced by the crimson of her wide sensitive mouth and the long, silken lashes and purple depths of the slightly slanting eyes which gave her face a piquant, oriental flavor.

"You say the message is repeated constantly, *Mademoiselle?*" asked Jules de Grandin, my diminutive French friend, as he cast a fleeting look of unqualified approval at the slim satin slipper and silk-sheathed leg the girl displayed as she sat with one foot doubled under her.

"Yes, it's most provoking when you're trying to get some inkling of the future, especially at such a time as this, to have the silly thing keep saying–"

"Alice, dear," Mrs. Hume remonstrated, "I wish you wouldn't trifle with such silly nonsense, particularly now, when–" She broke off with what would unquestionably have been a sniff in anyone less certainly patrician than Arabella Hume, and glanced reprovingly at her daughter.

De Grandin tweaked the needle-pointed tips of his little blond mustache and grinned the gamin grin which endeared him to dowager and debutante alike. "It is mysterious, as you have said, *Mademoiselle*,' he agreed, "but are you sure you did not guide the board–"

"Of course I am," the girl broke in. "Just wait: I'll show you." Placing her coffee cup upon the Indian mahogany tabouret, she leaped petulantly from the couch and hurried from the room, returning in a moment with a ouija board and table.

"Now watch," she ordered, putting the contrivance on the couch beside her. "John, you and Doctor Trowbridge and Doctor de Grandin put your hands on the table, and I'll put mine between them, so you can feel the slight tightening of my muscles. That way you'll be sure I'm guiding the thing, even unintentionally. Ready?"

Feeling decidedly sheepish, I rose and joined them, resting my finger tips on the little three legged table. Young Davisson's hand was next to mine, de Grandin's next to his, and between all rested Alice's slender, cream-white fingers. Mrs. Hume viewed the spectacle with silent disapproval.

For a moment we bowed above the ouija board, waiting tensely for some motion of the table. Gradually a feeling of numbness crept through my hands and wrists as I held them in the strained and unfamiliar pose. Then, with a sharp and jerky start the table moved, first right, then left, then in an ever-widening circle till it swung sharply toward the upper left-hand corner of the board, pausing momentarily at the A, then traveling swiftly the L, thence with constant acceleration back to I. Quickly the message was spelled out; a pause, once more the three-word sentence was repeated:

ALICE COME HOME

"There!" the girl exclaimed, a catch, half fright, annoyance, in her voice. "It spelled those very words three times today. I couldn't get it to say anything else!"

"Rot. All silly nonsense," John Davisson declared, lifting his hands from the table and gazing almost resentfully at his charming fiancée. "You may believe you didn't move the thing, dear, but you must have, for–"

"Doctor de Grandin, Doctor Trowbridge," the girl appealed, "you held my hands just now. You'd have known if I'd made even the slightest move to guide the table, wouldn't you?" We nodded silent agreement, and she hurried on:

"That's just what's puzzling me. Why should a girl who's going to be married tomorrow be telling herself, subconsciously or otherwise, to 'come home'? If the board had spelt 'go home,' perhaps it would have made sense, for we're going to our own place when we come back from our wedding trip; but why the constant repetition of 'come home,' I'd like to know. Do you suppose–"

The raucous hooting of an automobile horn broke through her question and a moment later half a dozen girls accompanied by as many youths stormed into the big hail.

"Ready, old fruit?" called Irma Sherwood, who was to be the maid of honor. "We'd better be stepping on the gas; the church is all lit up and Doctor Cuthbert's got the organ all tuned and humming." She threw a dazzling smile at us and added, "This business of getting Alice decently married is more trouble than running a man down for myself, Doctor Trowbridge. One more rehearsal of these nuptials and I'll be a candidate for a sanitarium."

St. Chrysostom's was all alight when we arrived at the pentice and paused beside the baptismal font awaiting the remainder of the bridal party; for, as it ever is with lovers, John and Alice had lagged behind the rest to exchange a few banalities of the kind relished only by idiots, little children and those engaged to wed.

"Sorry to delay the show, friends and fellow citizens," Alice apologized as she leaped from Davisson's roadster and tossed her raccoon coat aside. "The fact is, John and I had something of importance to discuss, and" – she raised both hands to readjust her hat – "and so we lingered by the way to–"

"*Alice!*" Mrs. Hume's voice betokened shocked propriety and hopeless protest at the antics of her daughter's graceless generation. "You're *surely* not going to wear that – that thing in church?" Her indignant glance indicated the object of her wrath. "Why, it's hardly decent", she continued, then paused as though vocabulary failed her while she pointed mutely to the silver girdle which was clasped about her daughter's slender waist.

"Of course, I shall, old dear," the girl replied. "The last time one of us was married she wore it, and the one before wore it, too. Hume women always wear this girdle when they're married. It brings 'em luck and insures fam–"

"*Alice!*" the sharp, exasperated interruption cut her short. "If you have to be indelicate, at least you might remember where we are."

"All right, Mater, have it your own way, but the girdle gets worn, just the same," the girl retorted, pirouetting slowly, so that the wide belt's polished bosses caught flashes from the chandelier and flung them back in gleaming, lance-like rays.

"*Mon Dieu, Mademoiselle*, what is it that you wear? May I see it, may I examine it?" de Grandin demanded excitedly, bending forward to obtain a closer view of the shining corselet.

"Of course," the girl replied. "Just a moment, till I get it off." She fumbled at a fastening in front, undid a latch of some sort and put the gleaming girdle in his hand.

It was a beautiful example of barbaric jewelry, a belt, perhaps a corset would be the better term, composed two curved plates of hammered silver so formed as to encircle the wearer's abdomen from front to hips, joined together at the back by a wide band of flexible brown leather of exquisitely soft texture. In front the stomach-plates were locked together by four rings with a long silver pin which went through them like a loose rivet, with a little ball at the top fastened by a chain of cold-forged silver links. The metal was heavily bossed and rather crudely set with a number of big red and yellow stones. From each plate depended seven silver chains, each terminating in a heart-shaped ornament carved from the same kind of stones with which the belt was jeweled, and these clanked and jingled musically as the little Frenchman held the thing up to the light and gazed at it with a look of mingled fascination and repulsion. "*Grand Dieu!*" he exclaimed softly. "It is! I can not be mistaken; it is assuredly one of them, but–"

Alice bent smilingly across his shoulder. "Nobody knows quite what it is or where it comes from," she explained, "but there's a tradition in the family that David Hume's mysterious bride brought it with her as a part of her marriage portion. For years every daughter of the house wore it to be married, and it's been known as 'the luck of the Humes' for goodness knows how long. The legend is that the girl who wears it will keep her beauty and her husband's love and have an easy time in child–"

"Alice!" Once more her mother intervened.

"All right, Mother, I won't say it," her daughter laughed, "but even nice girls know you don't find babies in a cabbagehead nowadays." Then, to de Grandin:

"I'm the first Hume girl in three generations, and the last of the family in the bargain; so I'm going to wear the thing for whatever luck there is in it, no matter what anybody says."

The answering smile de Grandin gave her was rather forced. "You do not know whence it comes, nor what its history is?" he asked.

"No, we don't," Mrs. Hume returned, before her daughter could reply, "and I'm heartily sorry Alice found the thing. I almost wish I'd sold it when I had the chance."

"Eh?" he turned upon her almost sharply. "How is that, *Madame*?"

"A foreign gentleman called the other day and said understood we had this thing among our curios and that it might be for sale. He was very polite, but quite insistent that I let him see it. When I told him it was not for sale, he seemed greatly disappointed and begged me to reconsider. He even offered to allow me to set whatever price I cared to, and assured me there would be no quibble over it, even though we asked a hundred times the belt's intrinsic worth. I fancy he was an agent with *carte blanche* from some wealthy collector, he seemed so utterly indifferent where money was concerned."

"And did he, by any chance, inform you what this belt may be, or whence it came?" de Grandin queried.

"Why, no; he merely described it, and begged to be allowed to see it. One hardly likes to ask such questions from a chance visitor, you know."

"*Precisement.* One understands, *Madame*," he nodded.

The procession was quickly marshaled, and attended by her maids, Alice marched serenely up the aisle. As she had no male relative to do the office, the duty of giving her in marriage was delegated to me, both she and her mother declaring that no one more deserved the honor than the one who had assisted her into the world and brought her through the measles, chickenpox and whooping cough.

"And we'll have Trowbridge somewhere in the first one's name old dear," Alice promised in a whisper as she patted my arm while we halted momentarily at the chancel steps.

"Now, when Doctor Bentley has pronounced the warning 'if no one offers an impediment to the marriage'," the curate who was acting as master of ceremonies informed us, "you will proceed to the communion rail and–"

Somewhere outside, faint and faraway-seeming, gaining quickly in intensity, there came a high, thin, whistling sound, piercing, but so high one could scarcely hear it. Rather, it seemed more like a screaming heard inside the head than any outward sound, and strangely, it seemed to circle round the three of us – the bride, the bridegroom and me – and to cut us definitely off from the remainder of the party.

"Queer," I thought. "There was no wind a moment ago, yet–" The thin, high whining closed tighter round us, and involuntarily I put my hands to my ears to shut out the intolerable sharpness of it, when with a sudden crash the painted window just above the altar burst as though a missile struck it, and through the ragged aperture came drifting a billowing yellow haze – a cloud of saffron dust, it seemed to me – which hovered momentarily above the unveiled cross upon the altar, then dissipated slowly, like steam evaporating in winter air.

I felt an odd sensation, almost like a heavy blow delivered to my chest, as I watched the yellow mist disintegate, then straightened with a start as another sound broke on my hearing.

"Alice! Alice, where are you?" the bridegroom called, and through the bridal party ran a wondering murmur.

"Where's Alice? She was right there a moment ago! Where *is* she? Where's she gone?"

I blinked my eyes and shook my head. It was so. Where the bride had stood, her fingers resting lightly on my arm, a moment before, there was only empty space.

Wonderingly at first, then eagerly, at last with a frenzy bordering on madness, we searched for her. Nowhere, either in the church or vestry room or parish house, was sign or token of the missing bride, nor could we find a trace of her outside the building. Her coat and motor gloves lay in a crumpled heap within the vestibule; the car in which she came to the church still stood beside the curb; an officer whose beat had led him past the door two minutes earlier declared he had seen no one leave the edifice – had seen no one on the block, for that matter. Yet, discuss and argue as we might, search, seek and call, then tell ourselves it was no more than a silly girl's prank, the fact remained: Alice Hume was gone – vanished as utterly as though absorbed in air or swallowed by the earth, and all within less time than the swiftest runner could have crossed the chancel, much less have left the church beneath the gaze of half a score of interested people for whom she was the center of attraction.

"She must have gone home," someone suggested as we paused a moment in our search and gazed into each other's wondering eyes. "Of course, that's it! She's gone back to Twelvetrees!" the others chorused, and by the very warmth of their agreement gave tokens of dissent.

At last the lights were dimmed, the church deserted, and the bridal party, murmuring like frightened children to each other, took up their way toward Twelvetrees, to which, we were agreed, the missing bride had fled.

But as we started on our way, young Davisson, with a lover's precense of evil to his loved one, gave tongue to the question which trembled silently on every lip. "Alice! he cried out to the unresponsive night, and the tremor in his voice was eloquent of his heart's agony, "Alice, beloved – *where are you?*"

## 2. "BULALA-GWAI"

"Coming?" I asked as the sorrowful little motorcade began its pilgrimage to Twelvetrees.

De Grandin shook his head in short negation. "Let them go on," he ordered. "Later, when they have left, we may search the house for *Mademoiselle* Alice, though I greatly doubt we shall find her. Meanwhile, there is that here which I would investigate. We can work more efficiently when there are no well-meaning nincompoops to harass us with senseless questions. Come." He turned on his heel and led the way back into the church.

"Tell me, Friend Trowbridge," he began as we walked up the aisle, "when that window yonder broke, did you see, or seem to see, a cloud of yellowness drift through the opening?"

"Why, yes, I thought so," I replied. "It looked to me like a puff of muddy fog – smoke, perhaps – but it vanished so quickly that–"

"*Très bien*," he nodded. "That is what I wished to know. None of the others mentioned seeing it and our eyes play strange tricks on us at times. I thought perhaps I might have been mistaken, but your testimony is enough for me."

With a murmuring of excuse, as though apologizing for the sacrilege, he moved the bishop's chair to a point beside the altar, mounted nimbly on its tall, carved back, and examined the stone casing of the broken window intently. From my station outside the communion rail I could hear him swearing softly and excitedly in mingled French and English as he drew a card from his pocket, scraped something from the window-sill upon the card, then carefully descended from his lofty perch.

"Behold, regard, attend me, if you will, Friend Trowbridge," he ordered. "Observe what I have found." As he extended the card toward me I saw a line of light, yellow powder, like pollen from a flower, gathered along one edge.

"*Regardez*!" he commanded sharply, raising the slip of pasteboard level with my face. "Now, if you please, what did I do?"

"Eh?" I asked, puzzled.

"Your hearing functions normally. What is it that I did?"

"Why, you showed me that card, and–"

"Precisely. And–?" He paused with interrogatively arched brows.

"And that's all."

"*Non*. Not at all. By no means, my friend," he denied. "Attend me: First I did, as you have said, present the card to you. Next, when it was fairly level with your nostrils, I did blow on it, oh so gently, so that some of the powder on it was inhaled by you. Next I raised my arms three times above my head, lowered them again, then capered round you like a dancing Indian. Finally. I did tweak you sharply by the nose."

"Tweak me by the nose!" I echoed aghast. "You're crazy!"

"Like the fox, as your slang so drolly expressed it," he returned with a nod. "My friend, it has been exactly one minute and forty seconds by my watch since you did inhale that so tiny bit of dust, and during all that time you were as utterly oblivious to all that happened as though you had been under ether. Yes. When first I saw I suspected. Now I have submitted it to the test and am positive it is so."

"What on earth are you talking about?" I asked.

"*Bulala-gwai*, no less."

"Bu – *what?*"

He seated himself in the bishop's chair, crossed his knees and regarded me with the fixed, unwinking stare which always reminded me of an earnest tom-cat. "Attend me," he commanded. "My duties as an army medical officer and as a member of *la Sureté*, have taken me to many places off the customary map of tourists. The Congo Francais, by example. It was there that I first met *bulala-gwai*, which was called by our *gendarmes* the snuff of death, sometimes *la petite mort*, or little death.

"*Barbe d'un rat vert*, but it is well named, my friend! A traveler journeying through the interior once lay down to rest on his camp bed within his tent. He meant to sleep for thirty minutes only. When he awoke he found that twenty-six hours had gone – likewise all his paraphernalia. Native robbers had inserted a tube beneath his tent flap, blown a minute pinch of their death snuff into the enclosure, then boldly entered and helped themselves to all of his effects. Again, a tiny paper torpedo of the stuff was thrown through the window of a locomotive cab while it stood on a siding. Both engineer and fireman were rendered unconscious for ten hours, during which time the natives denuded the machine of every movable part, So powerful an anaesthetic is *bulala-gwai* that so much of it as can be gotten on a penknife's point, if blown into a room fourteen feet square will serve to paralyze every living thing within the place for several minutes.

"The secret of its formula is close-guarded, but I have been assured by witch-men of the Congo that it can be made in two strengths, one to kill at once, the other to stupefy, and it is a fact to which I can testify that it is sometimes used successfully to capture both elephants and lions alive.

"I once went with the local inspector of police to examine premises which had been burglarized with the aid of this so powerful sleeping-powder, and on the window-sill we did behold a minute quantity of it. The inspector scooped it up on a card and called a native *gendarme* to him, then blew it in the negro's face. The stuff had lost much potency by exposure to the air, but still it was so powerful that the black was totally unconscious for upward of five minutes, and did not move a muscle when the inspector struck him a stinging blow on the cheek and even touched a lighted cigarette against his hand. Not only that, when finally he awakened he did not realize he had been asleep at all, and would not believe us till we showed him the blister where the cigarette had burned him.

"Very good. It is twenty years and more since I beheld this powder from the Devil's snuff-box, but when I saw that yellow cloud come floating through the broken window, and when I realized Mademoiselle Alice had decamped unseen by us before our very eyes, I said to me, 'Jules de Grandin, here, it seems, is evidence of *bulala-gwai*, and nothing else.'

"'You may be right, Jules de Grandin,' I answered me, 'but still you are not sure. Wait until the others have departed with their silly gabble-gabble, then ask Friend Trowbridge if he also saw the yellow cloud. He knows nothing of *bulala-gwai*, but if he saw that fog of yellowness, you may depend upon it there was such a thing.'

"And so I waited, and when you did agree with me, I searched, and having searched I found that which I sought and – forgive me, good friend! – as there was no other laboratory material at hand, I did test the stuff on you, and now I am convinced. Yes, I damn know how they spirited *Mademoiselle* Alice away while our eyes were open and unseeing. Who it was that stole her, and why he did it – that is for us to discover as quickly as may be."

He felt for his cigarette case and thoughtfully extracted a "Maryland" then, remembering where he was, replaced it. "Let us go," he ordered. "Perhaps the chatterers have become tired of useless searching at Twelvetrees, and we can get some information from Madame Hume."

"But if this *bulala* – this sleeping-powder, whatever its native name is – was used here, it's hardly likely Alice has gone back to Twelvetrees, is it?" I objected. "And what possible information, can Mrs. Hume give? She knows as little about it all as you or I."

"One wonders," he replied, as we left the church and climbed into my car. "At any rate, perhaps she can tell us more of that *sacre* girdle which *Mademoiselle* Alice wore."

"I noticed you seemed surprised when you saw it," I returned. "Did you recognize it?"

"Perhaps," he answered cautiously. "At least, I have seen others not unlike it."

"Indeed? Where?"

"In Kurdistan. It is a Yezidee bridal belt, or something very like it."

"A what?"

"A girdle worn by virgins who – but I forget, you do not know. "The work of pacifying subject people is one requiring all the white man's ingenuity, my friend, as your countrymen who have seen service in the Philippines will tell you. In 1922 when French authority was flouted in Arabia, I was dispatched there on a secret mission. Eventually my work took me to Deir-er-Zor, Anah, finally to Bagdad and across British Irak to the Kurdish border. There – no matter in what guise – I penetrated Mount Lalesh and the holy city of the Yezidees.

"These Yezidees are a mysterious sect scattered throughout the Orient from Manchuria to the Near East, but strongest in North Arabia, and feared and loathed alike by Christian, Jew, Buddhist, Taoist and Moslem, for they are worshippers of Satan.

"Their sacred mountain, Lalesh, stands north of Bagdad on the Kurdish border near Mosul, and on it is their holy and forbidden city which no stranger is allowed to enter, and there they have a temple, reared on terraces hewn from the living rock, in which they pay homage to the image of a serpent as the beguiler of man from pristine innocence. Beneath the temple are gloomy caverns, and there, at dead of night, they perform strange and bloody rites before an idol fashioned like a peacock, whom they call Malek Taos, the viceroy of Shaitan – the Devil – upon earth.

"According to the dictates of the Khitab Asward, or Black Scripture, their Mir, or pope, has brought to him as often as he may desire the fairest daughters of the sect, and these are his to do with as he chooses. When the young virgin is prepared for the sacrifice she dons a silver girdle, like the one we saw on *Mademoiselle* Alice tonight. I saw one on Mount Lalesh. Its front is hammered silver, set with semi-precious stones of red and yellow – never blue, for blue is heaven's color, and therefore is accursed among the Yezidees who worship the Arch-Demon. The belt's back is of leather, sometimes from the skin of a lamb untimely taken from its mother, sometimes of a kid's skin, but in exceptional cases, where the woman to be offered is of noble birth and notable lineage, it is made of tanned and carefully prepared human skin – a murdered babe's by preference. Such was the leather of Mademoiselle Alice's girdle. I recognized it instantly. When one has examined a human hide tanned into leather he can not forget its feel and texture, my friend."

"But this is dreadful – unthinkable!" I protested. "Why should Alice wear a girdle made of human skin?"

"That is precisely what we have to ascertain tonight, if possible," he told me. "I do not say Madame Hume can give us any direct information, but she may perchance let drop some hint that will set us on the proper track. No," he added as he saw protest forming on my lips, "I do not intimate she has wilfully withheld anything she knows. But in cases such as this there are no such things as trifles. Some bit of knowledge which she thinks of no importance may easily prove the key to this so irritating mystery. One can but hope."

Another car, a little roadster of modish lines, opulent with gleaming chromium, drew abreast of us as we halted at the gateway of the Hume house. Its driver was a woman, elegantly dressed, sophisticated, *chic* from the crown of her tightly fitting black felt hat to the tips of her black leather gloves. As she slackened speed and leaned toward us, our headlights' rays struck her face, illuminating it as an actor's features are picked out by the spotlight on a darkened stage. Although a black lace veil was drawn across her chin and cheeks after the manner of Western desperado's handkerchief mask, so filmy was the tissue that her countenance was alluringly shadowed rather than obscured. A beautiful face it was, but not a lovely one. Skin light and clear as any blond's was complemented by hair as black and bright as polished basalt, black brows circumflexed superciliously over eyes of almost startling blueness. Her small, petulant mouth had full, ardent lips of brilliant red.

There was a slightly amused, faintly scornful smile on her somewhat vixenish mouth, and her small teeth, gleaming like white coral behind the vivid carmine of her lips, seemed sharp as little sabers as she called to us in a rich contralto: "Good evening, gentlemen. If you're looking for someone, you'll save time and trouble by abandoning the search and going home."

The echo of a cynical, disdainful laugh floated back to us as she set speed to her car and vanished in the dark.

Jules de Grandin stared after her, his hand still halfway to the hat he had politely touched when she addressed us. Astonishingly, he burst into a laugh. "*Tiens*, my friend," he exclaimed when he regained his breath, 'it seems there are more locks than one for which we seek keys tonight."

## 3. "DAVID HUME HYS. JOURNAL"

Arabella Hume came quickly toward us as we entered the hall. Sorrow and hope – or the entreaty of hope – was in the gaze she turned on us. Also, it seemed to me, there deep in her eyes some latent, nameless fear, vague and definable as a child's dread of the dark, and as terrifying.

"Oh, Doctor Trowbridge – Doctor de Grandin – have you found out anything? Do you know anything? Do you know anything?" she quavered. "It's all so dreadful, so – so impossible! Can you – have you any explanation?"

De Grandin bent stiffly from the hips as he took her hand in his and raised it to his lips. "Courage, *Madame*," he exhorted. "We shall find her, never fear."

"Oh, yes, yes," she answered almost breathlessly, "she will be found. She *must* be found, with you and Doc Trowbridge looking for her, I know it. Don't you think a mother who has been as close to her child as I have been to Alice since Ronald was killed may have a sixth sense where she is concerned? I have such a sense. I tell you – I know – Alice is near."

The little Frenchman regarded her somberly. "I, too, have a feeling she is not far distant," he declared. "It is if she were near us – in an adjoining room, by example – but a room with sound-proof walls and a cleverly hidden door. It is for you to help us find that door – and the key which will unlock it – *Madame* Hume.'

"I'll do everything I can," she promised.

"Very good. You can tell us, to begin, all that you know, all you have heard, of David Hume, the founder of this family."

Arabella gave him a half-startled, half-disbelieving glance, almost as though he had requested her to state her views of the Einstein hypothesis or some similarly recondite and irrelevant matter. "I really don't know anything about him," she returned somewhat coldly. "He seems to have been a sort of Meichizadek, appearing from nowhere and without any antecedents."

"U'm?" De Grandin stroked his little wheat-blond mustache with affectionate thoughtfulness. "There are then no records – no family records of any kind – which one can consult? No deeds or wills or leases, by example?"

"Only the family Bible, and that–"

"*Eh bien, Madame*, we may do worse than consult the Scriptures in our present difficulty. By all means, lead us to it," he broke in.

The records of ten generations of Humes were spread upon the sheets bound between the Book of Malachi and the Apocrypha. Of succeeding members of the family there was extensive register, their births, their baptisms, their progeny and deaths, as well as matrimonial alliances being catalogued with painstaking detail. Of David Hume the only entry read: "*Dyed in ye hope of gloryous Ressurection aet yrs 81, mos 7, dys 20, ye 29th Sept. MDCLVII.*"

"*Nom d'un bouc,* and is that all?" De Grandin tugged so viciously at the waxed ends of his mustache that I felt sure the hairs would be wrenched loose from his lip. "Satan bake the fellow for a pusillanimous rogue! Even though he had small pride of ancestry, he should have considered future generations. He should have had a thought for my convenience, *pardieu*!"

He closed the great, cedar-bound book with a resounding bang and thrust it angrily back into the case. But as he shoved the heavy volume from him a hammered brass corner reinforcing the cover caught against the shelf edge, wrenching the tome from his hands, and the Bible fell crashing to the floor.

"Oh, *mille pardons!*" he cried contritely, stooping to retrieve the fallen book. "I did lose my temper, *Madame*, and – *Dieu de Dieu*, what have we here?"

The impact of the fall had split the brittle, age-worn cedar slabs with which the Bible had been bound, and where the wood had buckled gable-wise the glazed-leather inner binding had cracked in a long, vertical fissure, and from this opening protruded a sheaf of folded paper. Even as we leaned forward to inspect it we saw that it was covered with fine, crabbing writing in all but totally faded ink.

Bearing the manuscript to the reading-table de Grandin switched on all the lights in the electrolier and bent over the faded, time-obliterated sheets. For a moment he knit his brows in concentration; then:

"Ah-ha," he exclaimed' exultantly, "ah-ha-ha, my friends, we have at last flushed old Monsieur David's secret from its covert! Come close and look, if you will be so good."

He spread the sheets upon the polished tabletop and tapped the uppermost with the tip of a small, well-manicured forefinger. "You see?" he asked.

Although the passage of three hundred years had dimmed the ink with which the old scribe wrote, enough remained to let us read across the yellowed paper's top: "*David Hume hys Journal*" and below: "*Inscrybed at hys house at Twelvetrees in ye colonie of New–*"

The rest had faded out, but enough was there to tell us that some secret archive of the family had been brought to light and that the scrivener had been that mysterious ancestor of whom no more was known than that he once lived at Twelvetrees.

"May one trespass on your hospitality for pen and paper, *Madame?*" de Grandin asked, his little round blue eyes shining with suppressed excitement, the twin needles of his waxed mustache points twitching like the whiskers of an agitated tom-cat. "This writing is so faint it would greatly tax one to attempt reading it aloud, and by tomorrow it may be fainter with exposure to the air; but if you will give leave that I transcribe it while I yet may read, I will endeavor to prepare a copy and read you the results of my work when it is done."

Arabella Hume, scarcely less excited than we, nodded hasty assent, and de Grandin shut himself in the Ancestors' Room with pen and paper and a tray of cigarettes to perform his task.

Twice while we waited in the hall we saw the butler tiptoe into the closed room in answer to the little Frenchman's summons. His first trip was accompanied by a bowl of ice, a glass and a decanter of brandy. "He'll drink himself into a stupor," Arabella told me when the second consignment of liquor was borne in.

"Not he," I assured her with a laugh. "Alcohol's only a febrifuge with him. He drinks it like water when he's working intensively, and it never seems to affect him."

"Oh?" she answered somewhat doubtfully. "Well, I hope he'll manage to stay sober till he's finished."

"Wait and see," I told her. "If he's unsteady on his feet, I'll–"

De Grandin's entrance cut my promise short. His face was flushed, his little round blue eyes were shining as though with unshed tears, and his mustache fairly bristling with excitement and elation; but of alcoholic intoxication there was no slightest sign.

"*Voyez*," he ordered, flourishing a sheaf of rustling papers. "Although the writing was so faded that I did perforce miss much of the story of Monsieur the Old One, enough remained to give us information of the great importance. But yes. Your closest attention, if you please."

Seating himself on the table edge and swinging one small, patent leather shod foot in rhythm with his reading, he began:

"*...and now my case was truly worser than before, for though my Moslem captors had been followers of Mahound, these that had taken me from them were worshippers of Satan's self, and nightly bowed the knee to Beelzebub, whom they worshipped in the image of a peacock highte Melek Taos, whose favor they are wont to invoke with every sort of wickedness. For their black scriptures teach that God is good and merciful, and slow to take offense, while Shaitan, as they name the Devil, is ever near and ever watchful to do hurt to mankind, wherefore he must be propitiated by all who would not feel his malice. And so they work all manner of evil, accounting that as virtue which would be deemed most villainous by us, and confessing and repenting of good acts as though they were the deadliest of sins.*

"*Their chief priest is yclept the Mir, and of all their wicked tribe he is the wickedest, scrupling not at murder and finding great delight in* such vile acts as caused the Lord aforetimes to rain down fire and brimstone on the evil cities of the plain.

"Once as I stood without their temple gate by night I did espy a great procession entering with the light of torches and with every sound of minstrels and mirth, but in the middle of the revelers there walked a group of maidens, and these did weep continually. And when asked the meaning of this sight they told me that the girls, the very flower of the tribe, had been selected by the Mir for his delight and for the lust and cruelty of those who acted as his counsellors, for such is their religion that the pontifex may choose from out their womanhood as many as he pleases, and do unto them even according the dictates of his evil will, nor may any say him nay. Anu as I looked upon these woeful women I beheld that each was clasped about the middle by a stomacher of cunningly wrought silver, and this, they told me, was the girdle of a bride, for their women don such girdles when they are ready to engage in wedlock, or when they tread the path of sorrow which leads them to the Mir and degradation. For he who gives his daughter voluntarily to be devoured by the Mir acquires merit in the eyes of Satan, and to lie as paramour to the Devil's viceroy on earth is accounted honorable for any woman, yea, even greater than to enter into matrimony."

The little Frenchman laid his paper down and turned his quick, bird-like glance upon us. "Is it now clear?" he asked. "This old Monsieur David was undoubtlessly sold as slave unto the Yezidees by Moslems who had in some way captured him. It is, of Sheik-Adi, the sacred city of the Satanists, he writes, and his reference to the silver girdles of the brides in most illuminating. *N'est-ce-pas?* Consider what he has to say a little later."

Shuffling through the pile of manuscript, he selected a fresh sheet and resumed:

"Yet she, who was the daughter of this man of blood and sin, was fair and good as any Christian maid. Moreover, her heart was inclined toward me, and many a kind act she did for me, the Christian slave, who sadly lacked for kindness in that evil mountain city. And so, as it has ever been 'twixt man and maid, we loved, and loving knew that we could not be happy till our fates joined forever. And so it was arranged that we should fly to freedom in the south, where I could take her to wife, for she had agreed to renounce Satan and all his ways to follow in the pathway of the true religion.

"Now, in the falling of the year, when crops were gathered and the husbandry was through, these people were wont to gather in their temple of the peacock and make a feast wherewith they praised the power of evil, and on the altar would be offered beasts, birds and women devoted to the service of the arch-fiend. And thus did Kudejah and I arrange the manner of our flight:

"When all within the temple was prepared and we could hear the sound of drums and trumpets offering praise unto the Devil, we slipped quickly down the mountain pass, she closely veiled like any Moslem woman. I disguised as a man of Kurdistan, and with us were two mules well laden with gold and jewels of precious stones which she had filched from the treasury of the Mir, her sire. Nor did we loiter on the way, but hastened ever till we came to the border of the land of evil and were safe among the Moslems, who treated us right kindly, believing us co-religionists who were fleeing from the worshippers of Satan. And so we came at last to Busra, and thence by ship to Muskat, from whence we sailed again and finally came once more to England.

"But ere we breathed the English air again we had been wed with Christian rite; and Kudejah had dropped her heathen name and taken that of Mary, which had also been my mother's. And sure a sweeter bride or truer wife has no man ever had, e'en though she saw the light of day beneath the shadow of the Devil's temple. Yet, though she had accepted Christ and put behind her Lucifer and all his works, when we did stand before the parson to be wed my Mary wore about her the great silver belt which had been fashioned for her marriage when she dwelt on Satan's mountain, and this we have unto this day as a marriage portion for the women of our house.

"Most crafty are those devil men from whom we fled, and well were we aware of it, and so we came to this new land, where I did leave my olden name behind and take the name of Hume, that those who might come seeking us might the better be befooled; and yet, though leagues of ocean toss between us and the worshippers of Satan, a thought still plagues us as a naughty dream may vex a frightened child. The office of high priest to Melek Taos is hereditary in the family of the Mir. The eldest son ascends the altar to perform the rites of blood the moment that his sire has breathed his last, and if there be no son, then must the eldest daughter of the line be wedded unto Satan with formal ceremony and silver girdle, and serve as priestess in her father's stead until a son is born, whereupon she is led forth with all solemnity and put to death with horrid torment, for her sufferings are a libation unto Beelzebub. And thereupon a regency of under-priests must serve the King of Evil till the son is grown to man's estate.

"Wherefore, O ye who may come after me in this the family I have founded, I do adjure ye to make choice of death rather then submit unto the demands of the worshippers of Satan, for in the years to come it well may hap that the Mir and his line may be exhausted, and then those crafty men of magic who do dwell on Mount Lalesh may seek ye out and summon ye to serve the altar of the Devil. And so I warn ye, if the time should come when ye receive a message from ye know not where, bidding *ye simply to come home, that this shall be the sign, and straightway shall ye flee with utmost haste or if ye can not flee then take your life with your own hand, for better far is it to face an outraged God with the bloodstains of self-murder on your hands than to stand before the Seat of Judgment with your soul foredoomed for that ye were a priest and server of the Arch-Fiend in your days on earth.*

"I have—"

"Well?" I prompted as the silence lengthened. "What else?"

"There is no 'else,' my friend," he answered. "As I told you, the ink with which Monsieur l'Ancetre wrote was faded as an old belle's charms; the remainder of his message is but the shadow of a shadow, an angel out of Paradise could not decipher it."

We sat in silence for a moment, and it was Arabella Hume who framed our common thought in words: "He said, 'if the time should come when ye receive a message from ye know not where, bidding ye simply to come home, this shall be the sign' – the message Alice got on the ouija board today – you remember? You saw it repeated yourselves before we went to church!"

De Grandin bent a fixed, unwinking. stare on her. "*Madame,*" he asked, "can you not give us some description of the stranger who desired that you let him see the wedding girdle of Madame David? Was he, according to your guess, a Levantin?"

Mrs. Hume considered him a moment thoughtfully. Then: "No-o, I shouldn't think so," she replied. "He seemed more like a Spaniard, possibly Italian, though it's hard to say more than that he was dark and very clean-looking and spoke English with that perfect lack of accent which showed it was not his mother tongue. You know each word sharply defined, as though it might be the resuit of a mental translation."

"Perfectly," de Grandin nodded. "I should say—"

"Well, *I* should say it's all a lot of nonsense," I broke in. "It may be true old David Hume was sold as a slave to these Devil-Worshippers, and that he ran off with the high priest's daughter – and all the money he could get his hands on. But you know how superstitious people were in those days. The chances are he was filled full of fantastic stories by the Yezidees, and believed everything he heard and more that he imagined. I'd say his conscience was troubling him toward the last; perhaps his mind was failing, too. Look how carefully he hid what he'd written in the cover of the family Bible. Is that the action of a normal man, especially if he seriously intended future generations to profit by his warning?"

Arabella glanced at each of us in turn, finally gave vent to a sigh of relief and put her hand on mine. "Thank you Samuel," she said. "I knew there was some explanation for it all; but Alice's strange disappearance and all this has so upset me that I'm hardly normal." To de

Grandin she added:

"I'm sure Doctor Trowbridge's explanation is the right one. Old David must have been weak-minded when he wrote that senseless warning. He was eighty-one when died, and you know how old people are inclined to imagine things. Like children, really."

A stubborn, argumentative expression crossed de Grandin's face, but gave place instantly to one of his quick elfin grins. "Perhaps I have put too much trust in the vaporings of a senile old man's broken mind," he admitted. "Nevertheless, the fact remains that *Mademoiselle* Alice is not here, and the task remains for us to find her. Come, Friend Trowbridge, there is little we can do here and much we can do elsewhere. Let us go, if we have *Madame*'s permission to retire." He bowed with Continental grace to Arabella.

"Oh, yes; and thank you so much for what you've done already," Mrs. Hume returned. "I'm half inclined to think this is some madcap prank of Alice's, but" – her expression of false confidence gave way a moment, unmasking the panic fear which gnawed at her heart – "if we hear nothing by morning, I think we'd better summon the police, don't you?"

"By all means," he agreed, taking her hand in his and bending ceremoniously above it ere he turned to accompany me from the house.

"Thank you, my friend," he murmured as we began our homeward drive. "Your interruption was most timely and served to divert poor *Madame*'s mind from the awful horror I saw gathering round us."

"Eh?" I returned. "You don't mean to tell me you actually believe that balderdash you read us?"

He turned on me in blank amazement. "And was your avowal of disbelief in Monsieur David's tale not simulated?" he asked.

"Good Lord," I answered in disgust, "d'ye mean to say you swallowed that old dotard's story – all that nonsense about an hereditary priesthood of the Devil-Worshippers, and the possibility of – See here, don't you remember he said if the Mir's male line became extinct the eldest daughter had to serve, and that she must be married to the Devil? That might be possible – mystically speaking – but he specifically said she shall thereafter act as high priestess until a son is born. I know the legend of Robert the Devil, and it was probably implicitly believed in David Hume's day, for the Devil was a very real person then, but we've rather graduated from that sort of mediaevalism nowadays. How can a woman be married to the Devil, and bear him a son?"

There was more of sneer than smile in the mirthless grin he turned on me. "Have you been to India?" he demanded.

"India? Of course not, but what's that got to do with–"

"Then perhaps it is that you do not know of the *deva-dasis*, or wives of Siva. In that benighted land a father thinks he does acquire merit by giving up his daughter to be wedded to the god, and wedded to him she truly is, with all the formal pomp accompanying the espousal of a princess. Thereafter she is accounted honorable as consort of the great God of Destruction – but though her wedded lord is but a thing of carven stone she does not lack for offspring. No, *pardieu*, she is more often than not a mother before her thirteenth birthday, and several times mother when her twentieth year is reached – if she survives that long.

"Consider the analogy here. From what I have beheld with my own two eyes – and my sight is very keen – and from what I have been told by witnesses who had no need to lie or even stretch the truth, I know that Monsieur David's narrative is based on fact, and very ugly fact a that."

"But what about his hiding his 'warning' in the cover of the Bible?" I persisted. "Surely–"

"Three centuries have passed since he penned those words," de Grandin interrupted, "and in that time much may be forgotten. That David told his children where they might look for guidance if the need for guidance I rose make no doubt. But in the course of time his admonition was forgotten, or–" He broke off musingly, and I had to prompt him: "Yes? Or–?"

"Or the story of some secret warning *has* been handed down to each generation," he replied. "Did it not strike you more than once that *Madam*e Hume was not entirely honest – *pardon*, I should say frank – with us? The fear of something which she could or would not mention was plainly in her eyes when we came from the church, and earlier in the evening her efforts to direct the conversation from that obscure message which her daughter had from the ouija board were far more resolute than they would have been had she had nothing but a distaste for superstitious practice to excuse them. Also, when we did ask for information relative to Monsieur David she suddenly turned cold to us, and had I not persisted would undoubtlessly have turned us from examination of the family Bible. Moreover–"

Again he paused and again I prompted him.

"Jules de Grandin is experienced," he assured me solemnly. "As a member of *la Sureté* he has had much to do with questioned documents. He knows ink, he knows paper, he can scent a forgery or an attempt at alteration as far as he can recognize the symptoms of coryza. Yes."

"Yes? What then?"

"This, *cordieu*! I played the dolt, the simple, guileless fool, tonight, my friend, but this I say with half an eye as I made transcription of old David's story: Someone – I know not who – *some one has essayed to blot that writing out with acid ink eradicator*. Had the writing been in modem metallic ink the effort would have been successful, but *Monsieur l'Ancetre* wrote with the old vegetable ink of his time, and so the acid did not quite efface it. It is that to which I owed my ability to read the journal. But believe me, good friend, it was a man – or woman – and not time, which dimmed the writing on those pages and rendered illegible much which old David wrote to warn his descendants, and which would have greatly simplified our problems."

"But who could have done it – and why?" I asked.

He raised his narrow shoulders in an irritable shrug. "Ask the good God – or perhaps the Devil – as to that," I told me. "They know the answer; not I."

## 4. BY WHOSE HAND?

Threatening little flurries of snow had been skirmishing down from the cloud-veiled sky all evening; before we were halfway to my house the storm attacked in force, great feathery flakes following each other in smothering profusion, obscuring traffic lights, clinging to the wind-shield; clogging our wheels. Midnight was well past as we stamped up my front steps, brushed our feet on the doormat and paused a moment at the vestibule while I fumbled for my latch-key. As I swung back the door the office phone began a shrill, hysterical cachinnation which seemed to rise in terrified crescendo as I ran down the hall.

"Hullo?" I challenged gruffly.

"Doctor Trowbridge?" the high-pitched voice across the wire called.

"Yes; what–"

"This is Wilbur, sir, Mrs. Hume's butler, you know."

"Oh? Well, what's–"

"It's the missis, sir; she's – I'm afraid you'll be too late sir; but please hurry. I just found her, an' she's–" His voice trailed off in a wheeze of asthmatic excitement, and I could hear him gasping in a futile effort to regain his speech.

"Oh, all right; do what you can for her till we get there; we'll be right over," I called back. Attempting to ascertain the nature of the illness by questioning the inarticulate domestic would be only a waste of time, I saw, and obviously time was precious.

"Come on," I bade de Grandin. "Something's happened to Arabella Hume; Wilbur is so frightened he's gasping like a newly landed fish and can't give any information; so it may be anything from a broken arm to a stroke of apoplexy, but–"

"But certainly, by all means, of course," the Frenchman agreed enthusiastically. Next to solving a perplexing bit of crime he dearly loved a medical emergency. With deftness which combined uncanny speed with almost super-human accuracy of selection he bundled bandages and styptics, stimulants and sedatives, a sphygmomanometer and a kit of first-aid instruments into a bag, then: "Let us go," he urged. "All is ready."

Wilbur was pacing back and forth on the veranda when we arrived some half an hour later. His face was blue with cold, and his teeth chattered so he could scarcely form the hurried greeting which he gave us.

"Gawd, gentlemen," he told us tremblingly. "I thought you'd never get here!"

"*Eh bien*, so did we," de Grandin answered. "*Madame* your mistress, where is she, if you please?"

"Upstairs, sir, in her dressing-room. I found her like she is just before I called you. I'd finished lockin' up the house an' was going to my room by way of the back stairs when 1 heard the sound o' something heavy falling up the hall toward the front' o' the house, an' ran to see if I was wanted. She didn't answer when I knocked – indeed, it seemed so hawful quiet in 'er room that it fair gave me the creeps, sir. So I made bold to knock again; then, when she didn't hanswer, to look in, an'–"

"Lead on, *mon vieux*," de Grandin interrupted. "The circumstances of your discovery can wait, at present. It is *Madame* Hume that we would see."

The butler was a step or two ahead of us as we climbed the stairs, but as we approached Mrs. Hume's door his footsteps lagged. By the time we stood before the portal be had dropped back to de Grandin's elbow, and made no motion either to rap upon the panels or to turn the knob for us.

"Lead on," de Grandin repeated. "We would see her once, if you please."

"There's nothing you can do, of course," the servant answered, "but in a cyse like this it's best to have a doctor, so–"

The little Frenchman's temper broke beneath strain. "Damn yes!" he snapped, "but save your conversation till a later time, my friend. I do not care for it at present."

Without more ado he turned the latch and swung the door back, stepping quickly past the butler into Arabella's boudoir, but coming to a halt on the threshold.

Close behind him, I stepped forward, but stopped with a gasp at what I saw.

Suspended by a heavy silken curtain cord loop. about her neck, Arabella Hume hung from the iron curtain rod bridging the archway between her chamber and her dressing-room. A satin-upholstered boudoir-chair lay overturned on its back beneath her and a little to one side, her flaccid feet in their satin evening slippers swung a scant four inches from the floor, her hands draped limply at her sides, and her head was sharply bent forward to the left. Her lips were slightly parted and between them showed a quarter-inch of tongue, like the pale-pink pistil of a blossom protruding from the leaves. Her eyes were partly opened, and already covered with the shining gelatin-film of death, but not at all protuberant.

"Good heavens!" I exclaimed.

"My Gawd, sir, ain't it *hawful*?" whispered Wilbur.

"*Nom de Dieu de nom de Dieu; c'est une affaire du diable*!" said Jules de Grandin.

To Wilbur: "You say you first discovered her thus when you called Doctor Trowbridge?" he demanded.

"Ye-es, sir."

"Then why in the name of ten million small blue devils did you not cut her down? The chances are she was already dead, but–"

"You daren't cut a 'angin' person down till the coroner's looked at 'im, dast you, sir?" the servant replied.

"*Ohe; sacre nom d'un petit bonhomme!*" De Grandin wrenched savagely at the ends of his mustache. "This chimney-corner law; this smug wisdom of ignorance – it will drive me mad. Had you cut the cord by which she hung when you first saw her, it is possible there would have been no need to call the coroner at all, great stupidhead!" he stormed.

Abruptly he put his anger by as one might lay off a garment. "No matter," he resumed, "the mischief is now done. We must to work. Wilbur, bring me a decanter full – full, remember – of brandy."

"Yes, sir," the servant answered. "Thank you, sir."

"And, Wilbur–"

"Yes, sir?"

"Take a drink – or two – yourself before you serve me."

"Thank you sir!" The butler departed on his errand with alacrity.

"Quick, my friend," the Frenchman ordered, "we must examine her before he returns."

Snipping through the silken strangling cord with a pair of surgeon's scissors he eased the body down in his arms and bore it to the couch, then with infinite care loosened the ligature about the throat and slipped the noose over her head. "*Morbleu*," he murmured as he laid the cord upon the table, "who taught her to form a hangman's knot, one wonders?"

I took the curtain cord in my hand and looked at it. He was right. The loop which had been round Arabella's neck was no ordinary slipknot, but a carefully fashioned hangman's halter, several turns of end being taken round the cord above the noose, thus insuring greater freedom for the loop to tighten around the throat.

"It may be so," I heard him whisper to himself, "but I damn doubt it."

"What's that?" I asked.

He bent above the body, examining the throat first with his naked eye, then through a small but powerful lens which he drew from his waistcoat pocket.

"Consider," he replied, rising from his task to regard me with a fixed, unwinking stare. "Wilbur tells us that he heard a piece of furniture overturned. That would be the chair on which this poor one stood. Immediately afterward he ran to her room and knocked. Receiving no response, he knocked again; then, when no answer was forthcoming, he entered. With due allowance made for everything, not more than five minutes could have elapsed. Yet she was dead. I do not like it."

"She might not have been dead when he first saw her," I returned. "You know how quickly unconsciousness follows strangulation. She might have been unconscious and Wilbur assumed she was dead; then because of his fool notion that it was unlawful to cut a hanging body down, he left her strangling here while he ran to 'phone us and waited for us on the porch."

The little Frenchman nodded shortly. "How is death caused in hanging?" he demanded.

"Why – er – by strangulation – asphyxia – or fracture of the cervical vertebrae and rupture of the spinal cord.'

"*Precisement.* If Madame Hume had choked to death from yonder bar is it not nearly certain that not only her poor tongue, but her eyes, as well, would have been forced forward by pressure on the constricted blood vessels?"

"I suppose so, but–"

"The devil take all buts. See here–"

Drawing me forward he thrust his lens into my hand and pointed to the dead woman's throat. "Look carefully," he ordered. "You will observe the double track made by the wide silk noose with which poor Madame Hume was hanged."

"Yes," I nodded as my eye followed the parallel anemic band marked by the curtain cord. "I see it."

"Very good. Now look more closely – see, hold the glass so – and tell me if you see a third – a so narrow and deeper mark, a spiral track traced in slightly purple bruise beneath the wide, white marks made by the curtain cord?"

"By heaven!" I started as his slender finger pointed to the darker, deeper depression. "It's pretty faint, but still perceptible. I wonder what that means?"

"Murder, *pardieu*!" he spat the accusation viciously. "Hanged poor Madame Arabella undoubtlessly was, but *hanged after she was dead*.

"This so narrow, purple mark, I know him. Ha, do I not, *cordieu*? In the native states of India I have seen him more than once, and never can it be mistaken for other than itself. No. It is the mark of the *roomal* of the *thags*; the strangling cord of those who serve Bhowanee the Black Goddess. Scarcely thicker than a harp-string it is, yet deadly as a serpent's fang. See, those evil ones loop it quickly round their victim's neck, draw it tight with crossed ends, then with their knuckles knead sharply at the base of the skull where the atlas lies and, *pouf!* It is done. Yes. Certainly.

"You want more proof?" He rose and faced me with flashing eyes, his little, milk-white teeth bare beneath the line of his mustache. "Then look–" Abruptly he took Arabella's cheeks between his palms and drew her head forward, then rocked it sharply from side to side.

The evidence was indisputable. Such limber, limp flaccidity meant but one thing. The woman's neck was broken.

"But the drop," I persisted. "She might have broken her neck when she kicked the chair from under her, and–"

"Ah bah!" he countered hotly. That chair-seat is a scant half-meter high, her feet swung at least four inches from the floor; she could not possibly have dropped a greater-length then sixteen inches. Her weight was negligible – I lifted her a moment since – not more than ninety-five or ninety-eight pounds, at most. A drop so short such a light woman could not possibly have broken the spine. Besides, this fracture is high, not lower than the atlas or the axis; the ligature about her neck encompassed the second cervical vertebra. The two things do match. *Non*, my friend, this is no suicide, but murder cleverly dressed to simulate it."

"Your brandy, sir." Wilbur halted at the door, keeping his eyes averted resolutely from the quiet form couch.

"*Merci bien*," de Grandin answered. "Put it down, *mon vieux*; then call *Monsieur* the Coroner and await him. If the other servants have not yet been appraised of *Madame*'s death it will do no harm to let them wait till morning."

"Poor Arabella!" I murmured, staring with tear-dimmed eyes at the pathetic little body underneath the coverlet. "Who could have wanted to kill her?"

"*Eh bien*, who could have wanted to steal *Mademoiselle* Alice away? Who wanted to obtain the Devil-Worshippers' marriage belt? Who sent the strange veiled lady following after us to tell us that our quest was vain?" he answered, bitter mockery in his tones.

"Good heavens, you mean–"

"Precisely, exactly; quite so. I mean no more and certainly no less, my friend. This is assuredly the Devil's business, and right well have his servants done it. Certainly."

John Martin, county coroner and leading mortician of he city, and Jules ce Grandin were firm friends. At the little Frenchman's earnest entreaty he drove Parnell, the coroner's physician, to perform an autopsy which corroborated every assumption de Grandin had made. Death was due to coma induced by rupture of the myelon, not to strangulation, the post-mortem revealed. Moreover, though Parnell rebelled at the suggestion, Robert Hartley, chief bio-chemist at Mercy Hospital, was called in to make a decimetric test of Arabella's liver. Carefully, de Grandin, Martin and I watched him, he macerated a bit of the organ, mixed it with lampblack and strained it through a porcelain filter. While Parnell sulked in a corner of the laboratory the rest of us watched breathlessly as the serous liquid settled in the glass dish beneath the filter.

It was clear.

"Well, that's that," said Hartley.

"*Mais oui, c'est demontré,*" de Grandin nodded.

"Umpf!" Parnell grunted in disgust.

The ruddy-faced, gray-haired coroner looked interrogatively from one to the other. "Just what's been proved, gentlemen?" he asked.

"Absence of glycogen." Hartley answered.

"Murder, *parbleu*!" de Grandin added.

"Nothing – nothing at all." Parnell assured him.

"But–" the coroner began more bewildered than ever.

"*Monsieur*," de Grandin cut him short, "glycogen, or liver sugar represents the stored up energy of muscular strength in the machines we call our bodies. When it is plentiful we are strong, active, hearty – what you call filled with pep. As it is depleted we become weakened. When it is gone we are exhausted. Yes.

"Undoubtlessly a woman being strangled would make tremendous last muscular effort to fight off her assailant. Such an effort, lasting but a little minute, would burn this muscle-power we call glycogen from her liver. Her reservoir of strength would be drained.

"Am I not right?" he turned for confirmation to Hartley, who nodded slow agreement.

"Very well, then. Now, the experiment Doctor Hartley has just performed shows us conclusively that glycogen was practically absent from Madame Hume's liver. Had it been present in even small quantities the filtered liquid would have been cloudy. Yes. But it was clear, or nearly so, as you did observe with your own two eyes. What then?

"Simply this, *mordieu*: She fought – frenziedly, though futilely – for her life before the vile miscreant who killed her drew his *roomal* tight about her throat and with his diabolically skillful knuckles broke her neck. It was the tightening strangle-cord which prevented outcry, though the chair we found overturned was undoubtlessly turned over in the struggle, not kicked aside by her after she had adjusted the hangman's noose about her neck. No; by no means. Had she been self-hanged there would be ample store of glycogen found in her liver; as it is–" he paused, raising shoulders, elbows, and eyebrows in a shrug of matchless eloquence.

"I – see," said Mr. Martin slowly.

But the jury did not. Doctor Parnell's lukewarm reception of de Grandin's theory, Hartley's refusal to testify to anything save that there was a lack of glycogen found the liver, and the cleverness with which the stage had been set to give plausibility to suspicion of suicide combined to forge a chain of circumstantial evidence which the little Frenchman's fiery oratory could not break. Suicide – dead by her own hand while of unsound mind – was the consensus of the jury.

## 5. THE MISSING CHILD

Headlines screamed across the country: "Mother Slays Self as Cops Hunt Vanished Child" – "Broken Heart Makes Mother Seek Death" – "Love-Crazed Woman Suicides as Daughter Disappears" – these were among the more conservative statements which faced Americans from Maine to Oregon as they sat at breakfast, and for a time reporters from the metropolitan dailies were as thick in our town as hungry flies around an abattoir. At length the hue and cry died down, and Arabella's death and Alice's strange disappearance gave way on the front page to the latest tales of scandal in municipal administration.

Jules de Grandin shut himself in the study, emerging only at mealtime or after office hours for a chat with me, smoked innumerable vile-smelling French cigarettes, used the telephone a great deal and posted many letters; but as far as I could see, his efforts to find Alice or run down her mother's murderers were nil.

"I should think you'd feel better if you went out a bit," I told him at breakfast one day. "I know finding Alice is a hopeless task, and as for Arabella's murderer – I'm beginning to think she committed suicide, after all, but–"

He looked up from the copy of the *Morning Journal* he had been perusing and fixed me with a straight, unwinking stare. "The police are co-operating," he answered shortly. "Not a railway station or bus terminal lacks watchers, and no private cars or taxis leave the city limits without submitting to a secret but thorough inspection. What more can we do?"

"Why, you might direct the search personally, or check up such few clues as they may find–" I began, nettled by his loss of interest in the case, but he cut me short with a quick motion of his hand.

"My friend," he told me with one of his puckish grins, "attend me. When I was a little lad I had a dog, a silly energetic little fellow, all barks and jumps and wagging tail. He dearly loved a cat. *Morbleu*, the very sight of *Madame* Puss would put him in a frenzy! How he would rush at her, how he would show his teeth and growl and put on the fierce face! Then, when she had retired to the safety of a pear tree, how he would stand beneath her refuge and twitch his tail and bark! *Cordieu*, sometimes I would think he must surely burst with barking!

"And she, the scornful pussy, did she object? *Mille fois non.* Safe in her sanctuary she would eye him languidly, and let him bark. At last, when he had barked himself into exhaustion, he would withdraw to think upon the evils of times, and *Madame* Puss would leisurely descend the tree and trot away to safety.

"I would often say to him: 'My Toto, you are a great stupid-head. Why do you do it? Why do you not depart a little distance from the tree and lie *perdu*? Then *Madame* Puss may think that you have lost all interest and come down; then *pouf!* you have her at your mercy.' But no, that foolish little dog, he would not listen to advice, and so, though he expended great energy and made a most impressive noise, he never caught a cat.

"Friend Trowbridge, I am not a foolish little dog. By no means. It is not I who do such things. Here in the house I stay, with strict instructions that I be not called should any want me on the telephone; I am not ever seen abroad. For all of the display I make, I might be dead or gone away. But I am neither. Always and ever I sit here all watchful, and frequently I do call the *gendarmes* to find if they have discovered that for which we seek. I know – I see all that takes place. If any makes a move, I know it. But those we seek do not know I know. No, they think Jules de Grandin is asleep or drunk, or perhaps gone away. It is best so, I assure you. Anon, emboldened by my seeming lethargy, they will emerge from out their hiding-place; then–" His smile became unpleasant as he clenched one slender, strong hand with a gesture suggestive of crushing something soft within it. "Then *pardieu*, they shall learn that Jules de Grandin is not a fool, nor can they make the long nose at him with impunity!" He helped himself to a second portion of broiled mackerel from the hot-water dish and resumed his perusal of the *Journal*. Suddenly:

"*Ohe, misère, calamité, c'ect désastrieux!*" he cried. "Read here my friend, if you please. Read it and tell me that I am mistaken!"

Hands shaking with eagerness, he passed the paper to me, indicating a rather inconspicuous item in the lower left-hand corner of the third page.

CHILD VANISHES FROM BAPTIST HOME, the headline stated. Then:

*Shortly after one o'clock this morning Mrs. Maud Gordon, 47, a matron in the Harrisonville Baptist Home, was awakened by sounds of crying from the ward in which the younger children of the orphanage were quartered. Going quickly to the room the woman found some of the older children sitting up in bed and crying bitterly. Upon demanding what was wrong she was told that a man had just been in the place, flashed a flashlight in several of the children's faces, then picked Charles Eastman, eight months, from his crib which stood near the open window and made off with him.*

*The matron at once gave the alarm, and a thorough search of the premises was made, but no trace of the missing child or his abductor could be found. The gates of the orphanage were shut and locked, and the lodgekeeper, who was awakened by the searching party, declared it would have been impossible for anyone to pass in or out without his knowledge, as his were the only keys to the gates beside those in the main office of the* home, and the keys were in their accustomed place on his bureau in his bedroom when the alarm reached him. The home's extensive grounds are surrounded by a twelve-foot brick wall, with an overhang on either side, and climbing it either from the outside or from within would be almost impossible without extension ladders.

The Eastman child's parents are dead and, his only living relative so far as known is an uncle, lately released from the penitentiary. Police are checking up on this man's movements during the night, as it is thought he may have stolen the child to satisfy a grudge he had against the mother, now dead, whose testimony helped convict him on a charge of burglary five years ago.

"Well?" I asked as I laid the paper down. "Is that what you read?"

"*Helas*, yes. It is too true!"

"Why, what d'ye mean–" I began, but he cut in hurriedly.

"Perhaps I do mistake, my friend. Although I have lived in your so splendid country for upward of five years, there is still much which is strange to me. Is it that the sect you call the Baptists do not believe in infant baptism – that only those of riper years are given baptism by them?"

"Yes, that's so," I answered. "They hold that–"

"No matter what they hold, if that be so," he interrupted. "That this little one had not been accorded baptism is enough – *parbleu*, it is much. Come, my friend, the time for concealing is past. Let us hasten, let us rush; let us fly!"

"Rush?" I echoed, bewildered. "Where?"

"To that orphan home of the so little unbaptized Baptists, of course," he answered almost furiously. "Come, let us go right away, immediately, at once."

Maintained by liberal endowments and not greatly taxed by superfluity of inmates, the Baptist Home for Children lay on a pleasant elevation some five miles out of Harrisonville. Its spacious grounds, which were equipped with every possible device for fostering organized play among its little guests were, as the newspaper accounts described, surrounded by a brick wall of formidable height with projecting overhangs flanging T-wise, from the top. Moreover, in an excess of caution, the builder had studded the wall's crest with a fringe of broken bottle-glass set in cement, and anyone endeavoring to cross the barrier must be prepared not only with scaling ladders so long as to be awkward to carry, but with a gangway or heavy pad to lay across the shark-tooth points of glass with which the wall was armored. De Grandin made a rapid reconnaissance of the position, twisting viciously at his mustache meanwhile. "Ah, *helas*, the poor one!" he murmured as his inspection was completed. "Before, I had some hope;

now I fear the worst."

"Eh?" I returned. "What now?"

"Plenty, *pardieu* – a very damn great plenty!' he answered bitterly. "Come, let us interview the *concierge*. He is our only hope, I fear."

I glanced at him in wonder as we neared the pretty little cottage in which the gatekeeper maintained his home and office.

"No, sir," the man replied to de Grandin's question, "I'm sure no one could 'a' come through that gate last night. It's usually locked for th' night at ten o'clock, though I mostly sit up listenin' to th' radio a little later, an' if anything real important comes up, I'm on hand to open th' gates. Last night there wasn't a soul, man or woman, 'ceptin' th' grocery deliveryman, come in here after six o'clock – very quiet day it was, 'count th' cold weather, I guess. I wuz up a little later than usual, too, but turned in 'bout 'leven o'clock, I should judge. I'd made th' rounds o' th' grounds with Bruno a little after seven, an' believe me, I'm here to tell you no one could 'a' been hidin' anywhere without his knowin' it. No sir!

"Here, Bruno!" he raised his voice and snapped his fingers authoritatively, and a ponderous mastiff, seemingly big enough to drag down an elephant, ambled in and favored us with a display of awe-inspiring teeth as his black lips curled back in a snarl.

"Bruno slept right beside my bed, sir," the gatekeeper went on, "an th' winder wuz open; so if anyone had so much as stopped by th' gate to monkey with it, he'd 'a' heard 'em, an' – well, it wouldn't 'a' been so good for 'em, I'm tellin' you. I recollec' once when a pettin party across th' road from th' gate, Bruno got kind o' suspicious-like, an' first thing any of us knew he'd bolted through th' winder an made for 'em – like to tore th' shirt off th' feller 'fore I woke up an called 'im off."

De Grandin nodded shortly. "And may one examine your room for one little minute, *Monsieur*?" he asked courteously, "We shall touch nothing, of course, and request that you be with us at all times."

"We-ell—I don't – oh, all right," the watchman responded as the Frenchman's hand strayed meaningly toward his wallet. "Come on."

The small neat room in which the gatekeeper slept had a single wide window opening obliquely toward the gate and giving a view both of the portal and a considerable stretch of road in each direction, for the gatehouse was built into, and formed an integral part of the wall surrounding the grounds. From window-sill to earth was a distance of perhaps six feet, possibly a trifle less.

"And your keys were where, if you please?" de Grandin asked as he surveyed the chamber.

"Right on the bureau there, where I put 'em before I went to bed last night, an' they wuz in th' same place this mornin' when they called me from th' office, too. Guess they'd better 'a' been there, too. Any one tryin' to sneak in an' pinch 'em would 'a' had old Bruno to deal with, even if I hadn't wakened, which I would of, 'count of I'm such a light sleeper. You have to be, in a job like this."

"Perfectly," the Frenchman nodded understandingly as he walked to the window, removed the immaculate white linen handkerchief from his sleeve and flicked it lightly across the sill. "Thank you, *Monsieur*, we need not trouble you further, I think," he continued, taking a bill from his folder and laying it casually on the bureau before turning to leave the room.

At the gateway he paused a moment, examining the lock. It was a heavy snap-latch of modern workmanship, strong enough to defy the best efforts of a crew of journeymen safe-blowers.

"*C'est tres simple*," he murmured to himself as we left the gate and entered my car. "Behold, Friend Trowbridge."

Withdrawing the white handkerchief from his cuff he held it toward me. Across its virgin surface there lay, where he had brushed it on the watchman's window, a smear of yellow powder.

"*Bulala-gwai*," he told me in a weary, almost toneless voice.

"What, that devil-dust–"

"*Précisement*, my friend, that devil-dust. Was it not simple? To his window they did creep, most doubtlessly on shoes with rubber soles, which would make no noise upon the frozen ground. *Pouf!* the sleeping-powder tossed into his room, and he and his great mastiff are at once unconscious. They remove his keys; it is a so easy task. The gate is unlocked, opened; then made fast with a retaining wedge, and the keys replaced upon his bureau. The little one is stolen, the gate closed behind the kidnappers, and the spring-latch locks itself. When the alarm is broadcast *Monsieur le Concierge* can swear in all good conscience that no one has gone through the gate and his keys are in their proper place. But certainly; of course they were. By damn, but they are clever, those ones!"

"Whom do you mean? Who'd want to steal a little baby from an orphan's home?"

"A little *unbaptized* baby – and a boy," he interjected.

"All right, a little unbaptized boy."

"I would give my tongue to the cat to answer that," he told me solemnly. "That they are the ones who spirited *Mademoiselle* Alice away from before our very eyes we can not doubt. The technique of their latest crime has labeled them; but why they, whose faith is a bastardized descendant of the old religion of Zoroaster – a sort of disreputable twelfth cousin of the Parsees – should want to do this – *non*, it does not match, my friend. Jules de Grandin is much puzzled." He shook his head and pulled so savagely at his mustache that I feared he would do himself permanent injury.

"What in heaven's name–" I began. And:

"In heaven's name, *ha*! Yes, we shall have much to do in heaven's name, my friend," he cut in. "For a certainty we are aligned against a crew who ply their arts in *hell*'s name."

## 6. THE VEILED LADY AGAIN

Harrisonville's newest citizens, gross weight sixteen pounds, twelve ounces, delayed their advent past all expectations that night, but with their overdue arrival came trying complications, and for close upon three hours two nurses, a badly worried young house physician and I fought manfully to bring mother and her twins back across death's doorstep. It was well past midnight when I climbed my front steps, dog-tired, with hands that trembled from exhaustion and eyes still smarting from the ware of surgery lamps. "Half a gill of brandy, then bed – and no morning office hours tomorrow," I promised myself as I tiptoed down the hall.

I poured the spirit out into a graduate and was in the act of draining it when the sudden furious clamor of the night bell arrested my upraised hand. Acquired instinct will not be denied. Scarcely aware what I did, I put the brandy down untasted and stumbled, rather than walked, to the front door to answer the alarm.

"Doctor – Doctor, let me in – hide me. Quick, don't let them see us talking!" the fear-sharpened feminine whisper cut through the darkened vestibule and a woman's form lurched drunkenly forward into my arms. She was breathing in short, labored gasps, like a hunted creature.

"Quick – quick" – again that scarcely audible murmur, more pregnant with terror than a scream – "shut the door – lock it – bolt it – stand back out of the light! Please!"

I retreated a step or two, my visitor still clinging to me like a drowning woman to her rescuer. As we passed beneath the ceiling-light I took glance at her, I was vaguely conscious of her charm, of her beauty, of her perfume, so delicate that it was but the faint, seductive shadow of a scent. A tightly fitting hat of black was set on her head, and draped from this, from eartip to eartip, was stretched a black-mesh veil, its upper edge just clearing the tip of her nose but covering mouth, cheeks and chin, leaving the eyes and brow uncovered. Through its diaphanous gauze I could see the gleam of carmined lips and tiny, pearl-like teeth, seemingly sharp as little sabers as the small, childish mouth writhed back from them in panic terror.

"Why – why," I stammered. "it's the lady we saw when we–"

"Perfectly; it is *Mademoiselle l'Inconnue*, the lady of the veil," de Grandin finished as he descended the last three steps at a run, and in a lavender dressing-gown and purple kidskin slippers, a violet muffler draped round his throat, stepped nimbly forward to assist me with my lovely burden.

"What is it, Mademoiselle?" he asked, half leading, half carrying her toward the consulting-room; "have you perhaps come again to tell us that our search is vain?"

"No, no-o!" the woman moaned, leaning still more heavily upon us. "Help me, oh, help me, please! I'm wounded; they – he – oh, I'll tell you everything!"

"Excellent!" de Grandin nodded as he flung back the door and switched on the electric lights. "First let us see your hurt, then – *mon Dieu*, Friend Trowbridge, she had swooned!"

Even as he spoke the woman buckled weakly at the knees, and like a lovely doll from which the sawdust has been let, crumpled forward toward the floor.

I freed one hand from her arm, intent on helping place her on the table, and stared at it with an exclamation of dismay. The fingers were dyed to the knuckles with blood, and on the girl's dark motor-coat an ugly dull-red stain was sopping-wet and growing every moment.

"*Tres bien*, so!" de Grandin murmured, placing his hands beneath her arms and heaving her up the examination table. "She will be better here, for – *Dieu des chiens*, my friend, observe!"

As the heavy outdoor wrap the woman wore fell open we saw that it, a pair of modish patent leather pumps, her motor gloves and veil-draped hat were her sole wardrobe. From veil-swathed chin to blue-veined instep she was as nude as on the day she came into the world.

No wound showed on her ivory shoulders or creamy breast, but on her chest, immediately above the gently swelling breasts, was a medallion-shaped outline or cicatrix inside which was crudely tattooed the design of an inverted cross within a hexagram.

"Good heavens!" I exclaimed. "What *is* it?"

"*Précisement*, what is it – and what are these?" the little Frenchman countered, ripping aside the flimsy veil and exposing the girl's pale face. On each cheek, so deeply sunk into the flesh below the malar points that they could only be the result of branding, were two small, cruciform scars, perhaps three-quarters of an inch in height by half an inch in width, describing the device of a passion cross turned upside-down.

"Why, of all ungodly things–" I began, and:

"*Ha*, ungodly do you say, *mon vieux*? *Pardieu*, you call it by its proper name!" said Jules de Grandin. "An insult to *le bon Dieu* was intended, for this poor one wears upon her body–"

"I c-couldn't stand it!" moaned the girl upon the table. "Not that – not that! He looked at me and smiled and put his baby hand against my cheek! He was the image of my dear little – no, no, I tell you! You mustn't! O-o-oh, *no!*"

For a moment she sobbed brokenly, then: "Oh, *mea culpa, mea maxima culpa*! Remember not our offenses nor the offenses of our forefathers – spare us, good Lord – I will, I tell you! Yes I'll go to him and tell, if – Doctor de Grandin" – her voice sank to a sibilant whisper and she half rose from the table, glaring about with glazed, unseeing eyes – "Doctor de Grandin, watch for the chalk-signs of the Devil – follow the pointing tridents; they'll lead you to the place when – oh, *mea culpa, mea maxima culpa!* Have pity, Jesu!"

"Delirium," I diagnosed. "Quick, de Grandin, she's running a pretty high temperature. Help me turn her; the wound seems in her back."

It was. Puncturing the soft flesh a little to the left of the right shoulder, glancing along the scapula, then striking outward to the shoulder tip was a gunshot wound, superficial, but undoubtedly painful, and productive of extensive hemorrhage.

With probe and cotton and mercurochrome we sterilized the wound, then made a gauze compress liberally sprinkled with Senn's mixture and made it fast with cross-bandages of adhesive tape. Three-quarters of a grain of morphine injected in her arm provided a defense against recurring pain and sank her in a deep and peaceful sleep.

"I think she'd best be taken to a hospital," I told him when our work was finished. "We've given all the first aid that we can, and she'll be better tended there – we've no facilities for bed-rest here, or–"

"Agreed," He broke in, "To City Hospital, by all means. They have a prison ward there."

"But we can't put her there," I objected. "She's guilty of no crime, and besides, she's in no condition to go out alone for several days. She'll be there without the need of bars to keep her in."

"Not bars to keep her in," he told me. "Bars to *keep them out*, my friend."

"Them? Who–"

"The good God knows *who*, I only suspect *what*,' he answered. "Come, let us take her there without delay."

"Can't be done, son," Doctor Donovan told de Grandin when we arrived at City Hospital with our patient. "The prison ward's exclusively reserved for gents and ladies on special leave from the hoosegow, or those with some specific charge pending against 'em. You'd not care to place a charge against the lady, would you?"

De Grandin considered him a moment. "Murder is still a relatively serious offense, even in America," he returned thoughtfully. "Can not she be held as a material witness?"

"To whose murder?" asked the practical Donovan.

"The little Eastman boy's – he who was stolen from the Baptist Home last night," the Frenchman replied.

"Hold on, feller, be your age," the other cautioned. "Who says the little lad's been murdered? The police can't even find him alive, and till they find his body there's no *corpus delicti* to support a murder charge."

Once more the Frenchman gazed somberly, at him: "Whether you know it or not, my friend," he answered seriously, "that little one is dead. Dead as mutton, and died most unpleasantly – like the sinless little lamb was. Yes."

"Maybe you've got some inside dope on the case?" Donovan suggested hopefully.

"No – only reason and intuition, but they–"

"They won't go here," the other cut in. "We can't put this girl in the prison ward without a warrant of some sort, de Grandin: it's against the rules and as much as my job's worth to do it. There might be all sorts of legal complications: suits for false imprisonment, and that sort thing. But see here, she came fumbling at your door, mumbling all sorts of nonsense and clearly out of her head, didn't she?"

The Frenchman nodded.

"All right, then, we'll say she was batty, loony, balmy in the bean, as they say in classic Siamese. That'll give us an excuse for locking her up in H-3, the psychopathic ward. We've got stronger bars on those windows than we have in the prison ward. Plenty o' room there, too: no one but some souses sleeping off D.T.'s and the effects of prohibition whoopee. I'll move 'em over to make room for – by the way, what's your little playmate's name, anyhow?"

"We do not know," returned de Grandin. "She is *une innconnue*."

"Hell, I can't spell that," Donovan assured him. "We'll have to write her down unknown. All right?"

"Quite," the little Frenchman answered with a smile. "And now you will receive her?"

"Sure thing," the other promised.

"Hey, Jim!" he hailed an orderly lounging in the corridor, "bring the agony cart. Got another customer for H-3. She's unconscious."

"O.K. Chief," the man responded, trundling forward a wheeled stretcher.

Frightened, pitiful moans of voyagers in the borderland of horror sifted through the latticed doors of the cells facing the corridors of H-3 as we followed the stretcher down the hall. Here a gin-crazed woman sobbed and screamed in mortal terror at the phantoms of alcoholic delirium; there a sodden creature, barely eighteen, but with the marks of acute nephritis already on her face, choked and regurgitated in the throes of deathly nausea. "Three rousing cheers for the noble experiment," Doctor Donovan remarked, an ugly sneer gathering at the corners of his mouth. "I wish to God those dam' prohibitionists had to drink a few swigs of the kind of poison they've flooded the country with! If I had my way–"

"Jasus!" screamed a blear-eyed Irishwoman whose cell we passed. "Lord ha' mercy on us: 'tis she!" For a moment she clung to the wicket of her door like a monkey to the bars of its cage, staring horror-struck at the still form upon the stretcher.

"Take it easy, Annie," Donovan comforted. "She won't hurt you.".

"Won't hur-rt me, is it?" the woman croaked. "Won't har-rm me, wid th' Divil's silf mar-rchin' down th' hall beside her! Can't you see th' horns an' tail an' the flashin' fiery eyes of 'im as he walks beside her, Doctor darlin'? Oh, Lord ha' mercy; bless an' save us, Howly Mither!" She signed herself with the cross and stared with horror dazed, affrighted eyes at the girl on the litter till our pitiful procession turned the bend that shut us from her sight.

## 7. THE MUTTER OF A DISTANT DRUM

It was a windy night of scudding clouds which had brought a further fall of snow, and our progress was considerably impeded as we drove home from the hospital. I was nearly numb with cold and on the verge of collapse with fatigue when we finally stabled the car and let ourselves in the back door. "Now for that dose of brandy and bed," I promised myself as we crossed the kitchen;

"Yes, by blue," de Grandin agreed vigorously, "you speak wisdom, my friend. Me, I shall be greatly pleased to join you in both."

By the door of the consulting-room I halted. "Queer," I muttered. "I'd have sworn we turned the lights off when we left, but–"

"*S-s-sh!*" De Grandin's sibilant warning cut me short as he edged in front of me and drew the small but vicious automatic pistol, which he always carried, from its holster underneath his left armpit. "Stand back, Friend Trowbridge, for I, Jules de Grandin, will deal with them!" He dashed the door wide open with a single well-directed kick, then dodged nimbly back, taking shelter behind the jamb and leveling his pistol menacingly. "Attention, hands up – ! have you covered!" he called sharply.

From the examination table, where he had evidently been asleep, an under-sized individual bounced rather than rose, landing cat-like on both feet and glaring ferociously at the door where de Grandin had taken cover.

"Assassin!" he shouted, clenching his fists and advancing half a pace toward us.

"*Morbleu*, he has found us!" de Grandin almost shrieked. "It is the *apache*, the murderer, the robber of defenseless little ones and women! Have a care, monster!" – he leaped into the zone of light shed by the desk lamp and brandished his pistol – "stand where you are, if you would go on living your most evil life!"

Disdainful of the pistol as though it were a pointed finger the other advanced, knees bent in an animal-crouch, hands half closed, as though preparing for a death grip on de Grandin's throat. A single pace away he halted and flung wide his arms. "*Embrasse-moi!*" he cried, and in another moment they were locked together in a fond embrace like sweethearts reunited after parting.

"Oh Georges, *mon* Georges, you are the curing sight for tired eyes: you are truly heaven-sent!" de Grandin cried when he had in some measure regained his breath. "Between the sight of your so unlovely face and fifty thousand francs placed in my hand, I should assuredly have chosen you, *mon petit singe!*" To me he added:

"Assuredly you recall Monsieur Renouard, Friend Trowbridge? Georges Jean Jacques Joseph Marie Renouard, *Inspecteur du Service de la*

Sureté Generale?"

"Of course," I answered, shaking hands with the visitor. "Glad to see you again, Inspector." The little colonial administrator had been my guest some years before, and he, de Grandin and I had shared a number of remarkable adventures. "We were just about to take a drink," I added, and the caller's bright eyes lit up with appreciation. "Won't you join us?"

"*Parbleu*," Renouard assured me. "I do most dearly love your language, Monsieur Trowbridge, and most of all I love the words that you just said!"

Our liquor poured, we sat and faced each other, each waiting for the other to begin the conversation. At length:

"I called an hour or so ago," Renouard commenced, "and was admitted by your so excellent maid. She said that you were out, but bade me wait; then off she went to bed – nor do I think that she did count the silver first. She knows me. Yes, *bien alors*, I waited, and fell asleep doing so."

I looked at him with interest. Though shorter by some inches than the average American, Renouard could not be properly called under-sized. Rather, he was a giant in miniature. His very lack of height gave the impression of material equilibrium and tremendous physical force. Instinctively one felt that the thews of his arms were massive as those of a gladiator and that his torso was sheathed in muscles like that of a professional wrestler. A mop of iron-gray hair was brushed back in an uprearing pompadour from his wide, low brow, and a curling white mustache adorned his upper lip, while from his chin depended a white beard cut square across the bottom in the style beloved of your true Frenchman. But most impressive of all was his cold, pale face – a face with the pallor of a statue – from which there burned a pair of big, deep-set eyes beneath circumflexes of intensely bushy brows.

"*Eh bien, mon Georges*," de Grandin asked, "what storm wind blows you hither? You were ever the fisher in troubled water."

Renouard gulped down his brandy, stroked his mustache and tugged his beard, then drew forth a Russian leather case from which he extracted a "Maryland" cigarette. "Women, *parbleu*! One sometimes wonders why the good God made them." He snapped an English lighter into flame and with painstaking precision set his puissant cigarette aglow, then folded his big white hands demurely in his lap and glanced inquiringly at us with his bright dark eyes as though we held the answer to his riddle.

"*Tiens*, my friend." de Grandin laughed. "Had he not done so it is extremely probable that you and I would not be here indulging in this pleasant conversation. But women bring you here and why?"

Renouard expelled a double stream of acrid smoke from his nostrils, emitting a snort of annoyance at the same time. "One hardly knows the words to tell it," he replied.

"The trouble starts in Egypt. During the war, and afterward until the end of martial law in 1923, Egypt, apart from the Continental system of *maisons de tolerance*, was outwardly at least as moral as London. But since the strong clean hand of Britain has been loosed there has been a constantly increasing influx of white slaves to the country. Today hardly a ship arrives in Alexandria without its quota of this human freight. The trade is old, as old as Nineveh and Tyre, and to suppress it altogether is a hopeless undertaking, but to regulate it, ah, that is something different.

"We were not greatly exercised when the numbers of unfortunate girls going from Marseilles increased in Egypt, but when respectable young girls – *mais oui*, girls of more than mere *bourgeois* respectability, even daughters of *le beau monde*, were sucked beneath the surface, later to be boiled up as inmates of those infamous Blue Houses of the East – then we did begin to take sharp notice.

"They sent for me; 'Renouard,' they said, 'investigate and tell us what is which.'

"*Tres bon*, I did commence. The dossiers of half a dozen girls I took, and from the ground upward I did build their cases. Name of a little blue man!" He leaned forward, speaking in a low impressive tone scarce in a low, impressive tone scarce above a whisper: "There was devilment, literally, I mean, my friends, in that business. By example:

"Each one of these young girls was of an independent turn: she reveled in the new emancipation of her sex. Oh, but yes! So much she relished this new freedom that the ancient inhibitions were considered out of date. The good God, the gentle Christ Child, the Blessed Mother – *ah bah*, they were outmoded: she must follow after newer – or older – gods.

"*Eh bien*, exceedingly strange gods they were, too. In Berlin, Paris, London and New York there is a sect which preaches for its gospel 'Do What Thou Wilt; This Shall Be the Whole of the Law'. And as the little boy who eats too many bonbons inevitably achieves a belly-ache, so the the followers of this unbridled license reap destruction ultimately. But certainly.

"Each one of these young girls I find she has enlisted in this strange, new army of the freed. She has attended meetings where they made strange prayers to stranger gods, and – eventually she ends a cast-off plaything, eaten with drugs and surfeited with life, in the little, infamous Blue Houses of the East. Yes.

"I found them all. Some were dying, some were better dead, some had still a little way to tread the dreary, path of hell-in-life, but all – all, my friends – were marked with this device upon their breasts. See, I have seen him so often I can draw him from memory." Taking a black oil-cloth bound notebook from his pocket he tore out a leaf and scribbled a design upon it.

De Grandin and I stared at each other in blank amazement as he passed the sheet to us.

"Good Lord!" I ejaculated. "It's exactly like—"

"*Précisement; la même chose* — it is the same that Mademoiselle of the Veil displayed," de Grandin agreed. With shining eyes he turned to face Renouard. "Proceed, my friend," he begged. "When you have done we have a tale to tell."

"Ah, but I am far from done," the Inspector replied. "*Bien non*. I did investigate some more, and I found much. I discovered, by example, that the society to which these most unhappy girls belonged was regularly organized, having grand and subordinate lodges, like Freemasons, with a central body in control of all. Moreover, I did find that at all times and at all places where this strange sect met, there was a Russian in command, or very near the head. Does that mean anything to you? No?

"Very well, then, consider this: last year the Union of the Militant Godless, financed by the Soviet government, closed four thousand churches in Russia by direct action. Furthermore, still well supplied with funds, they succeeded in doing much missionary work abroad. They promoted all sorts of atheistic societies, principally among young people. In America on the one hand they gave much help to such societies as 'The Lost Souls' among college students, and on the other they greatly aided fanatical religious sects which aim at the abolition of innocent amusement — in the name of Christ. Associations for making the Sabbath Day unpleasant by closing of the cinemas, the shops and all places of recreation, have received large grants of money from the known agents of this Godless Union. Moreover, we know for certain that much of the legislation fostered by these bodies has been directly proposed by Russian agents posing as staunch upholders of fundamental religion. You see? On the one side atheism is promoted among the young, on the other religion's own ministers are whipped on by flattery or outright bribery to do such things as will make the churches hateful to all liberal-minded people. The scheme is beautifully simple, and it has worked well.

"Again: In England only half a year ago a clergyman was unfrocked for having baptized a dog, saying he would make it a good member of the Established Church. We looked this man's antecedents up and found that he was friendly with some Russians who posed as *emigrés* — refugees from the Bolshevik oppression. Now this man, who has no fortune and no visible means of support, is active every day in preaching radical atheism, and in weaning his former parishioners from their faith. He lives, and lives well. Who provides for him? One wonders.

"Defections in the clergy of all churches have been numerous of late, and in every instance one or more Russians are found on friendly terms with the apostate man of God.

"*Non*, hear me a little further," he went on as de Grandin was about to speak. "The forces of disorder, and of downright evil, are dressing their ranks and massing their shock troops for attack. Far in the East there is the mutter of a distant drum, and from the fastnesses of other lands the war-drum's beat is answered. Consider:

"In the Congo there is renewed activity by the Leopard Men, those strange and diabolical societies whose members disguise themselves as leopards, then seek and kill their prey by night, The authorities are taking most repressive measures, but still the Leopard Societies flourish more than ever, and the blacks are fast becoming unruly. There will be difficulties.

"In Paris, London and Berlin again and yet again churches are despoiled of sacred plate and blessed vestments, the host is stolen from the altar, and every kind of sacrilege is done. A single instance of this sort of thing, or even several, might be coincidence, but when the outrages are perpetrated systematically, not once, but scores of times, and always at about the same time, though in widely separated places, coincidences become statistics. There can no longer be a doubt; the black mass is being celebrated regularly in all the greater cities of the world; yet we do not think mere insult to God is all that is intended. No, there is some central, underlying motive for this sudden and widespread revival of satanism. One wonders what.

"And here another puzzle rises: in Arabia, north of Irak, in the Kurdish mountains, is the headquarters of a strange people called the Yezidees. About them we know little, save that they have served the Devil as their god time out of mind. Had they been strong numerically, they would have been a problem, for they are brave and fierce, and much given to killing, but they are few in number and their Moslem neighbors ring them round so thoroughly that they have been forced back upon themselves and seldom do they trouble those who do not trouble them. But" – he paused impressively – "on Mount Lalesh, where their great temple stands, strange things have been brewing lately. What it is we do not clearly know, but their members have been gathering from all parts of the East, from as far as Mongolia, in some instances, to celebrate some sort of mystic ceremony. Not only that, but strangers – Europeans, Africans, white, black and yellow men, who have no business being there, have been observed en route to Kurdistan, like pilgrims journeying to Mecca. Less than a month ago a party of brigands waylaid some travelers near Aleppo. Our *gendarmes* rescued them – they were a party of Americans and Englishmen, with several Spaniards as well and *all were headed for Kurdistan and Mount Lalesh*. Again one wonders why.

"Our secret agents have been powerless to penetrate the mystery.

We only know that many Russians have been sent to enter the forbidden city of the Yezidees: that the Yezidees, who once were poor, are now supplied with large amounts of ready cash; and that their bearing toward their neighbors has suddenly become arrogant.

"Wild rumors are circulated: there is talk of a revival of the cult of the Assassins, who made life terrible for the Crusaders and the Mussulmans alike. There are whispers of a prophetess to come from some strange land, a prophetess who will raise the standard of the Devil and lead his followers against the Crescent and Cross. Just what it is we do not surely know, but those of us who know the East can perceive that it means war. The signs are unmistakable; a revolution is fomenting. Some sort of unholy *jihad* will be declared, but where the blow will fall, or when, we can not even guess. India? Indo-China? Arabia? Perhaps in all at once. Who knows? London is preparing, so is Paris, and Madrid is massing troops in Africa – but who can fight a figure carved in smoke? We must know at whom to strike before we can take action, *n'est-ce-pas?*

"But this much I can surely tell: One single man, a so-mysterious man whose face I have not seen, but whose trail is marked as plainly as a snake's track in the dust, is always found at hand where the strings of these far-separated things are joined and knotted in a cord. He was a prime mover in the societies to which those wretched girls belonged; he was among those friendly with the unfrocked English clergyman; he was almost, but not quite, apprehended in connection with the rifling of the sanctuary of a church in Cologne; he has been seen in Kurdistan. Across France, England, Arabia and Egypt have I trailed him, always just a little bit too late, Now he is in America. Yes, *parbleu*, he is in this very city!

"*C'est tout!* I must find him, and finding him, I must achieve a method to destroy him, even if I have to stoop to murder. The snake may wiggle, even though his head has been decapitated, but God knows he can no longer bite when it is done. So do I."

Jules de Grandin leaned across the desk and possessed himself of Renouard's cigarette case, extracted from it a vile-smelling "Maryland" and lit it with a smile. "I know the answers to your problems – or some of them, at least – my friend," he asserted. "This very night there came to us – to this very house – a deserter from the ranks of the accursed, and though she raved in wild delirium, she did let fall enough to tell us how to find this man you seek, and when we find him–" The hard, cold light, which always reminded me of winter sunshine glinting on a frozen stream, came into his eyes, and his thin lips tightened in an ugly line. "When we have found him," he continued, "we shall know what to do. Name of an umbrella, we damn shall!

"The piecemeal information which you have fits admirably with what we already know and better yet with that which we suspect. Listen to me carefully—"

The sudden jangle of the telephone broke in.

"Doctor Trowbridge?" called a deep bass voice as I snatched up the instrument and growled a gruff "hullo?"

"Yes."

"Costello – Detective Sergeant Costello speakin'. Can you an' Doctor de Grandin be ready in five minutes to go wid me? I'd not be afther askin' ye to leave yer beds so early if it warn't important, sor, but—"

"That's all right, Sergeant, we haven't been to bed as yet," I told him. "We're pretty well done in, but if this is important—"

"Important: is it? Glory be to God, if th' foulest murther that iver disgraced th' Shtate o' Jersey ain't important, then I can't think what is. 'Tis out to th' Convent o' the Sacred Heart, by Rupleyville, sor, an' I'll take it kindly if ye'll go along wid me, sor. Th' pore ladies out there'll be needin' a docthor's services, I'm thinkin', an' St. Joseph knows I'm afther needin' all th' expert help that Doctor de Grandin can give me, too."

"All right, we'll be waiting for you," I replied as I put the monophone back in its hooks and turned to notify de Grandin and Renouard of our engagement.

# 8. "IN HOC SIGNO–"

The querulous crescendo of a squad car's siren sounded outside our door almost as I finished speaking, and we trooped down the front steps to join the big Irish policeman and two other plainclothes officers occupying the tonneau of the department vehicle. "Sure, Inspector Renouard," Costello greeted heartily as he shook hands, "'tis glad I am to see ye this mornin'. There's nothin' to do in this case but wor-rk like th' devil an' trust in God, an' th' more o' us there's here to do it, th' better our chances are. Jump in, gentlemen." To the uniformed chauffeur he ordered: "Shtep on it, Casey."

Casey stepped. The powerful Cadillac leaped forward like a mettlesome horse beneath the flailings of a lash, and the cold, sharp air of early winter morning was whipped into our faces with breathtaking force as we sped along the deserted road at nearly eighty miles an hour.

"What is it? What has happened?" de Grandin cupped his hands and shouted as we roared past the sleeping houses of the quiet suburb. Costello raised his gloved hand to his mouth, then shook his head. No voice was capable of bellowing above the screeching of the rushing wind.

Almost before we realized it we were drawn up before the tall graystone walls of the convent, and Costello was jerking vigorously at the bell-pull beside the gate. "From headquarters, Ma'am," he announced tersely, touching his hat as the portress drew back the little wicket in the door and gazed at us inquiringly.

Something more than ordinary silence seemed to brood above the big bare building as we followed our conductress down the clean-swept corridor to the public reception parlor: rather, it seemed to me, the air was charged with a sort of concentrated, apprehensive emanation of sheer terror. Once, when professional obligations required my attendance at an execution. I had felt some such eerie sensation of concentrated horror and anticipation as the other witnesses and I sat mute within the execution chamber, staring alternately with fright-filled eyes at the grim electric chair and the narrow door through which we knew the condemned man would soon emerge.

As we reached the reception room and seated ourselves on the hard, uncomfortable chairs, I suddenly realized the cause of the curiously anxious feeling which possessed me. From every quarter of the building – seemingly from floors and walls and ceilings – there came the almost mute but still perceptible soft sibilation of a whispered chorus. *Whisper, whisper, whisper*; the faint, half audible susurration persisted without halt or break, endless and untiring as the lisping of the tide upon the sands. It worried me, it beat upon my ears like water wearing on a stone: unless it stopped, I told myself, I would surely shout aloud with all my might for no other reason than to drown its everlasting monotonous reiteration.

The tap of light soled shoes and the gentle rustle of a skirt brought relief from the oppressive monotone, and the Mother Superior of the nunnery stood before us. Costello bowed with awkward grace as he stepped forward. De Grandin and Renouard were frigidly polite in salutation; for Frenchmen, especially those connected with official life, have not forgotten the rift between the orders and the Government of France existing since the disestablishment of 1903.

"We're from headquarters, Mother," Costello introduced: "we came as quickly as we could. Where is it – she – the body, if ye please?"

Mother Mary Margaret regarded him with eyes which seemed to have wept so much that not a tear was left, and her firm lips trembled as she answered: "In the garden, officer. It's irregular for men to enter there, but this is an emergency to which the rules must yield. The portress was making her rounds a little before matins when she heard somebody moving in the garden and looked out. No one was visible, but something looked strange to her, so she went out to investigate. She came to me at once, and I called your office on the 'phone immediately. Then we rang the bell and summoned all the sisters to the chapel. I told them what I thought they ought to know and then dismissed them. They are in their cells now, reciting the rosary for the repose of her soul."

Costello nodded shortly and turned to us, his hard-shaven chin set truculently. "Come on, gentlemen; lets git goin'," he told us. "Will ye lead us to th' gate?" he added to the Mother Superior.

The convent gardens stretched across a plot of level ground for several hundred feet behind the building. Tall evergreens were marshaled in twin rows about its borders, and neatly trimmed privet hedges marked its graveled paths. At the far end, by a wall of ivy-covered masonry some twelve feet high, was placed a Calvary, a crucifix, nine or ten feet high, set in a cairn, which overlooked the whole enclosure. It was toward this Costello led us, blue-black jaw set bellicosely. De Grandin swore savagely in mingled French and English as the light, powdery snow rose above the tops of his patent leather evening pumps and chilled his silk-shod feet. Renouard looked round with quick, appraising glances. I watched Costello's face, noting how the savage scowl deepened as he walked.

I think we recognized it simultaneously.

Renouard gave a short half-scream, half-groan.

"*Sacre nom de sacre nom de sacre nom!*" de Grandin swore.

"Jasus!" said Costello.

I felt a sinking in the middle of my stomach and had to grasp Costello's arm to keep from falling with the sudden vertigo of overpowering nausea. The lifeless figure on the crucifix was not a thing of plaster or of painted wood, it was human – flesh and blood!

Nailed fast with railway spikes through outstretched hands and slim crossed feet, she hung upon the cross, her slender, naked body white as carven ivory. Her head inclined toward her left shoulder and her long, black hair hung loosed across the full white breasts which were drawn up firmly by the outspread arms. Upon her head had been rudely thrust an improvised crown of thorns – a chaplet of barbed wire cut from some farmer's fence – and from the punctures that it made, small streams of coral drops ran down. Thin trickles of blood oozed from the torn wounds in her hands and feet, but these had frozen on the flesh, heightening the resemblance to a tinted simulacrum. Her mouth was slightly opened and her chin hung low upon her breast, and from the tongue which lay against her lower lip a single drop of ruby blood, congealed by cold even as it fell, was pendent like a ruddy jewel against the flesh.

Upon her chest, above her breasts, glowed the tattooed mark which we had seen when she appealed to us for help a scant four hours earlier.

Above the lovely, thorn-crowned head where the replica of Pontius Pilate's inscription had been set, another legend was displayed, an insulting, mocking challenge from the murderers: IN HOC SIGNO – "in this sign" – and then a grim, derisive picture of a leering devil's face.

"Ah, *la pauvre!*" de Grandin murmured. "Poor *Mademoiselle* of the Veil, were not all the bars and bolts of the hospital enough to keep you from them after all? I should have stayed with you, then they would not–" He broke off, staring meditatively at the figure racked upon the cross, his little, round blue eyes hardening as water hardens with a sudden frost.

Renouard tugged at his square-cut beard, and tears welled unashamed in his bright, dark eyes.

Costello looked a moment at the pendent figure on crucifix, then, doffing his hat, fell to his knees, signed himself reverently and began a hasty, mumbled prayer for the dying.

De Grandin neither wept nor prayed, but his little eyes were hard and cold as eyes of polished agate inlaid in the sockets of a statue's face, and round his small and thin-lipped mouth, beneath the pointed tips of his trim, waxed mustache, there gathered such a snarling grin of murderous hate as I had never seen. "Hear me, my friends," he ordered. "Hear me, you who hang so dead and lovely on the cross; hear me, all ye that dwell in heaven with the blessed saints," and in his eyes and on his face was the terrifying look of the born killer; "when I have found the one who did this thing, it had been better far for him had he been stillborn, for I shall surely give him that which he deserves. Yes, though he take refuge underneath the very throne of God Himself, I swear it upon this!" He laid his hand against the nail-pierced feet of the dead girl as one who takes a ritual oath upon a sacred relic.

It was grisly business getting her from the cross, but at last the spikes were drawn and the task completed. While Costello and Renouard examined every inch of trodden snow about the violated Calvary, de Grandin and I bore the body to the convent mortuary chapel, composed the stiffened limbs as best we could, then notified the coroner.

"This must by no means reach the press, *Monsieur*," le Grandin told the coroner when he arrived. "Promise you will keep it secret, at least until I give the word."

"H'm, I can't do that very well," Coroner Martin demurred. "There's the inquest, you know; it's my sworn duty to hold one."

"Ah, but yes; but if I tell you that our chances of capturing the miscreants who have done this thing depend upon our secrecy, then you will surely withhold publicity?" de Grandin persisted. "Can you not, by example, summon your jury, show them the body, swear them in, and then adjourn the public hearing pending further evidence?"

Mr. Martin lowered his handsome gray head in silent thought. "You'll testify the cause of death was shock and exposure to the cold?" he asked at length.

"Name of a small asparagus tree, I will testify to anything!" answered Jules de Grandin.

"Very well, then, We'll hush the matter up. I won't call Mother Mary Margaret at all, and Costello can tell us merely that he found her nude in the convent garden. Just how he found her is a thing we'll not investigate too closely. She disappeared from City Hospital psychopathic ward – the inference is she wandered off and died of exposure. It will be quite feasible to keep the jury from seeing the wounds in her hands and feet; I'll hold the official viewing in one of the reposing-rooms of my funeral home and have the body covered with a robe from the neck down. How's that?"

"*Monsieur*," de Grandin drew himself up stiffly and raised his hand in formal military salute, "permit me to inform you that you are a great man!

"*Allons*, speed, quickness, hurry, we must go!" he ordered when the pitiful body had been taken away and Costello and Renouard returned from their inspection of the garden.

"Where are we rushin' to now, sor?" the big detective asked.

"To City Hospital, *pardieu*! I would know exactly how it comes that one whose custody was given to that institution last night should thus be taken from her bed beneath their very noses and murderously done to death in this so foul manner."

"Say, de Grandin, was that gal you and Trowbridge brought here last night any kin to the late Harry Houdini?" Doctor Donovan greeted as we entered his office at City Hospital.

De Grandin favored him with a long, hard stare. "What is it that you ask?" he demanded.

"Was she a professional disappearing artist, or some thing of the kind? We saw her locked up so tight that five men and ten little boys couldn't have 'got her out, but she's gone, skipped, flown the coop; and not a soul saw her when she blew, either."

"Perfectly, we are well aware she is no longer with you," de Grandin answered. "The question is how comes it that you, who were especially warned to watch her carefully, permitted her to go."

"Humph, I wish I knew the answer to that one myself:' Donovan returned. "I turned in a few minutes after you and Trowbridge went, and didn't hear anything further till an hour or so ago when Dawkins, the night orderly in H-3, came pounding on my door with some wild story of her being gone. I threw a shoe at him and told him to get the devil away and let me sleep, but he kept after me till I finally got up in self-defense.

"Darned if he wasn't right, too. Her room was empty as a bass drum, and she was nowhere to be found, though we searched the ward with a fine-tooth comb. No one had seen her go – at least, no one will admit it, though I think someone's doing a piece of monumental lying."

"U'm?" de Grandin murmured non-committally. "Suppose we go and see."

The orderly, Dawkins, and Miss Hosskins, the night supervisor of the ward, met us as we passed the barred door. "No, sir," the man replied to de Grandin's quick: questions. "I didn't see or hear – gee whiz! I wonder if that could 'a' had anything to do with it – no, o' course it couldn't!"

"Eh?" de Grandin returned sharply. "Tell us the facts, *Monsieur*. We shall draw our own conclusions, if you please."

"Well sir," the man grinned sheepishly, "it was somewhere about five o'clock, possibly a bit later, an' I was sort o' noddin' in my chair down by th' lower end o' th' corridor when all of a sudden I heard a funny-soundin' kind o' noise – sort o' like a high wind blowin', or – let's see – well, you might compare it to the hum of a monster bee, only it was more of a whistle than a buzz, though there was a sort o' buzzin' sound to it, too.

"Well, as I was sayin', I'd been noddin', an' this sudden queer noise woke me up. I started to get up an' see what it was all about, but it didn't come again, so I just sat back an–"

"And went to sleep, eh?" Donovan cut in. "I thought you'd been lying, you swine. Fine chance we have of keeping these nuts in with you orderlies snoring all over the place!"

"*Monsieur* Donovan, if you please!" Renouard broke in with lifted hand. To Dawkins: "You say this was a high, shrill sound, *mon vieux*; very high and very shrill?"

"Yes, sir, it was. Not real loud, sir, but so awful shrill it hurt my ears to listen to it. It seemed almost as though it made me sort o' unconscious, though I don't suppose–"

"*Tiens*, but I do," Renouard broke in. "I think I understand." Turning to us he added seriously: "I have heard of him. Our agents in Kurdistan described him. It is a sound – a very high, shrill sound – produced by blowing on some sort of reed by those followers of Satan from Mount Lalesh. He who hears it becomes first deafened, then temporarily paralyzed. According to our agents' testimony, it is a refinement of the wailing of the Chinese screaming boys; that high, thin, piercing wail which so disorganizes the hearers' nervous system that his marksmanship is impaired, and often he is rendered all but helpless in a fight."

De Grandin nodded. "We know, my friend," he agreed. "The night *Mademoiselle* Alice disappeared we heard him – Friend Trowbridge and I – but that time they used their devil-dust as well, to make assurance doubly sure. It is possible that their store of *bulala-gwai* is low, or entirely exhausted, and so they now rely upon the stupefying sound to help them at their work.

"*Mademoiselle*," he bowed to Miss Hosskins, "did you too, by any chance, hear the strange sound?"

"I – I can't say I did," the nurse answered with embarrassment. "The fact is, sir, I was very tired, too, and was rather relying on Dawkins being awake to call me if anything were needed, so–" she paused, a flush suffusing her face.

"Quite so," de Grandin nodded. "But–"

"But I *did* wake up with a dreadful headache – almost as though something sharp had been thrust in my ears – just before Dawkins reported that the patient in 47 was missing," she added.

Again de Grandin nodded, "I fear there is nothing more to learn," he returned wearily. "Come, let us go."

"Doctor, Doctor darlin', they wuz here last night, like I told ye they'd be!" the drunken Irishwoman called to Donovan as we went past her door.

"Now, Annie," Donovan advised, "you just lie back and take it easy, and we'll have you in shape to go out and get soused again in a couple o' days."

"Annie th' divil, me name's Bridget O'Shay, an' well ye know it, bad cess to ye!" the woman stormed. "An' as fer shlapin' in this place again, I'd sooner shlape in hell, for 'tis haunted be divils th' house is!

"Last night, Doctor, I heard th' banshee keenin' outside me windy, an' 'Bridget O'Shay,' says I to mesilf, 'th' fairy-wife's come for ye!'

an' I lays down on th' floor wid both fingers in me ears to shtop th' sound o' her callin'.

"But prisently there comes a throop o' divils mar-rchin up th' corridor, th' one in front a-playin' on some sort o' divil's pipes which I couldn't hear a-tail, a-tail, fer havin' me fingers shtuck in me ears; an' walkin' clost behint him there wuz two others wans, an' they all wuz walkin' like they knew where they wuz goin'.

"I watched 'em till they tur-rned th' bend an' then took me finger from wan ear, but quick enough I shtuffed it back, fer there wuz th' horriblest screamin' noise in all th' place as would 'a' deafened me entirely if I hadn't shtopped me ears agin.

"Prisently they come again, th' foremost wan still playin' on 'is pipes o' hell, an' wan o' carryin' sumpin acrost 'is shoulders all wrapped up in a blanket, whilst th' other wuz a-lookin' round from right to left, an' 'is eyes wuz like peat-fires bur-rnin' in a cave, sor, so they wuz. I ducked me head as he wint past, for well I knowed they'd murder me if I wuz seen, and I know what it wuz, too. 'Twas Satan on earth come fer that woman ye brung in here last night, an' well I know she'll not be seen agin!"

"Gosh, that *was* some case of jimjams you had last night!" Donovan laughed. "Better see Father O'Connell and take the pledge again, Annie, or they'll be putting you in the bughouse for keeps some of these days. It's true the girl's wandered off, but we don't think anything has happened to her. We don't know where she is, even."

"*Eh bien*, my friend," de Grandin contradicted as we left the psychopathic ward, "you are most badly mistaken. We know quite definitely where the poor one is."

"Eh? The devil!" Donovan returned. "Where is she?"

"Upon a slab in Coroner Martin's morgue."

"For Pete's sake! Tell me about it; how'd it happen; I'm interested–"

"The papers will contain a story of her death," de Grandin answered as he suppressed a yawn. "I, too, am interested greatly – in five eggs with ham to match, ten cups of coffee and twelve hours' sleep. *Adieu, Monsieur*."

## 9. THOUGHTS IN THE DARK

I was too near the boundary line of exhaustion to do more than dally with the excellent breakfast which Nora McGinnis, my super-efficient household factotum, set before us, but Renouard, with the hardihood of an old campaigner, wolfed huge portions of cereal, fried sausages and eggs and hot buttered toast, washing them down with innumerable cups of well-creamed coffee, while de Grandin, ever ready to eat, drink or seek adventure, stowed away an amazing cargo of food.

"*Très bon*, now let us sleep," he suggested when the last evidence of food had vanished from the table. "*Parbleu*, me, I could sleep for thirty days unceasingly, and as for food, the thought of it disgusts me!"

"Madame Nora," he raised his voice and turned toward the kitchen, "would it be too much to ask that you have roast duckling and apple tart for dinner, and that you serve it not later than five this evening? We have much to do, and we should prefer not to do it on an empty stomach."

"No office hours today, Nora," I advised as I rose, swaying with sleepiness, "and no telephone calls for of any of us, either, please. Tell anyone who cannot wait to in touch with Doctor Phillips."

How long I slept I do not know, but the early dark of midwinter evening had fallen when I sat suddenly bolt-upright in my bed, my nerves still vibrating like telephone wires in a heavy wind. Gradually, insistently, insidiously, a voice had seemed commanding me to rise, don my clothes and leave the house. Where I should go was not explained, but that I go at once was so insistently commanded that I half rose from the bed, reluctance, fear and something close akin to horror dragging me back, but that not-to-be-ignored command impelling my obedience. Then, while I wrestled with the power which seemed dominating me, a sudden memory broke into my dream, a memory of other dreams of long ago, when I woke trembling in the darkened nursery, crying out in fright, then the stalwart bulk of a big body bending over me, hands firm yet tender patting my cheek reassuringly, and the mingled comforting smell of starched linen. Russian leather and good tobacco coming through the darkness while my father's soothing voice bade me not to be afraid, for he was with me.

The second dream dispelled the first, but I was still a-tremble with the tension of the summons to arise when I struggled back to consciousness and looked about the room.

Half an hour later, bathed, shaved and much refreshed, I faced de Grandin and Renouard across the dinner table.

"*Par l'amour d'un bouc*, my friends," de Grandin told us, "this afternoon has been most trying. Me, I have dreamed most unpleasant dreams – dreams which I do not like at all – and which I hope will not soon be repeated."

"*Comment cela?*" Renouard inquired.

"By blue, I dreamed that I received direct command to rise and dress and leave the house – and what is more, I should have done so had I not awakened!"

"Great Scott," I interjected, "so did I!"

"Eh, is it so?"

Renouard regarded each of us in turn with bright, dark eyes, shrewd and knowing as a monkey's. "This is of interest," he declared, tugging at his square-cut beard. "From what we know, it would seem that the societies to which the unfortunate young ladies who first did bring me in this case belong, are mixed in some mysterious manner with the Yezidees of Kurdistan, *n'est-ce-pas?*"

De Grandin nodded, watching him attentively.

"Very well, then. As I told you heretofore, I do not know those Yezidees intimately. My information concerning them is hearsay, but it comes from sources of the greatest accuracy. Yes. Now, I am told, stretching over Asia, beginning in Manchuria and leading thence across Tibet, westward into Persia, and finally clear to Kurdistan, there is a chain of seven towered temples of the Yezidees, erected to the glorifying of the Devil. The chiefest of these shrines stands upon Mount Lalesh, but the others are, as the electricians say, 'hooked up in series'. No, underneath the domes of each one of these temples there sits at all times a priest of Satan, perpetually sending off his thought-rays – his mental emanations. Oh, do not laugh, my friends, I beg, for it is so! As priests or nuns professed to the service of God offer up perpetual adoration and prayers of intercession, so do these servants of the archfiend continually give forth the praise and prayer of evil. Unceasingly they broadcast wicked influences, and while I would not go so far as to assert that they can sway humanity to sin, some things I know.

"I said I did not know the Yezidees, but that is only partly so. Of them I have heard much, and some things connected with them I have seen. For instance: when I was in Damascus, seeking out some answer to the riddle of the six women, I met a certain Moslem who had gone to Kurdistan and while there incurred the enmity of the Yezidee priests. What he had done was not entirely clear, although I think that he had in some way profaned their idols. However that may be, Damascus is a long and tiresome journey from the confines of Lalesh, where Satan's followers hold their sway, but–

"Attend me" – he leaned forward till the candle-light struck odd reflections from his deep-set eyes – "this man came to me one day and said he had received command to go out into the desert. Whence the command came he did not know, but in the night he dreamed, and every night thereafter he had dreamed, always the same thing, that he arise and go into the desert 'Was it a voice commanding?' I did ask, and 'No,' he said, 'it was rather like a sound unheard but felt – like that strange ringing in his ears we sometimes have when we have taken too much quinine for the fever.'

"I sent him to a doctor and the learned medical fool gave him some pills and told him to forget it. *Ha*, forget that never-ending order to arise and leave, which ate into his brain as a maggot eats in cheese? As well he might have told one burning in the fire to dismiss all thought of torment from his mind!

"There finally came a time when the poor fellow could no longer battle with the psychic promptings of the priests of Satan. One night he left the house and wandered off. Some few days later the desert patrol found his burnoose and boots, or what was left of them. The jackals, perhaps with the aid of desert bandits, had disposed of all the rest.

"Now we tread close upon these evil-doers' heels. I have followed them across the ocean. You, my Jules, and you, *Monsieu*r Trowbridge, have stumbled on their path, and all of us would bring them to account for their misdoings. What then?

"What, indeed, but that one of them, who is an adept at the black magic of their craft, has thrown himself into a state of concentration, and sent forth dire commands to us – such subtle, silent orders as the serpent gives the fascinated bird? You, my Jules, have it. So have you, *Monsieur* Trowbridge, for both of you are somewhat psychic. Me, I am the hard, tough-headed old policeman, practical, seeing little farther than my nose, and then seeing only what I do behold, no more. Their thought-commands, which are a species of hypnotism, will probably not reach me, or, if they do, will not affect my conduct.

"Your greatest danger is while you sleep, for then it is the sentry of your conscious mind will cease to go his guardian rounds, and the gateway to your inner consciousness will be wide open. I therefore think it wise that we shall share one room hereafter. Renouard is watchful; long years of practicing to sleep with one hand on his weapon and one eye open for attack have schooled him for such work. You cannot move without knowing, and when I hear you move I wake you. And when I wake you their chain is broken. Do you agree?"

The thought occurred to Jules de Grandin and me at once.

"Alice–" I began, and:

"Yes, *parbleu*, *Mademoiselle* Alice!" cried de Grandin. "That message which she had, that constant but not understood command: 'Alice, come home!' It was undoubtlessly so given her. Remember, a day or so before she first received a spy of theirs, pretending to be seeking curios for some collector, came to the house, and saw the marriage girdle of the

Yezidees. That was what he wanted, to assure himself that the Alice Hume their spies had run to earth was indeed the one they sought, the descendant of that high priest's daughter of the ancient days, she who had run off with the Christian Englishman. Yes, *par la barbe d'un chat*, no wonder that she could write nothing else upon her ouija board that day: no wonder she puzzled why she had that thought-impression of command to go. Already they had planted in her mind the order to abandon home and love and God and to join herself to their unholy ranks!

"By blue, my Georges, you have solved two problems for us. It was you who told us of the meaning of that shrilling cry which Friend Trowbridge and I did hear the night on which she disappeared and which made the hospital *attachés* unable to repel invasion of their ward; now you have thrown more light upon the subject, and we know it was that *Mademoiselle* Alice had that thought-command to leave before she could suspect that such things were.

"I think it would be wise if we consulted–"

"Detective Sergeant Costello," Nora McGinnis announced from the dining-room door.

"Ah, my friend, come in," de Grandin cried. "You are in time to share a new discovery we have made."

Costello had no answering smile for the little Frenchman's greeting. His eyes were set in something like a stare of horror, and his big, hard-shaven chin trembled slightly as he answered:

"An' ye're in time to share a discovery wid *me*, sor, if ye'll be good enough to shtep into th' surgery a moment."

Agog with interest we followed him into the surgery, watched him extract a paper parcel from his overcoat pocket and tear off the outer wrappings, disclosing a packed of oiled silk beneath.

"What is it? What have you found?" de Grandin questioned eagerly.

"This," the Irishman returned. "Look here!" He tore the silken folds apart and dumped their contents on the instrument table. A pair of little hands, crudely severed at the wrists, lay on the table's porcelain top.

## 10. WORDLESS ANSWERS

De Grandin was the first to recover from the shock. The double background of long practice as a surgeon and years of service with the secret police had inured him to such sights as would break the nerve of one merely a doctor or policeman. Added to this was an insatiable curiosity which drove him to examining everything he saw, be it beautiful or hideous. With a touch as delicate as though he had been handling some frail work of woven glass he took one of the little hands between his thumb and forefinger, held it up to the surgery light and gazed at it with narrowed eyes and faintly pursed lips. Looking at him, one would have said he was about to whistle.

"A child's?" I asked, shrinking from too close examination of the ghastly relic.

"A girl's," he answered thoughtfully. "Young, scarcely more than adolescent, I should say, and probably not well to do, though having inclination toward the niceties of life. Observe the nails."

He turned the small hand over, and presented it palm-downward for my scrutiny. "You will observe," he added, "that they are nicely varnished and cut and filed to a point, though the shaping is not uniform, which tells us that the treatment was self-done, and not the work of a professional manicurist. Again, they are most scrupulously clean, which is an indication of the owner's character, but the cuticle is inexpertly trimmed; another proof of self-attention. Finally" – he turned the hand palm-up and tapped the balls of the fingers Iightly – "though the digits are white and clean they are slightly calloused at the sides and the finger tips and the nail region are inlaid with the faintest lines of ineradicable soil-occupational discoloration which no amount of soap and scrubbing-brush will quite remove. Only acid bleacher or pumice stone would erase them, and these she either did not know of, or realized that their continued use would irritate the friction-skin. *Enfin*, we have here the very pretty hands of a young working girl possessing wholesome self-respect, but forced to earn her daily bread by daily toil. A factory operative, possibly, surely not a laundress or charwoman. There is too much work-soil for the first, too little for the second."

Again he held the hand up to the light. "I am convinced that this was severed while she was alive," he declared. "See it is practically free of blood; had death occurred some time before the severance, the blood would not have been sufficiently liquid to drain off – though the operation might have been made a short time after death," he added thoughtfully.

"Have you anything to add, my friend?" he asked Costello.

"No, sor. All we know is we found th' hands," the Irishman replied. "They wuz found layin' side by side, wid th' fingers touchin', like they might 'a' been clasped in prayer, but had fallen apart like, *just outside th' wall o' convent garden, sor.*"

"*Nom d'un miracle du bon Dieu*!" exclaimed de Grandin, with that near-blasphemous intimacy he affected for the Deity. "I had some other things in mind tonight but this must take precedence. Come, let us go, rush, hasten, fly to where you found them, then lay our course from there until she shall be found!"

The Convent of the Sacred Heart stood on an elevation from which it overlooked surrounding territory, and in the hollow to the east lay the little settlement of Rupleyville, a neat but unpretentious place comprised for the most part of homes of thrifty Italians who had been graduated from section gangs upon the Lackawanna's right of way to small truck-farming, huckstering or fruit-stand keeping. A general store, a bakery, a little church erected to Saint Rocco, and a shop in which two glass globes filled with colored water and the sign *Farmacia Italiana* proclaiming its owner's calling were the principal edifices of the place.

To the latter de Grandin led us, and introduced himself in a flood of voluble Italian. The little wrinkled pharmacist regarded him attentively, then replied torrentially, waving his hands and elevating shoulders and eyebrows till I felt sure both would be separated from their respective sub-structures. At length:

"*Perfetto; eccellente*!" de Grandin cried, raising his hat ceremoniously. "Many thanks, Signor. We go at once." To us: "Come, my friends; I think that we are on the trail at last."

"What did you find out, sor?" Costello asked as the little Frenchman led us hurriedly down the single street the hamlet boasted.

"Ah, but of course, I did forget you do not speak Italian," de Grandin answered contritely. "When we had looked upon the spot where you did find the little hands, I told me, 'It are useless to stand here staring at the earth. Either the poor one from whom those hands were cut are living or dead. In any event, she are not here. If she are alive, she might have wandered off though not far, for the bleeding from her severed wrists would be too extensive. If she are dead, she could not have moved herself, yet, since she are not here, some one must have moved her. Jules de Grandin, let us inquire.'

"And so I led the way to this small village, and first of all I see the pharmacist's shop. 'Very good,' I tell me, 'the druggist are somewhat of a doctor; injured persons frequently appeal to him for help. Perhaps he will know something.' And so I interrogate him.

"He knew nothing of a person suffering grievous hurt, but he informed me that a most respectable old woman living near had come to him some time ago in greatest haste and implored that he would sell her opium, as well as something which would staunch the flow of blood. The woman was not suffering an injury. The inference is then that she sought the remedies for someone else. *N'est-ce-pas?* Of course. Very well, it is to her house that we go all quickly."

We halted at the small gate of a cottage garden. The paling fence was innocent of paint, but nearly whitewashed, as were the rough plank sidewalls of the house. An oil-lamp burned dimly in the single room the cottage boasted, and by its feeble light we saw an old woman, very wrinkled, but very clean, bending over a low bed which lay in shadow.

De Grandin knocked imperatively on the whitewashed door, then, as no answer was forthcoming, pushed back the panels and stepped across the threshold.

The room was nearly bare of furniture, the bed, a small table and two rough unpainted chairs completing its equipment. The little kerosene lamp, a cheap alarm clock and two gayly colored pictures of religious scenes were the sole attempts at ornament. The aged woman, scrupulously neat in smooth black gown and cheap jet brooch, straightened on her knees beside the bed as we came in and raised a finger to her wrinkled lips. "Quiet pleez," she murmured. "She iss a-sleepa. I have give" – she sought the English word, then raised her shoulders in a shrug of impotence and finished in Italian – "I give *oppio*."

De Grandin doffed his hat and bowed politely, then whispered quickly in Italian. The woman listened, nodded once or twice, then rose slowly and beckoned us to follow her across the room. "*Signori*," she informed us in a whisper. "I am a poor woman, me; but I have the means to live a little. At night – what you call him? *si*, scrub – I scrub floors in the bank at the city. Sometimes I come home by the bus at morning, sometimes I walk for save the money. Last night – this morning – I walk.

"I pass the *convento* just when the dark is turning into light today, and I go for walk downhill and I hear somebody groan – *o-oh, a-ah!* – like that. I go for see who are in trouble, and find this *povera* lying in the snow.

"*Dio Santo*, what you think? Some devil he have cut her arms off close by the hand! She is bleeding fast.

"I call to her, she try for answer, but no can. What you think some more? That devil have cut out her tongue and blood run out her mouth when she try to speak!

"I go for look some more. *Santissima Madonna*, her eyes have been put out! Oh, I tell you, *Signori*, it is the sight of sadness that I see!

"I think at first I run for help; then I think 'no, while I am gone she may die from bleeding. I take her with me.' So I do.

"I am very strong, me. All my life, in old country, in new country, I worka verree hard. Yes, sure. So I put her on my back – so! – and make the run – not walk, run – all way downhill to my house here. Then I put clothes upon her where her hands should be and put her in my bed; then I run all the way by the *farmacia* for medicine. The drug man not like for sell me *oppio*, but I beg him on my knee and tell him it is for save a life. Then he give it to me. I come back with a run and make soup of it and from it feed her with a spoon. At first she spit it out again, but after time she swallow it, and now she not feel no more pain. She is asleep, and when she wake I give her more until her hurt all better. I not know who she is, *Signori*, but I not like for see her suffer. She iss so young, so pretty, so – what you say? – niza? Yes. Sure."

De Grandin twisted his mustache and looked at her appreciatively. At length: "*Madame*, you are truly one of God's good noblewomen," he declared, and raised her gnarled and work-worn fingers to his lips as though they had been the white jeweled fingers of a countess.

"Now, quick, my friends," he called to us. "She must have careful nursing and a bed and rest and the best medical attendance. Call for an ambulance from the pharmacy, my sergeant. We shall await you here."

Swiftly, speaking softly in Italian, he explained the need of expert nursing to the woman, adding that only in a hospital could we hope to revive the patient sufficiently to enable her to tell us something of her assailants.

"But no!" the woman told him. "That can not be, *Signor*. They have cut off her hands, they have cut out her tongue, they have put out her eyes. She can not speak or write or recognize the ones who did it, even though you made them arrest and brought them to her. Me, I think maybe it was the Mafia did this, though they not do like this before. They kill, yes; but cut a woman up like this, no. Sicilians verree bad men, but not bad like that, I think."

"*Ma mère*," de Grandin answered, "though all you say is true, nevertheless I shall find a way for her to talk and tell us who has done this thing, and how we best may find him. How I shall do it I cannot tell, but that I shall succeed I am assured. I am Jules de Grandin, and I do not fail. Most of my life has been devoted to the healing of the sick and tracking down the wicked. I may not heal her hurts, for only God's good self can grow new hands and replace her ruined eyes and tongue, but vengeance I can take on those who outraged her and all humanity when they did this shameful thing, and may Satan roast me on a spit and serve me hot in my own gravy with damned, detestable turnips as a garnish if I do not so, I swear it. She shall talk to me in hell's despite.

"*Mais oui*, you must accept it," he insisted as he tendered her a bill and the woman made a gesture of refusal. "Think of your ruined gown, your soiled bed-clothing, and the trouble you have been to. It is your due, not a reward, my old one."

She took the money reluctantly, but thankfully, and he turned impatiently to me. "Stand by, my friend," he ordered; "we must go with her when they have come, for every moment is of preciousness. Me, I do not greatly like the looks of things; the brutal way in which her hands were amputated, the exposure to the cold, the well-meaning but unhygienic measures of assistance which the kindly one has taken. Infection may set in, and we must make her talk before it is too late."

"Make her talk?" I echoed in amazement. "You're raving, man! How can she talk without a tongue, or—"

"*Ah bah*!" he interrupted. "Keep the eyes on Jules de Grandin, good Friend Trowbridge. The Devil and his servants may be clever, but he is cleverer. Yes, by damn, much more so!"

The clanging ambulance arrived in a few minutes, for the call Costello sent was urgent, and a bored young intern, collegiate raccoon coat slipped on over his whites, entered the cottage, the stretcher-bearers close behind him. "Hear you got a pretty bad case here—" he began, then straightened as he saw de Grandin. "Oh, I didn't know you were in charge here, Doctor," he finished.

The little Frenchman, whose uncanny skill at surgery had made his name a by-word in the local clinics, smiled amiably. "Quickly, *mon brave*," he ordered. "It is imperative that we should get her hence as rapidly as possible. I desire to converse with her."

"O.K., sir," the youngster answered. "What's wrong?" He drew out his report card and poised a pencil over it.

De Grandin nodded to the litter-bearers to begin their task as he replied: "Both hands amputated by transverse cuts incising the *pronator quadratus*; the tongue clipped across the apex, both eyes blinded by transverse knife cuts across the cornea and striking through the anterior chamber and crystalline lens."

"You – she's had all that done to her, an' you're going to *converse* with her?" the boy asked incredulously. "Don't you mean–"

"I mean precisely what I say, *mon vieux*," de Grandin told him positively. "I shall ask her certain questions, and she shall answer me. Come, make haste, or it may be too late."

At the hospital, de Grandin, aided by a wondering nurse and intern, removed the old italian woman's make-shift bandages from the girl's severed wrists, applied a strong anodyne liniment of aconite, opium and chloroform, and wound fresh wrappings on the stumps with the speed and skill of one who served a long and strenuous apprenticeship in trench dressing-stations and field hospitals.

Some time elapsed before the strong narcotic soup administered by the old Italian lost its effect, but at length the patient showed slight signs of consciousness.

"*Ma fille*," de Grandin said, leaning forward till his lips were almost against the maimed girl's bandaged face, "you are in great trouble. You are temporarily deprived of speech and sight, but it is necessary that you tell us what you can, that we may apprehend those who did this thing to you. At present you are in Mercy Hospital, and here you will be given every care.

"Attend me carefully, if you please. I shall ask you questions. You shall answer me by spelling. Thus" – he seated himself at the foot of the bed and placed his hand lightly on the blanket where her feet lay – "for *a* you will move your foot once, for *b* twice, and so on through the alphabet. You understand?"

A pause, then a slight movement underneath the bedclothes, twenty-five twitches of the foot, then five, finally nineteen: "Y-e-s."

"*Très bon*, let us start." Drawing a notebook from his pocket he rested it upon his knee, then poised a stylographic pen above it. "Leave us, if you will, my friends," he ordered. "We shall be better if alone.

"Now, *ma pauvre*?" he turned toward the mutilated girl, ready to begin his interrogatory.

Several hours later he emerged from the sickroom, tears gleaming in his eyes and a taut, hard look about his mouth. "It is finished – done – completed," he announced, sinking wearily into a chair and in defiance of every house rule drawing out an evil-smelling French cigarette and setting it alight.

"What's finished?" I demanded. "Everything; all!" he answered. "My questioning and the poor one; both together. Name of a miracle, I spoke truth when I told her that blond lie and said her loss of sight and speech was temporary, for now she sees and sings in God's own Paradise. The shock and loss of blood she suffered were too much – she is gone."

He drew a handkerchief from his cuff and wiped his eyes, then: "But not until she told me all did she depart," he added fiercely. "Give me a little time to put my notes in order, and I shall read them to you."

Three-quarters of an hour later he and I, Costello Renouard were closeted in the superintendent's office.

"Her name was Veronica Brady," he began, referring to his transcript of the notes he had taken in the dead girl's room, "and she lived beneath the hill the other side the convent. She was an operative in the Hammel factory, and was due at work at slightly after seven. In order to arrive in time she had to take an early bus, and as the snow was deep, she set out early to meet the vehicle on the highway. As she was toiling up the hill this morning she was attracted by a group of people skirting the convent wall, a woman and three men. The woman was enveloped in some sort of long garment – it seemed to her like a blanket draped round her – and seemed struggling weakly and pleading with the men, two of whom pushed and drove her onward, like a beast to slaughter, while the third one walked ahead and seemed to take no notice of the others.

"They reached the convent wall, and one of the men climbed upon another's shoulders, seized the woman and dragged her up, then leaped the wall. The second man mounted on the third one's shoulders, reached the wallcrest, then leaned down and assisted his companion up. As the last one paused a moment on the summit of the wall, preparatory to leaping over into the garden, he spied Mademoiselle Veronica, jumped down and seized her, then called to his companions. They bade him bring her, and he dragged her to the wall and forced her up to the villain waiting at the top. Thereafter they drew her to the garden, gagged her with handkerchiefs and ripped her stockings off, binding her hands and feet with them. Then, while she sat propped against the wall, she witnessed the whole vile scene. The base miscreants removed the effigy of Christ from the crucifix and broke it into pieces; then with railway spikes they nailed the woman upon the cross, and thrust a crown of barbed wire on her head and set an inscription over her. This done, they stood away and cursed her with all manner of vile oaths and pelted her with snowballs while she hung and died in torment.

"At length the coming of the dawn warned them their time was short, and so they gave attention to their second victim. Explaining that the one whom they had crucified had paid the penalty of talking, they then informed poor Mademoiselle Veronica that they would save her from such fate by making it impossible that she should betray them. And then they took the bindings from her wrists and ankles, made her resume her stockings and walk with them until they reached the wall. Across the wall they carried her; then in the snow outside they bade her kneel and clasp her hands in prayer while she looked her last upon the world.

"The poor child thought they meant to kill her. How little could she estimate their vileness! For, as she folded her hands in supplication, *zic!* a sudden knife-stroke hit her wrists, and scarcely realizing what she did, she found herself looking down at two small, clasped hands, while from her wrists there spurted streams of blood. The blow was quick and the knife sharp; she scarcely felt the stroke, she told me, for it was more like a heavy blow with a fist or club than a severing cut which deprived her of her hands.

"But before she realized what had befallen her she felt her throat seized by rough hands, and she was choked until her tongue protruded. A sudden searing pain, as though a glowing iron had been thrust into her mouth, was lowed by a blaze of flashing light; then – darkness – utter, impenetrable darkness, such as she had never known before, fell on her, and in the snow she writhed in agony of mind and body. Shut off from every trace of light and with her own blood choking back the screams for help she tried to give, in her ears was echoed the laughter of her tormentors.

"The next she knew she was lifted from the snow and borne on someone's shoulders to a house, bandages were wound about her wrists and yes, and anon a biting, bitter mixture was poured into her tortured mouth. Then merciful oblivion until she woke to find herself in Mercy Hospital with Jules de Grandin questioning her.

"Ah, it was pitiful to make her tell this story with her feet, my friends, and very pitiful it was to see her die, but far rather would I have done so than know that she must live, a maimed and blinded creature.

"*Ha*, but I have not done. No. She told me of the men who did this *sacre*, dastard thing. Their leader was a monstrous-looking creature, a person with an old and wrinkled face, not ugly, not even wicked, but rather sad and thoughtful, and in his wrinkled face there burned a pair of ageless eyes, all but void of expression, and his body was the lithe, well-formed body of a youth. His voice, too, was gentle, like his eyes, but gentle with the terrible gentleness of the hissing serpent. And though he dressed like us, upon his head was set a scarlet turban ornamented with a great greenish-yellow stone which shone and flickered, even in the half-light of the morning, like the evil eye of a ferocious tiger.

"His companions were similar in dress, although the turbans on their heads were black. One was tall, the other taller. Both were swarthy of complexion, and both were bearded.

"By their complexions and their beards, and especially by their noses, she thought them Jewish. The poor one erred most terribly and slandered a most great and noble race. We know them for what they truly were, my friends – Kurdish hellions, Yezidee followers and worshippers of Satan's unclean self!"

He finished his recital and lit another cigarette. "The net of evidence is woven," he declared. "Our task is now to cast it over them."

"Ye're right there, sor, dead right," Costello agreed. "But how're we goin' to do it?"

De Grandin looked at him a moment, then started as one who suddenly recalls a duty unperformed. "By blue," he cried, "we must at once to *Monsieur* the Coroner's; we must secure those photographs before it is too late!"

## 11. THE STRAYED SHEEP

"Hullo, Doctor de Grandin," Coroner Martin greeted as we entered the private office of his luxurious funeral home, "there's been a young man from Morgan's Photonews Agency hanging around here waiting for you for the last hour or so. Said you wanted him to take some pictures, but couldn't say what. It might be all right, then again, it mightn't, and he may be on a snooping expedition – you never can tell with those fellows – so I told him to wait. He's back in the recreation room with my boys now, smoking his head off and cussing you out."

The quick smile with which de Grandin answered was more a mechanical facial contortion then an evidence of mirth. "Quite yes," he agreed. "I greatly desire that you let us take some photographs of *Mademoiselle l'Inconnue* – the nameless lady whose body you took in charge at the convent this morning. We must discover her identity, if possible. Is all prepared according to your promise?"

Professional pride was evident as Mr. Martin answered, "Come and see her, if you will."

She lay upon a bedstead in one of the secluded "slumber rooms" – apartments dedicated to repose of the dead awaiting casketing and burial – a soft silk comforter draped over her, her head upon a snowy pillow, and I had to look a second time to make sure it was she. With a skill which put the best of Egypt's famed practitioners to shame, the clever-handed mortician had eradicated every trace of violent death from the frail body of the girl, had totally obliterated the naiI-marks from her slender hands and erased the cruel wounds of the barbed wire from her brow. Even the deeply burned cross-brands on her cheeks had been effaced, and on her calm, smooth countenance there was a look of peace which simulated natural sleep. The lips, ingeniously tinted, were slightly parted, as though she breathed in light, half-waking slumber, and so perfect was the illusion of life that I could have sworn I saw her bosom flutter with faint respiration.

"Marvellous, *parfait, magnifique!*" de Grandin pronounced, gazing admiringly at the body with the approval one artist may accord another's work. "If you will now permit the young man to come hither, we shall take the pictures; then we need trouble you no more."

The young news photographer set up his camera at de Grandin's orders, taking several profile views of the dead girl. Finally he raised the instrument till its lens looked directly down upon the calm, still face, and snapped a final picture.

Next day the photographs were broadcast to the papers with the caption:

"*Who Knows Her?* Mystery woman, found wandering in the streets of Harrisonville, N. J., was taken to the psychopathic ward of City Hospital, but managed to escape. Next morning she was found dead from exposure in a garden in the suburbs. Authorities are seeking for some clue to her identity, and any one who recognizes her is asked to notify Sergeant J. Costello, Detective Bureau, Harrisonville Police Dept. (Photo by Morgan's Photonews, Inc.)"

We waited several days, but no response came in. It seemed that we had drawn a blank.

At last, when we had about abandoned hope, the telephone called me from the dinner table, and Costello's heavy voice advised: "There's a young felly down to headquarters, sor, that says he thinks he recognizes that there now unknown gur-rI. Says he saw her picture in th' *Springfield Echo*. Will I take 'im over to th' coroner's?"

"Might as well," I answered. "Ask Mr. Martin to let him look at the body; then, if he still thinks he knows her, bring him over and Doctor de Grandin and I will talk with him."

"Right, sor," Costello promised. "I'll not be botherin' ye wid anny false alarrms." I went back to dessert, Renouard and Jules de Grandin.

Some three-quarters of an hour later while we sipped our postprandial coffee and liqueurs in the drawing-room, the doorbell shrilled and Nora ushered in Costello and a serious-faced young man. "Shake hands wid Mr. Kimble, gentlemen," the sergeant introduced. "He knows her, a'right. Identified her positively. He'll be claimin' th' remains in th' mornin', if ye've no objections."

De Grandin shook hands cordially enough, but his welcome was restrained. "You can tell us whence the poor young lady came, and what her name was, perhaps, *Monsieur?*" he asked, when the visitors had been made comfortable with cognac and cigars.

Young Mr. Kimble flushed beneath the little Frenchman's direct, unwinking stare. He was tall, stoop-shouldered, hatchet-faced, bespectacled. Such animation as he had seemed concentrated in his rather large and deep-set hazel eyes. Except for them he was utterly commonplace, a man of neutral coloring, totally undistinguished, doomed by his very nature to the self-effacement consequent upon unconquerable diffidence. "A clerk or bookkeeper," I classified him mentally, "possibly a junior accountant or senior routine worker of some sort." Beside the debonair de Grandin, the fiery and intense Renouard and the brawny, competent Costello he was like a sparrow in the company of tanagers.

Now, however, whatever remnant of emotion remained in his drab, repressed personality welled up as he replied: "Yes sir, I can tell you;

her name was Abigail Kimble. She was my sister."

'U'm,' de Grandin murmured thoughtfully, drawing at his cigar. Then, as the other remained silent:

"You can suggest, perhaps, how it came she was found in the unfortunate condition which led to her incarceration in the hospital, and later to her so deplorable demise?" Beneath the shadow of his brows he watched the young man with a cat-stare of unwinking vigilance, alert to note the slightest sign betokening that the visitor had greater knowledge of the case than the meager information in the newspaper supplied.

Young Kimble shook his head. "I'm afraid not," he replied. "I hadn't seen her for two years; didn't have the slightest idea where she was." He paused for a moment, fumbling nervously with his cigar; then: "Whatever I may say will be regarded confidentially?" he asked.

"But certainly," de Grandin answered.

The young man tossed his cigar into the fire and leaned forward, elbows on knees, fingers interlaced. "She was my sister," he repeated huskily. "We were born and reared in Springfield. Our father was–" He paused again and hunted for a word, then: "A tyrant, a good church-member and according to his lights a Christian, so righteous that he couldn't be religious, so pious that he couldn't find it in him to be kind or merciful. You know the breed. We weren't allowed to play cards or dance, or even go to parties, he was afraid we might play 'kissing games'. We had family prayers each night and morning, and on Sunday weren't allowed to play – my sister's dolls and my toys were put away each Saturday and not allowed outside the closet till Monday morning. Once when he caught me reading *Moby Dick* – I was a lad of fifteen, too, then – he snatched it from me and threw it in the fire. He'd 'tolerate no novel-reading in a Christian home,' he told me.

"I stood for it; I reckon it was in me from my Puritan ancestors, but Abigail was different. Our grandfather had married an Irish girl – worked her to death and broke her heart with pious devilishness before she was twenty-five – and Abigail took after her. Looked like her, too, they said. Father used to pray with her, pray that she'd be able to 'tear the sinful image of the Scarlet Woman' from her heart and give herself to Jesus. Then he'd beat her for her soul's salvation, praying all the time."

A bitter smile lit up his somber features, and something, some deep-rooted though almost eradicated spirit of revolt, flickered in his eyes a moment. "You can imagine what effect such treatment would have on a high-spirited girl," he added. "When Abby was seventeen she ran away.

"My father cursed her, literally. Stood in the doorway of our home and raised his hands to heaven while he called God's curse upon a wilful, disobedient child."

Again the bitter, twisted smile flickered across his face "I think his

God heard him," he concluded.

"But, *Monsieur*, are we to understand you did not again behold your so unfortunate sister until–" de Grandin paused with upraised brows.

"Oh, yes, I saw her," the young man answered caustically. "She ran away, as I said, but in her case the road of the transgressor was hard. She'd been brought up to call a leg a limb and to think the doctors brought babies in their satchels. She learned the truth before a year had gone.

"I got a note from her one day, telling me she was at farmhouse outside town and that she was expecting a baby. I was working then and making fairly good money for a youngster, keeping books in a hardware store, but my father took my wages every Saturday night, and I was allowed only a dollar a week from them. I had to put that on the collection plate on Sunday.

"When Abby's letter came I was almost frantic. hadn't a nickel I could use, and if I went to my father he would quote something from the Bible about the wages of sin being death, I knew.

"But if you're driven far enough you can usually manage to make plans. I did. I deliberately quit my job at Hoeschler's. Picked a fight with the head bookkeeper, and made 'em discharge me.

"Then I told my father, and though I was almost twenty-one years old, he beat me till I thought I'd drop beneath the torture. But it was all part of my plan, so I gritted my teeth and bore it.

"I got the promise of another job before I quit the first one, so I went to work at the new place immediately; but I fooled the old man. My new salary was twenty dollars a week, twice as much as I'd received before, but I told him I had to take a cut in pay, and that they gave me only ten. I steamed the pay envelope open and took out ten dollars, then resealed it and handed it to him with remaining ten each Saturday. He never knew the difference.

"As quickly as I could I went to see my sister, told her not to worry, and engaged a doctor. I paid him forty dollars on account and signed notes for the balance. Everything was fixed for Abigail to have the proper care.

"He was a pretty little fellow, her baby; pretty and sweet and innocent as though he hadn't been a" – he halted, gagging on the ugly word, then ended lamely – "as if his mother had been married.

"Living was cheaper in those days, and Abby and the baby made out nicely at the farm for 'most two years. I'd had two raises in pay, and turned the increase over to her, and she managed to pick up some spare change at odd work, too, so everything went pretty well–" He stopped again, and the knuckles of his knitted hands showed white and bony as the fingers laced together with increased pressure.

"Yes my friend, until–" de Grandin prompted softly.

"Till she was taken sick," young Kimble finished. "It was influenza. We'd been pretty hard hit up Springfield way that spring, and Abigail was taken pretty bad. Pneumonia developed, and the doctor didn't hold out much hope to her. Her conscience was troubling her for running out on the old man and on account of the baby, too. I guess. Anyhow, she asked to see a minister.

"He was a young man, just out of the Methodist seminary, with a mouth full of Scriptural quotations and a nose that itched to get in other people's business. When she'd confessed her sin he prayed with her a while, then came hot-foot to the city and spilled the story to my father. Told him erring was human, but forgiveness divine, and that he had a chance to bring the lost sheep back into the fold – typical preacher's cant, you know.

"I was of age, then, but still living home. The old man came to me and taxed me with my perfidy in helping Abby in her life of shameful sin, and – what was worse! – holding back some of my salary from him. Then he began to pray, likening himself to Abraham and me to Isaac, and asking God to give strength to his arm that he might purge me of all sin, and tried to thrash me.

"I said tried, gentlemen. The hardware store I worked in had carried a line of buggy-whips, but the coming of the motor car had made them a back number. We hadn't had a call for one in years, and several of the men had brought the old things home as souvenirs. I had one. My father hit me, striking me in the mouth with his clenched fist and bruising my lips till they bled. Then I let him have it. All the abuse I'd suffered from that sanctimonious old devil since my birth seemed crying out for redress right then, and, by God, it got it! I lashed him with that whip till it broke in my hands, then I beat him with the stock till he cried for mercy. When I say 'cried', I mean just that. He howled and bellowed like a beaten boy, and the tears ran down his face as he begged me to stop flogging him.

"Then I left his house and never entered it again, not even when they held his funeral from it.

"But that didn't help my sister. The old man knew where she was living, and as soon as his bruises were healed he went out there, saw the landlady and told her he was the baby's grandfather and had come to take it home. My sister was too sick to be consulted, so the woman let him take the boy. He took him to an orphanage, and the child died within a month. Diphtheria immunization costs money, and the folks who ran that home – it was proof of a lack of faith in Providence to vaccinate the children for diphtheria, they said; but when you herd two hundred children in a place and one of 'em comes down with the disease, there's bound to be some duplication. Little Arthur died and they were going to bury him in Potter's Field, but I heard of it and claimed the body and gave it decent burial.

"My sister lay half-way between life and death for weeks. Finally she was well enough to ask for her son, and they told her he had gone off with his grandfather. She was almost wild with fear of what the old man might do to the child, but still too weak to travel, and the nervous strain she labored under set her back still further. It was nearly midsummer when she finally went to town.

"She went right to the house and demanded that he give her back her child – told him she'd never asked him for a cent and never would, and every penny that he'd paid out for the little boy would be refunded to him.

"He'd learned his lesson from me, but my sister was a mere woman, weak from a recent illness; no need to guard his tongue while he talked with her. And so he called her every vile name imaginable and that her hope of heaven was gone, for she was living with a parent's curse upon her. Finally he told her that her child was dead and buried in a pauper's grave. He knew that was a lie, but he couldn't forego the joy of hurting her by it.

"She came to me, half crazed with grief, and I did what I could to soothe her. I told her that the old man lied, and knew he lied, and that little Arthur had been buried in Graceland, with a tombstone set above his grave. Then, of course, she wanted to go see the place."

Tears were falling from the young man's eyes as he concluded: "I never shall forget that afternoon, the last time that I ever saw my little sister living. It was nearly dark when we reached the grave, and she had to kneel to make out the inscription on the stone. Then she went down like a mother bending by a crib, and whispered to the grass above her baby's face. 'Good-night little son; good-night and happy dreams, I'll see you early in the morning.' Then realization seemed to come to her. 'Oh, God,' she cried, 'there won't be any morning! Oh, my baby; my little baby boy! They took you from me and killed you, little son – they and their God!'

"And then beside her baby's grave she rose and held her hands up to the sky and cursed the father who begot her and who had done this thing to her; she cursed his church and his religion, cursed his God and all His works, and swore allegiance to the Devil! I'm not a religious man, gentleman. I had too big an overdose of it when I was a child, and I've never been in church since I left my father's house; but that wild defiance of hers and her oath of fealty to everything we'd been taught to hate and fear fairly gave me the creeps.

"I never saw her from that night to this. I gave her a hundred dollars, and she took the evening train to Boston where I understand she got mixed up with all sorts of radical movements. The last I heard of her before I saw her picture in the paper yesterday was when she wrote me from New York saying she'd met a Russian gentleman who was preaching a new religion; one she could subscribe to and accept. I didn't quite understand what it was all about, but I gathered it was some sort of New Thought cult, or something of the kind. Anyway, 'Do What Thou Wilt. This Shall Be the Whole of the Law' was its gospel, as she wrote it to me."

De Grandin leaned forward, his little round blue eyes alight with interest and excitement. "Have you, by any chance, a picture of your little nephew, *Monsieur*!" he asked.

"Why, yes, I think so," young Kimble answered. "Here's a snapshot I took of him and Abigail out at the farm the winter before her illness. He was about eight or nine months old then." From an inner pocket he drew a leather wallet and from it took a worn and faded photograph.

"*Morbleu*, I damn knew it; of course, that is the explanation!" de Grandin cried as he looked at the picture. "Await me, my friends, I shall return at once!" he shouted, leaping from his seat and rushing from the room. In a moment he was back, another picture in his hand. "Compare," he ordered sharply; "put them together, and tell me what it is you see."

Mystified but eager, Renouard, Costello and young Kimble leaned over my shoulder as I laid the photographs side by side upon the coffee table. The picture to the right was the one Kimble furnished us. It showed a woman, younger than the one we knew, and with the light of happiness upon her face, but indisputably the beautiful veiled lady whose tragic death had followed her visit to us. In her arms nestled a pretty, dimpled little boy with dark curling hair clustering in tendrils round his baby ears, and eyes which fairly shone with life and merriment.

The picture to the left was one de Grandin had obtained from the Baptist Home of the little Eastman boy who vanished. Though slightly younger, his resemblance to the other child was startling. Line for line and feature for feature, each was almost the perfect duplicate of the other.

De Grandin tweaked his mustache as he returned the snapshot to young Kimble. "Thank you, *Monsieur*," he said; "your story has affected us profoundly. Tomorrow, if you will make formal claim to your sister's body, no obstacle to its release will be offered by the coroner, I promise you." Behind the visitor's back he made violent motions to Costello, indicative to our wish to be alone.

The Irishman was quick to take the hint, and in a few minutes had departed with young Mr. Kimble. Half an hour later he rejoined us, a frown of deep perplexity upon his brow.

"I'll bite, Doctor de Grandin, sor," he confessed. "What's it all about?"

## 12. THE TRAIL OF THE SERPENT

"But it is obvious," the little Frenchman answered. "Do not you see it, Renouard, Trowbridge?" he turned his bright bird-like gaze on us.

"I'm afraid not," I replied. "Just what connection there is between the children's resemblance and–"

"*Ahe bah!*" he interrupted. "It is elementary. Consider, if you please. This poor Mademoiselle Abigail, she was hopelessly involved with the Satanists, is it not so?"

"Yes," I agreed. "From what her brother told us, there's not much doubt that the sect with which she was connected is the same one Renouard told us about, but–"

"But he roasted on the grates of hell! Can you think no farther back than the hinder side of your own neck, great stupid one? What did she say when she came rushing to this house at dead of night and begged us for protection? Think, remember, if you can."

"Why, she was raving incoherently; it's rather hard to say that anything she told us was important, but–"

"*Dites* – more of your *sacre* buts! Attend me: She came to us immediately after the small Baptist one had been abducted, and she did declare: 'He was the image of my dear little–' Her statement split upon that word, but in the light of what we now know, the rest is obvious. The little Eastman child resembled her dead baby; she could not bear to see him slaughtered, and cried out in horror at the act. When they persisted in this fiendishness she threatened them with us – with me, to be exact – and ran away to tell us how they might be found. They shot at her and wounded her, but she won through to us, and though she raved in wild delirium, she told enough to put us on the trail. But certainly. Did she not say, 'Watch for the chalk-signs of the Devil – follow the pointed trident'? But yes."

He turned to Sergeant Costello and demanded: "And have your men been vigilant, *mon vieux*? Do they keep watch for childish scrawls on house or fence or sidewalk, as I bade?"

Costello eyed him wonderingly. "Sure, they are," he answered. "Th' whole force has its orders to look out for 'em though th' saints know that ye're after wantin' wid 'em when ye find 'em."

"Very good," de Grandin nodded. "Attend me, I have known such things before. You, too, Renouard. Only a word was needed to put me on the trail. That word was furnished by the poor young woman whom they crucified.

"In Europe, when the Satanists would gather for their wicked rites they send some secret message to their members, but never do they tell the place of the meeting. No, the message might be intercepted and the police come. What then?

"Upon the walls of houses, on sidewalks, or on fences they draw a crude design of Satan, a foolish childish thing which will escape notice as scrawling of naughty little boys, but each of these drawings differs from the others, for whereas one will have the Devil's pitchfork pointing one way, another will point in a different direction. The variation will not be noticed by one who does not know the significance of the scrawls, but to those who know for what they look the pointing tridents are plain as markers on a motor highway. One need but follow the direction of the pointing tridents from picture to picture in order to be finally led right to the door of Satan's temple. Yes; of course. It is so."

"Indubitably," Renouard accorded, with a vehement nod.

"But what's th' little Eastman boy to do wid it!" Costello asked.

"Everything, *parbleu*," de Grandin and Renouard replied in sober chorus.

"It was undoubtlessly for the Black Mass – the Mass of Saint Secaire – the little one was stolen. Satan is the *singe de Dieu* – the impudent imitator of God and in his service is performed a vile parody of the celebration of the mass. The celebrant is, when possible, an unfrocked priest, but if such a one can not be found to do the office, any follower of the Devil may serve.

"In the latter case a wafer already consecrated must he stolen from the monstrance of the church or impiously borne from communion in the mouth of a mock-communicant. Then, robed as a priest, the buffoon who officiates ascends the Devil's altar and mouths the words prescribed in the missal, but reverses all the ritual gestures, kneeling backward to the altar, signing himself with the cross upside down and with his left hand, reciting such prayers as he pleases backward. At the end he holds aloft the sacred Host, but instead of veneration the wretched congregation shrieks out insults, and the elements are then thrown to the ground and trampled underfoot.

"*Ha*, but if a renegade priest can be persuaded to officiate, there is the foulest blasphemy of all, for he still has the words of power and the right to consecrate the elements, and so he says the mass from start to finish. For greater blasphemy the altar is the naked body of a woman, and when the rubric compels the celebrant to kiss the sanctuary, his lips are pressed against the human fair-cloth. The holy bread is consecrated, likewise the wine, but with the wine there is mingled the lifeblood of a little unbaptized baby boy. The celebrant, the deacon and sub-deacon partake of this unholy drink, then share it with the congregation, and also they accept the wafer, but instead of swallowing it in reverence they spit it forth with grimaces of disgust and every foul insult.

"You apprehend? The Mass of Saint Secaire was duly celebrated on the night poor *Mademoiselle* Abigail came knocking at our door, and the little Eastman boy had been the victim. You noticed that she wore no clothing. save her outdoor wraps? Was that mere eccentricity? No, *parbleu*, it was evidence no less. Evidence that she quit the nest of devils as she was and came forthwith to us with information which should lead to their undoing. She had undoubtlessly served as altar cloth that night, my friends, and did not tarry for an instant when she fled – not even long enough to clothe herself. The little victim of that night so much resembled her dead babe that the frozen heart within her was softened all at once, and she became once more a woman with a woman's tender pity, instead of the cold instrument of evil which her pious devil of a father had made her. Certainly. The strayed sheep had come back into the fold."

He tore the end from a blue packet of French cigarettes, set one of the vile-smelling things in his eight-inch amber holder, and thoughtfully ignited it. "Renouard, *mon vieux*," he said, "I have thought deeply on what you told us. I was reluctant at the first to credit what the evidence disclosed, but now I am convinced. When the small Eastman boy was stolen I could not fit the rough joints of the puzzle to each other. Consider–" He spread his fingers fanwise and checked the items off on them – "*Mademoiselle* Alice disappears, and I find evidence that *bulala-gwai* was used. 'What are the meaning of this?' I ask me. 'This snuff-of-sleep, he is much used by savage Africans, but why should he be here? It are a puzzle.'

"Next we find proof that *Mademoiselle* Alice is the lineal descendant – presumably the last one – of that Devil's priest of olden days whose daughter married David Hume. We also see that a spy of the Yezidees has proved her identity to his own satisfaction before she is abducted. The puzzle is more mystifying.

"Then we do find poor Madame Hume all dead. The outward evidence says 'suicide!' but I find the hidden proof of murder. Murder by the *roomal* of the *Thags* of India. *Que diable*? The *Thags* are worshippers of Kali, the Black Goddess, who is a sort of female devil, a disreputable half-sister of the Evil One, and in her honor they commit all sorts of murders. But what, I ask to know, are they doing here? Already we have Yezidees of Kurdistan, witch-doctors from Central Africa, now *Thags* from India injected in this single case. *Mon Dieu*; I suffer *mal de tête* from thinking, but nowhere can I find one grain of logic in it. *Non*, not anywhere, *cordieu*!

"Anon the little Eastman baby disappears. He is a Baptist; therefore, unbaptized. Time was, I know, when such as he were wanted for the mass of wickedness, but how can he be wanted by the Yezidees? They have no dealings with the Mass of Saint Secaire, the aping of a Christian rite is not a part of their dark ceremonies; yet here we have *bulala-gwai* again, and *bulala-gwai* was also used when the Yezidees – presumably –

stole *Mademoiselle* Alice from before our very eyes.

"'Have the Yezidees, whose cult is rooted in obscure antiquity, and dates back far beyond the Christian Era, combined the rites of medieval Satanists?' I ask. It are not likely, yet what is one to think?

"Then comes this poor young woman and in her delirium lets fall some words which, in the light of what we know tonight, most definitely connects the stolen baby – the baby stolen even as *Mademoiselle* Alice was – with the sacrifice of the Mass of Saint Secaire.

"Now I think of you and what you tell us. How you have found unfortunate young women, all branded on the breast like Mademoiselle Abigail, all of them once members of the sect of Satanists, each chapter of which unclean cult is led or inspired by one from Russia. And you tell us of this League of Godlessness which is a poisonous fungus spreading through the world from that cellar of unclean abominations we call Russia.

"'Pains of a most dyspeptic bullfrog,' I inform me. 'I see a little, so small light!' And by that light I read the answer to my riddle. It is this: as businessmen may take a dozen old and bankrupt enterprises possessed of nothing but old and well-known names, and weld them into one big and modern corporation which functions under a new management, so have these foes of all religion seized on the little, so-weak remnants of diabolism and welded them together in a formidable whole. In Africa, you say, the cannibal Leopard Men are on the rampage. The emissaries of Moscow are working with them – have they not brought back the secret of *bulala-gwai* to aid them in their work? In Kurdistan the Yezidees, an obscure sect, scarce able to maintain itself because it is ringed round by Moslems, is suddenly revived, shows new activity. Russia, which prays the world for charity to feed its starving people, can always find capital to stimulate its machinations in other lands. The Arabian *gendarmerie* find European pilgrims *en route* to Mount Lalesh, the stronghold of the Yezidees; such things were never known before, but–"

"'*Ha*, another link in this so odious chain!' I tell me. 'In Europe and in America the cult of Satanism, almost dead as witchcraft, is suddenly revived in all its awful detail. That it is growing rapidly is proved by the number of renegade clergymen of all faiths, a number never paralleled before in such short time. From all sides comes evidence of its activities; from London, Paris and Berlin we hear of violated churches; little children – always boys – are stolen in increasing numbers and are not held to ransom; they merely disappear. The connection is most obvious. Now we have proof that this vile cult is active in America – right here in Harrisonville, *parbleu*."

"My friends, upon the crumbling ruins of the ancient Yezidee religion and the time-obliterated relics of witchcraft and demonism of the

Middle Ages, this Union of the Godless are rearing a monstrous structure designed to crush out all religion with its weight. The trail of the serpent lies across the earth; already his folds are tightening round the world. We must annihilate him, or he will surely strangle us. Yes. Certainly."

"But Alice–" I began. "What connection has she with all this–"

"Much – all – everything," he cut in sharply. "Do you not recall what the secret agents of France have said, that in the East there is talk of a white prophetess who shall raise the Devil's standard and lead his followers on to victory against the Crescent and the Cross? That prophetess is Alice Hume! Consolidated with the demonology of the West, the Devil-Worship of the East will take new force. She has been sought – she has been found, *cordieu*! – and anon she will be taken to some place appointed for her marriage to the Devil; then, with the fanaticism of the Yezidees and the fervor of the atheistic converts as a motivating force, with the promise of the Devil's own begotten son to come eventually as a result of this marriage. with the gold of Soviet Russia and the contributions of wealthy ones who revel in the freedom to do wickedness this new religion gives, they will advance in open warfare. The time to act is now. If we can rescue *Mademoiselle* Alice and exterminate the leaders of this movement, we may succeed in stemming the tide of hell's rebellion. Failing that–" he spread his hands and raised his shoulders in a shrug of resignation.

"All right," I countered, "how do we go about it? Alice has been gone two weeks – ten days to be exact – and we haven't the slightest clue to her location. She may be here in Harrisonville, she may have gone to Kurdistan, for all we know. Why aren't we looking for her?"

He gazed at me a moment, then: "I do not lance an abscess till conditions warrant it." he answered. "Neither do we vent our efforts, fruitlessly in this case. *Mademoiselle* Alice is the focal point of all these vile activities. Where she is, there are the leaders of the Satanists – and where they are, there is she.

"From what *Mademoiselle* Abigail told us, we may assume there will be other celebrations of the Mass of Wickedness – when we find one of these and raid it, our chances of finding Alice are most excellent. Costello's men are on the lookout, they will inform us when the signs are out; until that time we jeopardize our chances of success by any move we make. I feel – I know – the enemy is concentrated here, but if we go to search for him he will decamp, and instead of the city which we know so well, we shall have to look for him only God knows where. *Alors*, our best activity is inactivity."

"But," I persisted, "what makes you think they're still in the city? Common sense would have warned them to get out before this, you'd think, and–"

"*Non*: you mistake," he told me bluntly. "The safest hiding-place is here. Here they logically should not be, hence this is the last place in which we should be thought to look for them. Again, temporarily at least, this is their headquarters in America. To carry out such schemes as they plan requires money, and much money can be had from converts to their cult. Wealthy men, who might fear to follow nothing but the dictates of their unconscionable consciences, will be attracted by the freedom which their creed permits, and will join them willingly – and willingly contribute to their treasury. It is in hope of further converts that they linger here, as well as to await the blowing over of the search for Alice. When the hue and cry has somewhat abated, when some later outrage claims the public interest, they can slip out all unnoticed. Until that time they are far safer in the shadows of police headquarters than if they took to hasty flight, and–"

*Br-r-r-ring!* The telephone's sharp warning shut him off.

"Costello? Yes, just a moment," I answered, passing the instrument to the sergeant.

"Yeah, sure – eh? Glory be to God!" Costello said, responding to the message from across the wire. To us: "Come on, gentlemen; it's time to get our feet against the pavement," he admonished. "Two hours ago some murderin' hoodlums beat up a nursemaid wheelin' a baby home from a visit wid its grandmother, an' run off wid it. An' the boys have found th' chalk-marks on th' sidewalks. It looks–"

"*Nom d'un chou-fleur*, it looks like action!" de Grandin cried exultantly. "Come, Friend Trowbridge; come, my Renouard, let us go at once, right away, immediately!"

Renouard and he hurried up the stairs while I went to the garage for the car. Two minutes later they joined us, each with a pair of pistols belted to his waist. In addition to the firearms, de Grandin wore a long curve-bladed Gurkha knife, a wicked, razor-bladed weapon capable of lopping off a hand as easily as a carving-knife takes off the wing of a roast fowl.

Costello was fuming with impatience. "Shtep on it, Doctor Trowbridge sor.' he ordered. "Th' first pitcher wuz at twenty-eighth an' Hopkins Streets; if ye'll take us there we'll be after follyin' th' trail – I've tellyphoned to have a raidin' party meet us there in fifteen minutes."

"But it is grand, it is immense; it is magnificent, my friend!" de Grandin told Renouard as we slipped through the darkened streets.

"It is superb!" Renouard assured de Grandin.

"Bedad, here's where Ireland declares war on Kur-rdistan!" Costello told them both.

## 13. INSIDE THE LINES

A large, black and very shiny limousine was parked at the curb near the intersection of 28$^{th}$ and Hopkins Streets, and toward it Costello led the way when we halted at the corner. The vehicle had all the earmarks of hailing from some high-class mortician's garage, and this impression was heightened by a bronze plate displayed behind the windshield with the legend *Funeral Car* in neat block letters. But there was nothing funereal – except perhaps potentially – about the eight passengers occupying the tonneau. I recognized Officers Hornsby, Giffigan and Schultz, each with a canvas web-belt decorated with a service revolver and nightstick buckled outside his blouse, and with a vicious-looking sub-machine gun resting across his knees. Five others, similarly belted, but equipped with fire axes, boathooks and slings of tear-bombs, huddled out of sight of casual passers-by on the seats of the car. "Camouflage," Costello told us with a grin, pointing to the funeral sign; then: "All Set. Hornsby? Got ever'thing, axes, hooks, tear-bombs, an–"

"All jake, sir. Got th' works," the other interrupted. "Where's th' party?"

The sergeant beckoned the patrolman loitering at the corner. "Where is it?" he demanded.

"Right here, sir," the man returned, pointing to a childish scrawl on the cement sidewalk.

We examined it by the light of the street lamp. Unless warned of its sinister connotation, no one would have given the drawing a second glance, so obviously was it the mark of mischievous but not exceptionally talented children. A crudely sketched figure with pot-belly, triangular head and stiffly jointed limbs was outlined on the sidewalk in white chalk of the sort every schoolboy pilfers from the classroom. Only a pair of parentheses sprouting from the temples and a pointed beard and mustache indicated the faintest resemblance to the popular conception of the Devil, and the implement the creature held in its unskilfully drawn hand might have been anything from a fishing-pole to a pitchfork. Nevertheless, there was one fact which struck us all. Instead of brandishing the weapon overhead, the figure pointed it definitely toward 29th Street. De Grandin's slender nostrils twitched like those of a hunting dog scenting the quarry as he bent above the drawing. "We have the trail before us," he whispered. "Come, let us follow it. *Allons!*"

"Come on, youse guys; folly us, but don't come too close unless we signal." Costello ordered the men waiting in the limousine.

Down Hopkins Street, shabby, down-at-the-heel thoroughfare that it was, we walked with all the appearance of nonchalance we could master, paused at 29th Street and looked about. No second guiding figure met our eye.

"Damn!" de Grandin swore. "*C'est singulier*. Can we have – *ah, regardez-vous, mes amis*!" The tiny fountain-pen searchlight he had swung in an ever-widening circle had picked out a second figure, scarcely four inches high, scribbled on the red-brick front of a vacant house. The trident in the demon's hand directed us down 29th Street toward the river.

A moment only we stopped to study it, and all of us were impressed at once with one outstanding fact; crudely drawn as it was, the second picture was a duplicate in miniature of the first, the same technique, if such a word could be applied to such a scrawl, was evident in every wavering line and faulty curve of the small picture. "*Morbleu*," de Grandin murmured, "he was used to making these, the one who laid this trail. This is no first attempt."

"*Mais non*," Renouard agreed.

"Looks that way," I acquiesced.

"Sure," said Costello. "Let's get goin'."

Block after block we followed the little sprawling figures of the Devil scrawled on sidewalk, wall or fence, and always the pointing tridents led us toward the poorer, unkempt sections of the city. At length, when we had left all residential buildings and entered a neighborhood of run-down factories and storehouses, de Grandin raised his hand to indicate a halt.

"We would better wait for reinforcements," he cautioned; "there is too great an opportunity for an ambuscade in his deserted quarter, and – *ah, par la barbe d' un poisson rouge*!" he cried. "We are in time, I think. Observe him, if you please."

Fifty or a hundred yards beyond us a figure moved furtively. He was a shadow of a man, sliding noiselessly and without undue movement, though with surprising speed, through the little patch of luminance cast by a flickering gas street-lamp. Also he seemed supremely alert, perceptive and receptive with the sensitiveness of a wild animal of the jungle stalking wary prey. The slightest movement of another in the semi-darkness near him would have needed to be more shadow-silent than his own to escape him.

"This," remarked Renouard, "will bear investigating. Let me do it, my Jules, I am accustomed to this sort of hunting." With less noise than a swimmer dropping into a darkened stream he disappeared in the shadow of a black-walled warehouse, to emerge a moment later halfway down the block where a street lamp stained the darkness with its feeble light. Then he melted into the shadow once again.

We followed, silently as possible, lessening the distance between Renouard and ourselves as quickly as we could, but making every effort at concealment.

Renouard and the shadow-man came together at the dead-end of a cross-street where the oil-stained waters of the river lapped the rotting piles.

"Hands up, my friend!" Renouard commanded, emerging from the darkness behind his quarry with the suddenness of a magic-lantern view thrown on a screen. "I have you under cover; if you move, your prayers had best be said!" He advanced a pace, pressing the muzzle of his heavy pistol almost into the other's neck, and reached forward with his free hand to feel, with a trained policeman's skill, for hidden weapons.

The result was surprising, though not especially pleasing. Like an inflated ball bounced against the floor, Renouard rose in the air, flew over the other's shoulder and landed with a groan of suddenly-expelled breath against the cobblestones, flat upon his back. More, the man whose skill at *ju-jitsu* accomplished his defeat straightened like a coiled steel spring suddenly released, drew an impressively large automatic pistol and aimed it at the supine Frenchman. "Say *your* prayers, if you know any, you–" he began, but Costello intervened.

Lithe and agile as a tiger, for all his ponderous bulk, the Irishman cleared the space between them with a single leap and swung his club in a devastating arc. The man sagged at the knees and sank face forward to the street, his pistol sliding from his unnerved hand and lying harmless in the dust beside him.

"That's that," remarked the sergeant. "Now, let's have a look at this felly."

He was a big man, more lightly built, but quite as tall as the doughty Costello, and as the latter turned him over, we saw that though his hair was iron-gray, his face was young, and deeply tanned. A tiny, dark mustache of the kind made popular by Charlie Chaplin and British subalterns during the war adorned his upper lip. His clothes were well cut and of good material, his boots neatly polished, and his hands, one of which was ungloved, well cared for – obviously a person with substantial claims to gentility, though probably one lacking in the virtue of good citizenship, I thought.

Costello bent to loose the buttons of the man's dark overcoat, but de Grandin interposed a quick objection. "*Mais non, mon sergent*," he reproved, "our time is short. Place manacles upon his hands and give him into custody. We can attend to him at leisure; at present we have more important pots upon the fire."

"Right ye are, sor." the Irishman agreed with a grin, locking a pair of handcuffs on the stunned man's wrists. He raised his hand in signal, and as the limousine slid noiselessly alongside: "Keep an eye on this bur-r-d, Hornsby," he ordered. "We'll be wantin' to give 'im th' wor-rks at headquarters – afther we git through wid this job, y'understand."

Officer Hornsby nodded assent, and we returned to our queer

game of hare and hounds.

It might have been a half-hour later when we came to our goal. It was a mean building in a mean street. The upper floors were obviously designed for manufacturing, for half a dozen signs proclaimed that desirable lofts might be rented from as many agents: "Alterations Made to Suit Tenant for a Term of Years". The ground floor had once been occupied by an emporium dispensing spirituous, malt and vinous liquors, and that the late management had regarded the law of the land with more optimism than respect was evident from the impressive padlock on the door and the bold announcement that the place was "Closed by Order of U.S. District Court".

Beside the door of what had been the family entrance in days gone by was a sketch of Satan, his trident pointing upward – the first of the long series of guiding sketches to hold the spear in such position. Undoubtedly the meeting place was somewhere in the upper portion of the empty-seeming building, but when we sought an entrance every door was closed and firmly barred. All, indeed, were furnished with stout locks on the outside. The evidence of vacancy was plain and not to be disputed, whatever the Satanic scrawl might otherwise imply.

"Looks like we're up agin a blank wall, sor," Costello told de Grandin. "This place is empty as a bass drum – probably ain't had a tenant since th' prohibition men got sore 'cause someone cut off their protection money an' slapped a padlock on th' joint."

De Grandin shook his head in positive negation. "The more it seems deserted the more I am convinced we are arrived at the right place," he answered. "These locks, do they look old?"

"H'm," the sergeant played his searchlight on the nearest lock and scratched his head reflectively. "No, sor, I can't say they do," he admitted. "If they'd been here for a year – an' th' joint's been shut almost that long – they ought to show more weather-stain, but what's that got to do wid–"

"*Ah, bah,*" de Grandin interrupted, "to be slow of perception is the policeman's prerogative, but you abuse the privilege, my friend! What better means of camouflage than this could they desire? The old locks are removed and new ones substituted. Each person who is bidden to the rendezvous is furnished with a key; he follows where the pointing spears of Satan lead, opens the lock and enters. *Voila tout!*"

"Wallah me eye," the Irishman objected. "Who's goin' to lock up afther 'im? If–"

A sudden scuffle in the dark, a half-uttered, half-suppressed cry, and the sound of flesh colliding violently with flesh cut him off.

"Here's a bird I found layin' low acrost th' street, sir," Officer Hornsby reported, emerging from the darkness which surrounded us, forcing an undersized individual before him. One of his hands was firmly twisted in the prisoner's collar, the other was clamped across his mouth, preventing outcry.

"I left th' gang in th' car up by th' entrance to th' alley," he continued, "an' come gum-shoein' down to see if I wuz needed, an' this gink must 'a' seen me buttons, for he made a pass at me an' missed, then started to let out a squawk, but I choked 'im off. Looks like he wuz planted as a lookout for th' gang, an–"

"Ah?" de Grandin interrupted. "I think the answer to your question is here, my sergeant." To Hornsby: "You say that he attempted an assault?"

"I'll tell th' cock-eyed world," the officer replied. "Here's what he tried to ease into me." From beneath his blouse he drew a short, curve-bladed dagger, some eight inches in length, its wicked keen-edged blade terminating in a vicious vulture's-beak hook. "I'd a' made a handsome-lookin' corpse wid that between me ribs," he added grimly.

De Grandin gazed upon the weapon, then the captive. "The dagger is from Kurdistan," he declared. "This one" – he turned his back contemptuously on the prisoner – "I think that he is Russian, a renegade Hebrew from the Black Sea country. I know his kind, willing to sell his ancient, honorable birthright and the god of his fathers for political preferment. What further did he do, if anything?"

"Well, sir, he kind of overreached his self when he drove at me wid th' knife – I reckon I must 'a' seen it comin', or *felt* it, kind of. Anyhow, he missed me, an' I cracked 'im on the wrist wid me nightstick, an' he dropped his sticker an' started to yell. Not on account o' the pain, sir – it warn't that sort o' yell – but more as if he wuz tryin' to give th' tip-off to 'is pals. Then I claps me hand acrost 'is trap an' lets 'im have me knuckles. He flings sumpin – looked like a bunch o' keys, as near as I could make out – away an' – well, here we are, sir."

"What'll I do wid 'im, Sergeant?" He turned inquiringly to Costello.

"Put th' joolry on 'im an' slap 'im in th' wagon wid th' other guy," the sergeant answered.

"I got you," Hornsby replied, saluting and twisting his hand more tightly in the prisoner's collar. "Come on, bozo," he shook the captive by way of emphasis, "you an' me's goin' bye-bye."

"And now, my sergeant, for the strategy," de Grandin announced. "Renouard, Friend Trowbridge and I shall go ahead. Too many entering at once would surely advertise our coming. The doors are locked and that one threw away the keys. He had been well instructed. To search for them would take up too much time, and time is what we cannot well afford to waste. Therefore you will await us here, and when I blow my whistle you will raid the place. And oh, my friend, do not delay your coming when I signal! Upon your speed may rest a little life. You understand?"

"Perfectly, sor," Costello answered. "But how're ye goin' to crack th' crib – git in th' joint, I mean?"

De Grandin grinned his elfish grin. "Is it not beautiful?" he asked, drawing something from the inside pocket of his sheepskin reefer. It was a long instrument of tempered steel, flattened at one end to a thin but exceedingly tough blade.

The Irishman took it in his hand and swung it to and fro, testing its weight and balance. "Bedad, Doctor de Grandin, sor," he said admiringly, "what an elegant burglar was spoilt when you decided to go straight!"

De Grandin motioned to Renouard and me, and crept along the base of the house wall. Arrived at a soiled window, he inserted the thin edge of his burglar tool between the upper and lower casings and probed and twisted it experimentally. The window had been latched, but a little play had been left between the sashes. Still, it took us but a moment to determine that the casings, though loose, were securely fastened.

"*Allons*," de Grandin murmured, and we crept to another window. This, too, defied his efforts, as did the next two which we tested, but success awaited us at our fifth trial. Persistence was rewarded, and the questing blade probed and pushed with gentle persuasion till the rusty latch snapped back and we were able to push up the sash.

Inside the storehouse all was darker than a cellar, but by the darting ray of de Grandin's flashlight we finally descried a flight of dusty stairs spiraling upward to a lightless void. We crept up these, found ourselves in a wide and totally empty loft, then, after casting about for a moment, found a second flight of stairs and proceeded to mount them.

"The trail is warm – *pardieu*, it is hot!" he murmured. "Come, my friends, forward, and for your lives, no noise!'

The stairway terminated in a little walled-off space, once used as a business office by the manufactory which had occupied the loft's main space, no doubt. Now it was hung with draperies of deep-red velours realistically embroidered with the figure of a strutting peacock some six or eight feet high. "Melek Taos – the Peacock Spirit of Evil. Satan's viceroy upon earth," de Grandin told us in a whisper as we gazed upon the image which his flashing searchlight showed. "Now do you stand close beside me and have your weapons ready, if you please. We may have need of them."

Across the little intervening space he tiptoed, put aside the ruddy curtains and tapped timidly on the door thus disclosed. Silence answered his summons, but as he repeated the hail with soft insistence the door swung inward a few inches and a hooded figure peered cautiously through the opening.

"Who comes?" the sentinel whispered. "And why have ye not the mystic knock?"

"The knock, you say?" de Grandin answered almost soundlessly. "*Morbleu*, I damn think that we have one—do you care for it?" Swiftly he swung the steel tool with which he had forced the windows and caught the hooded porter fairly on the cranium.

"Assist me, if you please," he ordered in a whisper, catching the man as he toppled forward and easing him to the floor. "So. Off with his robe, while I insure his future harmlessness."

With the waist-cord from the porter's costume he bound the man's hands and ankles, then rose, donned the red cassock and tiptoed through the door.

"*Ss-s-st!*" His low, sharp hiss came through the dark and we followed him into the tiny ante-room. A row of pegs was ranged around the wall, and from them hung hooded gowns of dark-red cloth, similar to that worn by the sentinel. Obedient to de Grandin's signaled order, Renouard and I arrayed ourselves in gowns, pulled the hoods well forward to obscure our features, and, hands clasped before us and demurely hidden in our flowing sleeves, crept silently across the vestibule, paused a moment at the swinging curtains muffling the door, then, with bowed heads, stepped forward in de Grandin's wake.

We were in the chapel of the Devil-Worshippers.

## 14. THE SERPENT'S LAIR

Hangings of dark-red stuff draped loosely from the ceiling of the hall, obscuring doors and windows, their folds undulating eerily, like fluttering cerements of unclean phantoms. Candles like votive lights flickered in cups of red glass at intervals round the walls, their tiny, lambent flames diluting rather than dispelling the darkness which hovered like vapor in the air. Only in one spot was there light. At the farther end of the draped room was an altar shaped in imitation of the Gothic sanctuary of a church, and round this blazed a mass of tall black candles which splashed a luminous pool on the deep red drugget covering the floor and altar-steps. Above the altar was set a crucifix, reversed, so that the thorn-crowned head was down, the nail-pierced feet above, and back of this a reredos of scarlet cloth was hung, the image of a strutting peacock appliquéd on it in flashing sequins. On the table of the altar lay a long cushion of red velvet, tufted like a mattress. Two ranks of backless benches had been set transversely in the hail, a wide center aisle between them, smaller aisles to right and left, and on these the congregation sat in strained expectancy, each member muffled in a hooded gown so that it was impossible to distinguish the features, or even the sex, of a given individual.

A faint odor of incense permeated the close atmosphere; not sweet incense, such as churches use, but something with a bitter, pungent tang to it, and – it seemed to me – more than a hint of the subtle, maddening aroma of burnt cannabis, the *bhang* with which fanatics of the East intoxicate themselves before they run amok. But through the odor of the incense was another smell, the heavy smell of paraffin, as though some careless person had let fall an open tank of it, soaking the thick floor-covering before the error could be rectified.

Somewhere unseen to us, perhaps behind the faintly fluttering draperies on the walls, an organ was playing very softly as Renouard, de Grandin and I stole quickly through the curtained doorway of the anteroom and, unobserved, took places on the rearmost bench.

Here and there a member of the congregation gave vent to a soft sigh of suppressed anticipation and excitement, once or twice peaked cowls were bent together as their wearers talked in breathless whispers; but for the most part the assemblage sat erect in stony silence, motionless, yet eager as a flock of hooded vultures waiting for the kill which is to furnish them their feast.

An unseen gong chimed softly as we took our seats, its soft resonant tones penetrating the dark room like a sudden shaft of daylight let into a long-closed cellar, and the congregation rose as one, standing with hands clasped before them and heads demurely bowed. A curtain by the altar was pushed back, and through the opening three figures glided.

The first was tall and gaunt, with a Slavic type of face, wild, fantastic eyes and thick, fair hair; the second was young, still in his early twenties, with the lithe, free carriage, fiery glance and swarthy complexion of the nomadic races of southeastern Europe or western Asia. The third was a small, frail, aged man – that is, he seemed so at first glance. A second look left doubt both of his frailty and age. His face was old, long, thin and deeply etched with wrinkles, hard-shaven like an actor's or a priest's and in it burned a pair of big, sad eyes – eyes like Lucifer's as he broods upon the high estate from which he fell. His mouth was tight-lipped, but very red, drooping at the corners, the mouth of an ascetic turned voluptuary. His body, in odd contrast to his face, seemed curiously youthful, erect and vigorous in carriage, a strange and somehow terrifying contrast, it seemed to me. All three were robed in gowns of scarlet fashioned like monks' habits, with hooded capes pendant at the back and knotted cords of black about the waist. On the breast of each was emblazoned an inverted passion cross in black; each had a tonsure shaven on his head: each wore red leather sandals on his feet.

A gentle rustling sounded as the trio stepped into the circle of light before the altar, a soughing of soft sighs as the audience gave vent to its pent-up emotion.

The old-young man moved quickly toward the altar, his two attendants at his elbows, sank to one knee before it it in humble genuflection; then, like soldiers at command to wheel, they turned to face the congregation. The two attendants folded hands before them, bringing the loose cuffs of their sleeves together; the other advanced a pace, raised his left hand as though in benediction and murmured: "*Gloria tibi, Lucifero!*"

"*Gloria tibi, Lucifero!*" intoned the congregation in low-voiced chant.

"Praise we now our Lord the Peacock, Melek Taos, Angel Peacock of our Lord the Prince of Darkness!" came the chanted invocation of the red priest.

"Hail and glory, laud and honor, O our Lord, great Melek Taos!" responded the auditors.

"Let us not forget the Serpent, who aforetime in the Garden undertook the Master's bidding and from bondage to the Tyrant freed our parents, Eve and Adam!" the red priest admonished.

"Hail thee, Serpent, who aforetime in the Garden men call Eden, from the bondage of the Tyrant freed our parents Eve and Adam!" cried the congregation, a wave of fervor running through them like fire among the withered grass in autumn.

The red priest and his acolytes wheeled sharply to the left and marched beyond the limits of the lighted semi-circle made by the altar candles, and suddenly the hidden organ, which had been playing a sort of soft improvisation, changed its tune. Now it sang a slow *andante* strain, rising and falling with persistent, pulsating quavers like the almost tuneless airs which Eastern fakirs play upon their pipes when the serpents rise to "dance" upon their tails.

And as the tremulous melody burst forth the curtains parted once again and a girl ran out into the zone of candlelight. For a moment she poised on tiptoe, and a gasp of savage and incredulous delight came from the company. Very lovely she was, violet-eyed, daffodil-haired, with a body white as petals of narcissi dancing in the wind. Her costume gleamed and glittered in the flickering candlelight, encasing her slim frame from hips to armpits like a coiled green hawser. It was a fifteen-foot live boa constrictor!

As she moved lithely through the figures of her slow, gliding dance to the sensuous accompaniment of the organ, the great reptile loosed its hold upon her torso and waved its hideous, wedge-shaped head back and forth in perfect time. Its glistening, scaly head caressed her cheek, its lambent forked tongue shot forth to meet her red, voluptuous mouth.

Gradually the wailing minor of the organ began to quicken. The girl spun round and round upon her toes, and with that odd trick which we have of noting useless trifles at such times, I saw that the nails of her feet had been varnished to a gleaming pink, like the nails of a hand, and as she danced they cast back twinkling coral-toned reflections of the candles' flames. The great snake seemed to waken. Silently, swiftly, its sleek body extended, flowing like a stream of molten green metal about the girl, slithering from her bare white breast to her bare white feet, then knotting once again about her hips and waist like a gleaming girdle of death. Round and round she whirled like a lovely animated top, her grisly partner holding her in firm embrace. Finally, as the music slowed once more, she fell exhausted to the carpet, and the snake again entwined itself about her body, its devilish head raised above her heaving shoulders, its beady eyes and flickering tongue shooting silent challenge to the world to take her from it.

The music still whined on with insistent monotone, ann the girl rose slowly to her knees, bowed to the altar till her forehead touched the floor and signed herself with the cross – in reverse, beginning at her breast and ending at her brow. Then, tottering wearily beneath the burden of the great snake's weight, she staggered through the opening between the swaying curtains.

The organ's wailing ceased, and from the shadow-shrouded rear of the hall there came the low intoning of a chant. The music was Gregorian, but the words were indistinguishable. Then came the high, sweet chiming of a sacring bell, and all the audience fell down upon their knees, heads bowed, hand clasped, as a solemn, robed procession filed up the aisle.

First marched the crucifer, arrayed in scarlet cassock and white surplice – and what a crucifix he bore! The rood was in reverse, the corpus hung head-downward, and at the staff-head perched the image of a strutting peacock, its silver overlaid with bright enamel, simulating the natural gaudy colors of the bird. Next came two men in crimson cassocks, each with a tall black candle flickering in his hand, and then a man who bore a staff of silver bells, which chimed and tinkled musically. Two other surpliced acolytes came next, walking slowly backward and swinging censers which belched forth clouds of pungent smoke. Finally the red priest, now clothed in full canonicals, chasuble, alb and amice, while at his elbows walked his two attendants in the dalmatic and tunicle of deacon and sub-deacon.

Two by two behind the men there came a column of girls garbed in a sort of conventual habit – long, loose-cuffed sleeves, full skirts reaching to the ankle, high, cope-like collars – all of brilliant scarlet embroidered with bright orange figures which waved like flickering flames as the garments swayed. The gowns were belted at the waist, but open at the throat, leaving chest and bust uncovered and disclosing on each breast the same symbol we had seen on Abigail Kimble's white flesh. Upon their heads they wore tall caps of stiff red linen, shaped somewhat like a bishop's miter and surmounted by the silver image of a peacock. As they walked sedately in the wake of the red priest their bare white feet showed with startling contrast to the deep red of their habits and the dark tones of the carpet.

A brazen pot of glowing charcoal was swung from a long rod borne by the first two women, while the next two carried cushions of red plush on which there lay some instruments of gleaming metal. The final members of the column were armed with scarlet staves which they held together at the tips, forming a sort of open arbor over a slight figure swathed in veils which marched with slow and faltering steps.

"*Morbleu*," de Grandin whispered in my ear, "*une proselyte*! Can such things be?"

His surmise was correct. Before the altar the procession halted, spread out fanwise, with the veiled girl in their midst. The women set their firepot on the altar steps and blew upon the embers with a bellows till they glowed with sudden life. Then into the red nest of coals they put the shining instruments and stood back, waiting, a sort of awful eagerness upon their faces.

"Do what thou wilt; this shall be the whole of the law!" the red priest chanted.

"Love is the law; love free and unbound," the congregation

intoned.

"Do what thou wilt shall be the law," the priest repeated; "therefore be ye goodly, dress ye in all fine raiment, eat rich foods and drink sweet wines, even wines that foam. Also take thy fill of love, when and with whom ye will. Do what thou wilt; this is the law."

The women gathered round the kneeling convert, screening her from view, as the red priest called:

"Is not this better than the death-in-life of slaves who serve the Slave-God and go oppressed with consciousness of sin, vainly striving after tedious virtues? There is no sin – do what thou wilt; that is the law!"

The red-robed women started back and left the space before the altar open. In the candle-lighted clearing, the altar-lights reflected in the jewels which glimmered in her braided hair, knelt the convert, stripped of her enshrouding veils, clad only in her own white beauty. The red priest turned, took something from the glowing fire-pot–

A short, half-strangled exclamation broke from the kneeling girl as she half started to her feet, but three watchful red-robed women sprang upon her, seized her wrist and head, and held her rigid while the priest pressed the glowing branding-iron tight against her breast, then with a deftness which denoted practise, took a second tool and forced it first against one cheek, and then the other.

The branded girl groaned and writhed within her guardians' grasp, but they held her firmly till the ordeal was finished, then raised her, half fainting to her feet and put a crimson robe on her, a yellow sash about her waist and a crimson miter on her head.

"Scarlet Women of the Apocalypse, behold your sister – Scarlet Woman, you have put behind your consciousness of right and wrong, look on the others of your sisterhood!" the red priest cried. "Show them the sign, that all may know that which ye truly are!"

Now pride, perhaps the consciousness that all connection with religious teaching had been cut, seemed to revive the almost swooning girl. Though tears still glinted on her eyelids from the torment she had undergone, a wild, bold recklessness shone in her handsome face as she stood forth before the other wearers of the brand and pridefully, like a queen, drew back her ruddy robe. displaying the indelible signs of evil stamped upon her flesh. Her chin was raised, her eyes glowed through their tears with haughty pride as she revealed the symbols of her covenant with hell.

The little silver bells burst forth into a peal of admonition. Priest and people dropped upon their knees as the curtains by the altar were drawn back and another figure stepped into the zone of candlelight.

Slowly, listlessly, almost like one walking in a dream she stepped. A long and sleeveless smock of yellow satin, thickset with red figures of dancing demons, hung loosely from her shoulders. A sort of ureus fashioned like a peacock was set crown-like on her head, rings set with fiery gems glowed on every toe and finger, great ruby pendants dangled from her ears. She seemed a very Queen in Babylon as she proceeded to the altar between the ranks of groveling priests and women and sank to her knees, then rose and signed herself with the cross, beginning at the breast and ending at the brow.

A whispered ripple which became a wave ran rapidly from lip to lip: "It's she; the Queen, the Prophetess, the Bride-Elect! She has graced us with her presence!"

De Grandin murmured something in my ear, but I did not hear him. My other senses seemed paralyzed as my gaze held with unbelieving horror to the woman standing at the altar. The Queen – the Devil's Bride-Elect – was Alice Hume.

## 15. THE MASS OF ST. SECAIRE

Preparations for the sacrilegious sacrament had been carefully rehearsed. For a long moment Alice stood erect before the altar, head bowed, hands clasped beneath her chin; then parting her hands and raising them palm-forward to the level of her temples, she dropped as though forced downward by invincible pressure, and we heard the softly thudding impact as she flung herself prostrate and beat her brow and palms against the crimson altar-carpet in utter self abasement.

"Is all prepared?" the red priest called as, flanked deacon and sub-deacon, he paused before the altar steps.

"Not yet; we make the sanctuary ready!" two of scarlet-robed women returned in chorus as they stepped forward, bent and raised Alice Hume between them. Quickly, like skilled tiring women working at their trade, they lifted off her yellow robe with its decorations of gyrating devils, drew the glinting ruby rings from her toes and fingers, unhooked the flashing pendants from the holes bored through her ears. Then they unloosed her hair, and as the cloven tide of silken tresses rippled down, took her by the hands and led her slowly up the stairway to the altar. There one of them crouched to the floor, forming herself into a living stepping-stone, while, assisted by the other, Alice trod upon her back, mounted to the altar and laid her white form supine on the long, red cushion. Then, ankles crossed and hands with upturned palms laid flaccidly beside her, she closed her eyes and lay as still as any carven statue. They put the sacred vessels on her breast, the golden chalice thick-inlaid with gems, the heavy, hand-chased paten with its freight of small, red wafers, and the yellow plate shone brightly in the candlelight, its reflection casting halos of pale gold upon the ivory flesh.

The red priest mounted quickly to the altar, genuflected with his back to it, and called out: *Introibo ad altare Dei* – I will go up into the altar of God."

Rapidly the rite proceeded. The fifty-second Psalm – *quid gloriaris* – was said, but blasphemously garbled, God's name deleted and the Devil's substituted, so that it read: "Why boastest thou thyself, thou tyrant, that thou canst do mischief, whereas the evilness of Satan endureth yet daily?"

Then came confession, and, as *oremus te Domine* was intoned the priest bowed and kissed the living altar as provided by the rubric. Again repeating *Dominus vobiscum*, he pressed a burning kiss upon the shrinking flesh.

The sub-deacon took a massive black-bound book and bore it to the deacon, who swung the censer over it; then, while the other held it up before him, he read aloud:

"In the beginning God created seven spirits as a man lighteth one lamp from another, and of these Lucifer, whose true name is forbidden to pronounce, was chiefest. But he, offended by the way in which God treated His creations, rebelled against the Tyrant, but treachery was overthrown.

"Therefore was he expelled from heaven, but seized dominion of the earth and air, which he retaineth to this day. And those who worship him and do him honor will have the joys of life all multiplied to them, and at the last shall dwell with him in that eternal place which is his own, where they shall have dominion over hosts of demons pledged to do their will.

"Choose ye, therefore, man; choose ye whether ye will have the things of earth added to an endless authority in hell, or whether ye will submit to the will of the Tyrant of the Skies, have sorrow upon earth and everlasting slavery in the world to come."

The deacon and sub-deacon put the book aside, crossing themselves in reverse, and the call came mockingly: "May our sins be multiplied through the words contained in this Gospel."

The red priest raised the paten high above the living altar, intoning: "*Suscipe sancte Pater hanc immaculatum hostiam–*"

De Grandin fumbled underneath his robe. "Renouard, my friend," he whispered, "do you go tell the good Costello to come quickly. These cursed curtains round the walls, I fear they will shut in my whistle's sound, and we must have aid at once. Quickly, my friend, a life depends on it!"

Renouard slipped from his place and crept toward the door, put back the curtain with a stealthy hand, and started back dismayed. Across the doorway we had entered a barrier was drawn, an iron guard-door intended to hold back flames should the building catch afire.

What had occurred was obvious. Recovered from the blow de Grandin dealt him, the seneschal had struggled from his bonds and barred the portal, then – could it be possible that he had gone unseen behind the screen of curtains hanging from the walls and warned the others of our presence?

De Grandin and Renouard reached for their firearms, fumbling with the unfamiliar folds of their disguises

Before a weapon could be drawn we were assaulted from behind, our elbows pinioned to our sides, lengths of coiling cords wound tightly around our bodies. In less than half a minute we were helpless, firmly bound and set once more in our places on the bench. Silently and swiftly, as a serpent twines its coils about a luckless rabbit our assailants did their work, and only they and we, apparently, knew what occurred. Certainly the hellish ritual at the altar never faltered, nor did a member of the congregation turn round to see what passed behind.

Two women of the Scarlet Sisterhood had crept back of the curtains by the altar. Now they emerged, bearing between them a little, struggling boy, a naked, chubby little fellow who fought and kicked and offered such resistance as his puny strength allowed and called out to his "Daddy" and his "Mamma" to save him from his captors.

Down on the altar steps they flung the little boy; one woman seized his little, dimpled hands, the other took his feet, extending his small body to its greatest length. The deacon and sub-deacon had stepped forward.

I shut my eyes and bowed my head, but my ears I could not stop, and so I heard the red priest chant: "*Hic est enim calix sanguins mea* – this is the chalice of my blood–" I smelled the perfume of the incense, strong, acrid, sweet yet bitterly revolting, mounting to my brain like some accursed Oriental drug; I heard the wail which slowly grew in volume, yet which had a curiously muffled quality about it, the wail which ended in a little strangling, suffocated bleat!

I knew! Though not a Catholic, I had attended mass with Catholic friends too often not to know. The priest had said the sacred words of intention, and in a church the deacon would pour wine, the sub-deacon water in the chalice. But this was not a church: this was a temple dedicated to the Devil, and mingled with the red wine was not water... A bitter memory of my childhood hurried back across the years: they'd given me a lamb when I was five years old, all summer I had made a pet of it. I 'loved' the gentle, woolly thing. Then autumn came, and with it came the time for slaughter... that agonizing, strangling bleat! That blood-choked cry of utter anguish!

Another sound cut in. The red priest once again was chanting, this time in a language which I could not understand, a ringing, sonorous tongue, yet with something wrong about it. Syllables which should have been noble in their cadences were clipped and twisted in their endings.

And now *another voice* – an abominably guttural voice with a note of hellish chuckling laughter in it – was answering the priest, still in that unknown tongue. It rose and fell, gurgled and chuckled obscenely, and though its volume was not great it seemed to fill the place as rumbling thunder fills the summer sky. Sweat broke out on my forehead. Luckily for me I had been seated by my captors; otherwise I should have fallen where I stood. As surely as I knew my heart was hammering against my ribs, I knew the voice of incarnate evil was speaking in that curtained room – with my own ears I heard the Devil answering his votary!

Two red-robed priestesses advanced, one from either side of the altar. Each bore an ewer of heavy hammered brass, and even in the candles' changing light I saw the figures on the vessels were of revolting nastiness, beasts, men and women in attitudes of unspeakable obscenity.

The deacon and sub-deacon took the vessels from the women's hands and knelt before the priest, who dropped upon his knees with outspread hands and upturned face a moment, then rose and took the chalice from the human altar's gently heaving breast and held it out before him as a third red nun came forward, bearing in her outstretched hands a queer, teapot-like silver vessel.

I say a teapot, for that is what it most resembled when I saw it first. Actually, it was a pitcher made of silver, very brightly polished, shaped to represent a strutting peacock with fanned-out tail and erected crest, its neck outstretched. The bird's beak formed the spout of the strange pitcher, and a funnel-shaped opening in the back between the wings permitted liquids to be poured into it.

The contents of the chalice, augmented and diluted by ruby liquors from the ewers which the women brought, were poured into the peacock-pitcher – a quart or so, I estimated – and the red priest flung the chalice by contemptuously and raised the new container high above his head, so that its polished sides and ruby eyes flung back the altar candles' lights in myriad darting rays.

"Vile, detestable wretches – miscreants!" de Grandin whispered hoarsely. "They mingled blood of innocents, my friends; the wine which represents *le precieux sang de Dieu* and the life-blood of that little baby boy whose throat they cut and drained a moment ago! *Parbleu*, they shall pay through the nose for this if Jules de Grandin–"

The red priest's deep voice boomed an invitation: "Ye who do truly and earnestly repent you of all your good deeds, and intend to lead a new life of wickedness, draw nigh and take this unholy sacrament to your souls' damnation, devoutly kneeling!"

The congregation rose and ranged themselves upon their knees in a semi-circle round the altar. From each to each the red priest strode, thrusting the peacock's hollow beak into each opened mouth, decanting mingled wine and blood.

"You see?" de Grandin's almost soundless whisper came to me. "They study to give insult to the end. They make the cross-sign in reverse, the crucifix they have turned upside-down; when they administer their sacrament of hell they give the wine before the wafer, mocking both the Angelican and Latin rites. *Saligauds!*"

The ceremony proceeded to "*ite missa est*", when the celebrant suddenly seized a handful of red, triangular wafers from the paten and flung them broadcast out upon the floor. Pandemonium best describes the scene that followed. Those who have seen a group of urchins scrambling for coins tossed by some prankish tourist can vision how that audience of gowned and hooded worshippers of Satan clawed and fought for fragments of the host, groveled on the floor, snatching, scratching, grasping for the smallest morsel of the wafer, which, when obtained, they popped into their mouths and chewed with noisy mastication, then spat forth with exclamations of disgust and cries of foul insult.

As the guards who stood behind us joined the swinish scramble for the desecrated host, de Grandin suddenly lurched forward, hunched his shoulders, then straightened like a coiling spring released from tension. Supple as an eel – and as muscular – he needed but the opportunity to wriggle from the ligatures which lashed his elbows to his sides.

"Quick, my friends, the haste!" he whispered, drawing his sharp Gurkha knife and slashing at our bonds. "We must–"

"*Les gendarmes* – the police!"

The fire-door leading to the ante-room banged back as the hooded warder rushed into the hall, screaming his warnings. He turned, slammed the door behind him, then drew a heavy chain across it, snapping a padlock through its links. "They come – *les gendarmes*!" he repeated hysterically.

The red priest barked a sharp command, and like sailors trained to spring to quarters when the bugles sound alarm, some half-dozen Satanists rushed to the walls, upset the guttering votive lamps, then scuttled toward the altar. Their companions already had disappeared behind the curtains hanging round the shrine.

"*Qui est–*" Renouard began, but de Grandin cut him short.

"Quickly, for your lives!" he cried, seizing us by the elbows and forcing us before him.

Now we understood the heavy, sickening smell of kerosene which hovered in the room. From top to hem the shrouding curtains at the walls were soaked in it, requiring but the touch of fire to burst into inextinguishable flame. Already they were blazing fiercely where the upset lamps had lighted them, and the heavy, suffocating smoke of burning oil was spreading like mephitic vapor through the room. In a moment the place would be a raging hell of fire.

Beyond the heavy fire-door we heard Costello's peremptory hail: "Open up here: open in th' law's name, or we'll break th' door!" Then the thunder of nightsticks on the steel-sheathed panels; finally the trap-drum staccato of machine-gun bullets rattling on the metal barricade.

Too late to look for help that way, we knew. The door was latched and bolted, and barred with a locked chain, and a geyser of live flame was spurting upward round it, for the wooden walls were now ablaze, outlining the fireproof door in a frame of death.

Now the oil-soaked carpet had begun to burn; red tongues of flame and curling snakes of smoke were darting hungrily about our feet.

"On!" cried de Grandin, "it is the only way! They must have planned this method of defense in case of raid; surely they have left a rathole for their own escape!"

His guess seemed right, for only round the altar were the flames held back, though even there they were beginning to make progress.

Sleeves held before our faces for such poor protection as they gave, we stumbled toward the altar through the choking smoke. A big, cowled man rose out of nowhere in my path, and aimed a blow at me. Scarce knowing what I did I struck at him, felt the sharp point of my hunting knife sink into the soft flesh of his axilla, felt the warm blood spurt upon my hand as his artery was severed, and rushed on. I was no longer Samuel Trowbridge, staid, middle-aged practitioner of medicine, I was not even a man, I was a snarling, elemental beast, alive to only one desire, to save myself at any cost; to butcher anything that barred my path.

We lurched and stumbled up the stairway leading to the altar, for there the smoke was somewhat thinner, the flames a trifle less intense. "*Succes*," de Grandin cried, "the way lies here, my friends – this is the exit from their *sacre* burrow! Follow on; I can already see– *qui diable?*" He started back, his pistol flashing in the firelight.

Behind the altar, looming dimly through the swirling smoke, a man's shape bulked. One glance identified him. It was the big, young, white-haired man Costello had knocked unconscious to save Renouard an hour or so before.

In his arms he held the fainting form of Alice Hume.

## 16. FRAMED

"Hands up!" de Grandin barked. "Elevate your hands, or–"

"Don't be an utter ass," the other advised tartly. "Can't you see my hands are full?" Displaying no more respect for the Frenchman's pistol than if it had been a pointed finger, he turned on his heel, then flung across his shoulder as a sort of afterthought, "if you want to save your hides a scorching you'd best be coming this way. There's a stairway here – at least, there was fifteen minutes ago."

"*Fanons d' un corbeau*, he is cool, this one!" de Grandin muttered with grudging admiration, treading close upon the stranger's heels.

Sandwiched between our building and the next was a narrow, spiral stairway, a type of covered fire escape long since declared illegal by the city. Down this the stranger led us, de Grandin close behind him, his pistol ready, his flashlight playing steadily on the other's back. "One false step and I fire," he warned as we descended the dark staircase.

"Oh be quiet," snapped our guide. "One false step and I'll break my silly neck! Don't talk so much, you make me nervous."

Two paces ahead of us, he paused at the stairway's bottom, kicked a metal firedoor open, then drew aside to let us pass. We found ourselves in a narrow alleyway, darker than a moonless midnight, but with a single feeble spot of light diluting the blackness at its farther end, where the weak rays of a flickering gas street lamp battled with the gloom.

"Now what?" the little Frenchman asked. "Why do we stand here like a flock of silly sheep afraid to enter through a gate? Why–"

"*S-s-st!*" our guide's sharp hiss shut him off. "I think they're waiting for us out there, they – *ha?* I knew it!"

The faintly glowing reflection of the street lamp's light was shut off momentarily as a man's form bulked in the alley exit.

De Grandin tapped me on the arm. "*Elle est nue* – she has no protection from the chill," he whispered with a nod toward Alice. "Will you not put your robe upon her? I shall require mine for disguise a little longer, or–"

"All right," I answered, slipping off my scarlet cassock and draping it about the girl's nude loveliness while the man who held her in his arms assisted me with quick, deft hands.

"Dimitri-Franz?" a voice called cautiously from the alley entrance. "Are you there? Have you brought the Bride?"

For a moment we were silent, then: "Yes," our companion answered thickly, as though he spoke with something in his mouth, "she's here, but–"

His answer broke abruptly, and I felt rather than saw him shift the girl's weight to his left arm as he fumbled under his coat with his right hand.

"But what?" the hail came sharply. "Is she injured? You know the penalty if harm comes to her. Come here!"

"Here, take her," the stranger whispered, thrusting Alice into my arms. To de Grandin: "How about that pistol you've been so jolly anxious to shoot off, got it ready?"

"*Certainement. Et puis?*" the Frenchman answered.

"All right; look lively – this way!"

Silently as shadows the three of them, de Grandin, the stranger and Renouard, crept down the alley, leaving me to follow with the fainting girl as best I could.

Just inside the entrance to the passageway the stranger spoke again: "The Bride is safe, but–" Once more his thick speech halted; then, "Franz is hurt; he can not walk well, and–"

"Then kill him, and be quick!" the sharp command came back. "None must fall into their hands alive. Quick; shoot him, and bring the Bride, the car is waiting!"

A muffled shot sounded, followed by a groan, then:

"Bring the Prophetess at once!" came the angry command. "What are you waiting for–"

"Only for you, old thing!" With a booming shout of mingled exultation and hilarity, the strange man leaped suddenly from the shadow of the alley's mouth, seized his interrogator in his arms and dragged him back to the shelter of the passageway's arched entrance.

"Hold him, Frenchy!" he commanded. "Don't let him get away; he's–"

A spurting dart of flame stabbed through the darkness and a sharp report was followed by the vicious *whin-n-ng!* of a ricocheting bullet which glanced from the vaulted roof and whined past me in the dark.

I crouched to the cement pavement, involuntarily putting myself between the firing and the girl in my arms. A second report sounded, like an echo of the first, followed by a screaming cry which ended in a choking groan, then the sound of running feet.

"That's one who'll never slit another throat,"the stranger remarked casually.

I waited for a moment, then, as there seemed no further danger to my unconscious charge, rose and joined the others. "What happened?" I asked.

"Oh, as we were escaping from the fire up there this poor fellow came to help us, and this other one shot him," the unknown man replied coolly. "Rankest piece of cold-blooded murder I ever saw. Positively revoltin'. Eh, Frenchy?"

"But certainly," de Grandin agreed. "He shot the noble fellow down *a'froid*. Oh, yes; I saw it with my own two eyes."

"I, too," Renouard supplemented.

"Are you crazy?" I demanded. "I saw one of you grapple with this man, then when the other shot at you, you returned his fire, and–"

A kick which nearly broke my tibia was delivered to my shin. "*Ah bah*, how could you see, my friend?" de Grandin asked me almost angrily. "You were back there with *Mademoiselle* Alice, and the night is dark. I tell you this so estimable, noble fellow would have aided us, had not this vile miscreant assassinated him. He would have killed us, too – all three of us – had not *Monsieur* – er – this gentleman, gallantly gone forth and pulled him down with his bare hands at peril of his life. Yes, of course. That is how it was. See, here is the weapon with which the wicked murder was committed."

"Right-o, and ain't it unfortunate that it's a German gun?" the stranger added. "They'll never be able to trace it by its serial number, now. However, we're all eye-witnesses to the crime, and any ballistics expert will be able to match the bullet and the gun. So–"

"But you fired that shot!" I accused.

"I?" his tone was pregnant with injured innocence. "Why, I didn't have a weapon–"

"*Mais certainement*," de Grandin chimed in eagerly, "the sergeant took his weapon from him when they had their so unfortunate misunderstanding in the street." In a fierce whisper he added: "Learn to hold your tongue in matters not concerning you, my friend. *Regardez*!" He turned his flashlight full upon the prisoner's face.

It was the red priest.

The bellowing halloo of a fire engine's siren sounded from the other street, followed by the furious clanging of a gong. "Come," de Grandin ordered, "the fire brigade has come to fight the flames, and we must find Costello. I hope the noble fellow came to no harm as he tried to rescue us."

"Glory be, Doctor de Grandin, sor!" Costello cried as we rounded the corner and returned to the street from which we had entered the devil-worshippers' temple an hour or so earlier. "We waited for ye till we figgered ye'd been unable to signal, then went in to git ye; but th' murtherin' divils had barred th' door an' set th' place afire – be gob, I thought ye'd a'been cremated before this?"

"Not I," de Grandin answered with a chuckle. "It is far from so, I do assure you. But see, we have not come back empty-handed. Here, safe in good friend Trowbridge's arms, is she whom we did seek, and here" – he pointed to the red priest who struggled futilely in the big stranger's grasp – "here is one I wish you to lock up immediately. The charge is murder. Renouard and I, as well as this gentleman, will testify against him."

"Howly Moses! Who the divil let *you* out?" the sergeant demanded, as he caught sight of our strange ally. "I thought they put the bracelets on ye, an'–"

"They did," the other interrupted with a grin, "but I didn't think such jewelry was becoming to my special brand of homeliness, so I slipped 'em off and went to take a walk–"

"Oh, ye did, eh? Well, young felly me lad, ye can be afther walkin' right, straight back, or–"

"But no!" de Grandin cut in quickly, "I shall be responsible for him, my sergeant. He is a noble fellow. It was he who guided us from the burning building, and at the great peril of his life seized this wicked one and wrenched his pistol from him when he would have killed us. Oh, yes; I can most confidently vouch for him.

"Come to Doctor Trowbridge's when you have put that so wicked man all safely in the jail," he added as we made off toward my car. "We shall have much to tell you."

"But it was the only way, *mon vieux*," de Grandin patiently explained as we drove homeward. "Their strategy was perfect – or almost so. But for good luck and this so admirable young man, we should have lost them altogether. Consider: when they set fire to. that old building it burned like tinder; even now the fire brigade fights in vain to save it. With it will be utterly destroyed all evidences of their vile crimes, the paraphernalia of their secret worship – even the bones of their little victims.

"When their leader fell into our hands we had no single shred of evidence to hold him; he had simply to deny all we said, and the authorities must let him go, for where was proof of what he did? Nowhere, *parbleu* – it was burned up! Of course. But circumstances so fell out that we killed one of his companions. *Voila*, our chance had come! We had been wooden-heads not to have grasped it. So we conspire to forswear his life. As the good Costello would express it, we have put the frame around him. It is illegal, I admit, yet it is justice. You yourself know he did slay a little baby boy, yet you know we can not prove he did it; for none of us beheld the little corpse, and it is now but a pile of ashes mixed with other ashes. How many more like it there may be we do not surely know, but from what poor *Mademoiselle* Abigail told us, we know of one, at least.

"And must they die all unavenged? Must we stand by and see that spawn of hell, that devil's priest go free because as the lawyers say, the *corpus deliciti* of his crimes can not be established for want of the small corpses? Non, *cordieu*, I say it shall not be! While he may not suffer legally for the murders which he did, the law has seized him – and *pardieu*, the law will punish him for a crime he did not do. It may not be the law, my friend; but it is justice. Surely, you agree?"

"I suppose so," I replied, "but somehow it doesn't seem–"

"Of course it does," he broke in smilingly, as though a simple matter had been settled. "Our next great task is to revive *Mademoiselle* Alice, make her as comfortable as may be, then notify her grieving fiance that she is found. *Parbleu*, it will be like a tonic to see that young man's face when we inform him we have found her!"

## 17. "HIJI"

Alice was regaining consciousness as de Grandin and I carried her upstairs and laid her on the guest-room bed. More accurately, she was no longer in a state of actual swoon, for her eyes were open, but her whole being seemed submerged in a state of lethargy so profound that she was scarcely able to move her eyes and gaze incuriously about the room.

"*Mademoiselle*," de Grandin, whispered soothingly, "you are with friends. Nothing can harm you now. No one may order you to do that which you do not wish to do. You are safe."

"Safe," the girl repeated. It was not a query, not an assertion; merely a repetition, parrot-wise, of de Grandin's final word.

She gazed at us with fixed, unquestioning eyes, like a new-born infant, or an imbecile. Her face was blank as an unwritten sheet.

The little Frenchman gave her a quick, sharp glance, half surprised, half speculative. "But certainly," he answered. "You know us, do you not? We are your friends. Doctor Trowbridge, Doctor de Grandin."

"Doctor Trowbridge, Doctor de Grandin." Again that odd, phonographic repetition, incurious, disinterested, mechanical, meaningless.

She lay before us on the bed, still as she had lain upon the devil's altar, only the gentle motion of her breast and the half-light in her eyes telling us she was alive at all.

The Frenchman put his hand out and brushed the hair back from her cheeks, exposing her ears. Both lobes had been bored to receive the golden loops of the earrings she had worn, and the holes pierced through the flesh were large enough to accommodate moderately thick knitting-needles; yet the surrounding tissue was not inflamed, nor, save for a slight redness, was there any sign of granulation round the wounds. "Electrocautery," he told me softly. "They are modern in their methods, those ones, at any rate. Observe here, also, if you please–"

Following his tracing forefinger with my eyes, I saw a row of small, deep-pitted punctures in the white skin of her forearms. "Good heavens!" I exclaimed. "Morphine? Why, there are dozens of incisions! They must have given her enough to–"

He raised his hand for silence, gazing intently at the girl's expressionless, immobile face.

"*Mademoiselle*," he ordered sharply, "on the table yonder you will find matches. Rise, go to them, take one and light it; then hold your finger in the flame while you count three. When that is done, you may come back to bed. *Allez!*"

She turned her oddly lifeless gaze on him as he pronounced his orders. Somehow, it seemed to me, reflected in her eyes his commands were like writing appearing supernaturally, a spirit-message on a medium's blank slate. Recorded, somehow, in her intelligence – or, rather, perceptivity – they in nowise altered the paper-blankness of her face.

Docilely, mechanically and unquestioningly, like one who walks in sleep, she rose from the bed, paced slowly across the room, took up the tray of matches and struck one.

"Hold!" de Grandin cried abruptly as she thrust her finer in the flame, but the order came a thought too late.

"One," she counted deliberately as the cruel fire licked her ivory hand, then obedient to his latest order removed her finger, already beginning to glow angry-red with exposure to the flame, blew out the match, turned slowly, and retraced her steps. Not a word or inarticulate expression, not even by involuntary wincing, did she betray rebellion at his orders or consciousness of the sharp pain she must have felt.

"No, my friend," he turned to me, as though answering an unspoken question, "it was not morphine – then. But it must be so now. Quick, prepare and give a hypodermic of three-quarters of a grain as soon as is convenient. In that way she will sleep, and not be able to respond to orders such as mine – or worse."

Wonderingly I mixed the opiate and administered it, and de Grandin prepared a soothing unguent to bandage her burned finger. "It was heroic treatment," he apologized as he wound the surgical gauze deftly round her hand, "but something drastic was required to substantiate my theory. Otherwise I could not have rested."

"How do you mean?" I asked curiously.

"Tell me, my friend," he answered irrelevantly, fixing me with his level, unwinking stare, "have not you a feeling – have not you felt that *Mademoiselle* Alice, whatever might have been her provocation, was at least in some way partly guilty with those murderers who killed the little helpless babes in Satan's worship? Have not you–"

"Yes!" I interrupted. "I *did* feel so, although I hesitated to express it. You see, I've known her all her life, and was very fond of her, but – well, it seemed to me that though she were in fear of death, or even torture, the calm way in which she accepted everything, even the murder of that helpless child – confound it, that got under my skin! When we think how poor Abigail Kimble sacrificed her life rather than endure the sight of such a heartless crime, I can't help but compare the way Alice has taken everything, and–"

"*Precisement*," he broke in with a laugh. "I, too, felt so, and so I did experiment to prove that we were wrong. *Mademoiselle* Abigail – the good God rest her soul! – was herself, in full possession of her faculties, while *Mademoiselle* Alice was the victim of *scopolamin apomophia*."

"*Scopolamin apomophia?*" I repeated blankly.

"*Mais certainement*; I am sure of it."

"Isn't that the so-called 'truth serum'?"

"*Precisement.*"

"But I thought that had been discredited as a medical imposture–"

"For the purpose for which it was originally advertised; yes." he agreed. "Originally it was claimed that it could lead a criminal to confess his crimes when questioned by the officers, and in that it failed, but only because of its mechanical limitations.

"*Scopolamin apomophia* has a tendency so to throw the nervous system out of gear that it greatly lessens what we call the inhibitions, tearing down the warning signs which nature puts along the road of action. Subjected to its action, the criminal's caution, that cunning which warns him to refrain from talking lest he betray himself, is greatly lessened, for his volition is practically nullified. But that is not enough. No. Under *scopolamin apomophia*, if the injection be strong enough, he will repeat what is said to him, but that is not 'confession' as the law demands it. It is but parroting the accusation of the officers. So it has been discredited for judicial use.

"But for the purpose which those evil ones desired it was perfect. With a large dose of *scopolamin apomophia* injected in her veins, *Mademoiselle* Alice became their unresisting tool. She had no will nor wish nor consciousness except as they desired. Her mind was but a waxen record on which they wrote directions, and as the record reproduces words when placed upon the phonograph, so she reacted blindly to their orders.

"*Par exemple*: they dose her with the serum of *scopolamin apomophia*. They say to her, 'You will array yourself in such a way, and when the word is given you will stand thus before the altar, you will abase yourself in this wise, you will cross yourself so. Then you will permit the women to disrobe you until you stand all nude before the people, but you will not feel embarrassed. No. You will thereon mount the altar and lay yourself upon it as if it were a bed and stay there till we bid you rise.'

"And as they have commanded, so she does. Did you not note the similarity of her walk and general bearing when she crossed the room a moment ago and when she stood before the altar of the devil?"

"Yes," I agreed, "I did."

"*Tres bon.* I thought as much. Therefore, when I saw those marks upon her arms and recognized them as the trail of hypodermic needles, I said to me: 'Jules de Grandin, it are highly probably that *scopolamin apomophia* has been used on her.' And I replied, 'It are wholly likely, Jules de Grandin.'

"Very well, then. Let us experiment. It has been some time since she was dosed with this medicine which steals her volition, yet her look and bearing and the senseless manner she repeats our words back at us reminds me greatly of one whom I had seen in Paris when the *gendarmes* had administered *scopolamin apomophia* to him.

"*Bien alors*, I did bid her rise and hurt herself. Only a person whose instinct of self-preservation has been blocked would go and put his hand in living flame merely because another told him to, *n'est-ce-pas?*

"Yet she did do it, and without protest. As calmly though I requested that she eat a bonbon, she rose and crossed the room and thrust her so sweet finger into searing flame. *La pauvre*! I did hate myself to see her do it, yet I knew that unless she did I must inevitably hate her. The case is proved, good Friend Trowbridge. We have no need to feel resentful toward her. The one we saw bow down before the devil's altar, the one we saw take part in their vile rites, was not our *Mademoiselle* Alice. No, by no means, It was but her poor image, the flesh which she is is clothed in. The real girl whom we sought, and who we brought away with us, was absent, for her personality, her consciousness and volition were stolen by those evil men exactly as they stole the little boys they slew upon the altar of the devil."

I nodded, much relieved. His argument was convincing, and I was eager to be convinced.

"Now we have sunk her in a sleep of morphine, she will rest easily," he finished. "Later we shall see how she progresses, and if conditions warrant it, tomorrow young John Davisson shall once more hold his *amoureuse* against his heart. Yes. That will be a happy day for me.

"Shall we rejoin the others? We have much to talk about; and that Renouard, how well I know him! The bottle will be empty if we do not hasten!"

"So I hanged the blighters out of hand," the stranger was telling Renouard as de Grandin and I rejoined them in the study.

"Admirable. Superb. I approve," Renouard returned, then rose and bowed with jack-knife formality to the stranger, de Grandin and me in turn. "Jules, Doctor Trowbridge," he announced, "permit that I make you acquaint with Monsieur le Baron Ingraham, late of His Majesty's *gendarmerie* in Sierra Leone – Monsieur le Baron, Doctor Jules de Grandin, Doctor Trowbridge. I am Inspector Renouard of the *Service-Sureté*."

Smilingly the stranger acknowledged the introductions, adding: "It ain't quite as bad as the Inspector makes it out, gentlemen. My pater happened to leave me a baronetcy – with no money to support the title – but you'd hardly call me a baron, I fear. As to the *gendarmerie*, I was captain in the Sierra Leone Frontier Police, but–"

"Exactly, precisely, quite so," Renouard interjected. "It is as I said. Monsieur le Baron's experiences strangely parallel my own. Tell them, if you please *Monsieur le Bar–*"

"Give over!" cried the other sharply. "I can't have you *Monsieur le Baron*ing me all over the place, you know – it gives me the hump! My sponsors in baptism named me Haddingway Ingraham Jameson Ingraham – H-I-J-I, you know – and I'm known in the service as 'Hiji'. Why not compromise on that – we're all policemen here, I take it?"

"All but Doctor Trowbridge, who has both the courage and the wit to qualify," de Grandin answered. "Now, *Monsieur* Hiji, you were about to tell Inspector Renouard–" He paused with upraised eyebrows.

The big Englishman produced a small, black pipe and a tin of Three Nuns, slowly tamped tobacco in the briar and eyed us quizzically. He was even bigger than I'd thought at first, and despite his prematurely whitened hair, much younger than I'd estimated. Thirty-one or two at most, I guessed. "How strong is your credulity?" he asked at length.

"*Parbleu*, it is marvelous, magnificent," declared de Grandin. "We can believe that which we know is false, if you can prove it to us!"

"It'll take a lot of believing," Ingraham answered, "but it's all true, just the same.

"A year or so ago, about the time Inspector Renouard was beginning to investigate the missing girls, queer rumors began trickling back to Freetown from the Reserved Forest Areas. We've always had leopard societies in the back country – gangs of cannibals who disguise themselves as leopards and go out stalking victims for their ritual feasts – of course, but this seemed something rather new. Someone was stirring up the natives to a *poro* – an oath-bound resistance to government. The victims of the latest leopard outrages were men who failed to subscribe to the rebellion. Several village headmen and sub-chiefs had been popped into the pot by the leopard men, and the whole area was getting in an awful state of funk.

"Nobody wants to go up in the Reserved Forests, so they sent me. 'Let good old Hiji do it; Hiji's the lad for this show!' they said; so I took a dozen Houssa policemen, two Lewis guns and ten pounds or so of quinine and set out.

"Ten days back in the brush we ran across the leopards' spoor. We'd stopped at a Mendi village and I sent word forward for the headman to come out. He didn't come.

"That wasn't so good. If I waited too long for him outside the place I'd lose face; if I went in to him after summoning him to come to me; he would have 'put shame on me'. Finally I compromised by going in alone.

"The chief lolled before his hut with his warriors and women around him, and it didn't take more than half an eye to see he'd placed no seat for me.

"'I see you, Chief,' I told him, swaggering forward with the best assurance I could summon. I also saw that he was wearing a string of brummagem beads about his neck, as were most of his warriors, and wondered at it, for no license had been issued to a trader recently, and we'd had no reports of white men in the section for several years.

"'I see you, white man,' he replied, but made no move to rise or offer me a seat.

"'Why do you thus put shame upon the King-Emperor's representative?' I demanded.

"'We want no dealings with the Emperor-King, or any of his men,' the fellow answered. 'The land is ours, the English have no right here; we will have no more of him.' The patter rattled off his tongue as glibly as though he had been a soap-box orator preaching communism in Hyde Park.

"This was rank sedition, not at all the sort of thing to be countenanced, you know, so I went right for the blighter. 'Get up from there, you unholy rotter,' I ordered, 'and tell your people you have spoken with a crooked tongue, or-'

"It was a lucky thing for me I'm handy with my feet. A spear came driving at me, missing me by less than half an inch, and another followed it, whistling past my head so close I felt the wind of it.

"Fortunately, my men were hiding just outside, and Bendingo, my half-caste Arab sergeant, was a willing worker with the Enfield. He shot the foremost spearman through the head before the fellow had a chance to throw a second weapon, and the other men began to shoot before you could say 'knife'. It was a gory business, and we'd rather killed half the poor beggars before they finally called it quits.

"The chief was most apologetic when the fracas ended, of course, and swore he had been misled by white men who spoke with crooked tongues.

"This was interesting. It seemed, from what the beggar told me, there has been several white men wandering at large through the area distributing what would be equivalent to radical literature at home – preaching armed and violent rebellion to government and all that sort of thing. Furthermore, they'd told the natives the brummagem beads they gave 'em would act as 'medicine' against the white man's bullets, and that no one need fear to raid a mission station or refuse to pay the hut-tax, for England had been overthrown and only a handful of Colonial administrators remained – no army to come to their rescue if the natives were to rise and wipe 'em out.

"This was bad enough, but worse was coming. It appeared these playful little trouble-makers were preaching miscegenation. This was something new. The natives had never regarded themselves as inferior beings, for it's strictly against regulations to say or do anything tending to do more than make 'em respect the whites as agents of the government, but they'd never – save in the rarest instances – attempted to take white women. Oh, yes they killed 'em sometimes, often with torture, but that was simply part of the game – no chivalry, you know. But these white agitators were deliberately urging the Timni, Mendis and Sulima to raid settlements and mission stations and spare the women that they might be carried off as prizes.

"That was plenty. Right there the power of the British rule had to be shown, so I rounded up all the villagers who hadn't taken to the woods, told 'em they'd been misled by lying white men whom I'd hang as soon as caught, then strung the chief up to the nearest oil-palm. His neck muscles were inordinately strong and he died in circumstances of considerable elaboration and discomfort, but the object lesson was worthwhile. There be no more defiance of a government agent by *that* gang.

"We were balked at every turn. Most of our native informers had been killed and eaten, and the other blacks were sullen. Not a word could we get from 'em regarding leopard depredations, and they shut up like a lot of clams when we asked about the white trouble makers.

"We'd never have gotten anywhere if it hadn't been for Old Man Anderson. He was a Wesleyan missionary who ran a little chapel and clinic way up by the French border. His wife and daughter helped him. He might have loved his God; he certainly had a strange love for his womenfolk to bring 'em into that stinkin' hellhole.

"It was a month after our brush with the Mendi when we crashed through the jungle to Anderson's. The place was newly raided, burned and leveled to the ground, ashes still warm. What was left of the old man we found by the burned chapel – all except his head. They'd taken that away for a souvenir. We found the bodies of several of his converts, too. They'd been flayed, their skins stripped off as you'd turn off a glove. His wife and daughter were nowhere to be found.

"They hadn't taken any special pains to cover up their tracks, and we followed at a forced march. We came upon 'em three days later.

"The blighters had eaten 'emselves loggy, and drunk enough trade-gin to float the *Berengaria*, so they didn't offer much resistance when we charged. I'd always thought a man who slaughtered unresisting enemies was a rotten beast, but the memory of old Anderson's dismembered body and those pink, skinless corpses made me revise my notion. We came upon 'em unawares, opened with the Lewis guns from both sides of the village and didn't sound cease firin' till the dead lay round like logwood corded in a lumber camp. Then, and not till then, we went in.

"We found old Mrs. Anderson dead, but still warm. She'd – I think you can imagine what she'd been through, gentlemen.

"We found the daughter, too. Not quite dead.

"In the four days since her capture she'd been abused by more than a hundred men, black and white, and was barely breathing when we came on her. She–"

"White and black, *Monsieur*?" de Grandin interrupted.

"Right-o. The raiding party had been led by whites. Five of 'em. Stripped off their clothes and put on native ornaments, carried native weapons, and led the blacks in their hellish work. Indeed, I don't believe the poor black beggars would have gone out against the 'Jesus Papa' if those white hellions hadn't set 'em up to it.

"They'd regarded Rebekah Anderson as good as dead, and made no secret of their work. The leader was a Russian, so were two of his assistants. A fourth was Polish and the last some sort of Asiatic – a Turk, the poor child thought.

"They'd come up through Liberia, penetrated the Protectorate and set the natives up to devilment, finally organizing the raid on Anderson's. Now their work was done, and they were on their way.

"She heard the leader say he was going to America, for in Harrisonville, New Jersey, the agents of his society had found a woman whom they sought and who would lead some sort of movement against organized religion. The poor kid didn't understand it all – no more did I – but she heard it, and remembered.

"The white men had left the night before, striking east into French Guinea on their way to the coast, and leaving her as a plaything for the natives.

"Before the poor child died she told me the Russian in command had been a man with a slender, almost boyish body, but with the wrinkled face of an old man. She'd seen him stripped for action, you know, and was struck by the strange contrast of his face and body.

"One other thing she told me: when they got to America they intended holding meetings of their damned society, and the road to their rendezvous would be directed by pictures of the Devil with his pitchfork pointing the way the person seeking it should take. She didn't understand, of course, but – I had all the clues I wanted, and as soon as we got back to Freetown I got a leave of absence to hunt that foul murderer down and bring him to justice."

The young man paused a moment to relight his pipe, and there was something far from pleasant in his lean and sun-burned face as he continued: "Rebekah Anderson went to her grave like an old Sumerian queen. I impounded every man who'd had a hand in the raid and put 'em to work diggin' a grave for her, then a big, circular trench around it. Then I hanged 'em and dumped their carcasses into the trench to act as guard of honor for the girl they'd killed. You couldn't bribe a native to go near the place, now.

"I was followin' the little pictures of the Devil when Renouard set on me. I mistook him for one of 'em of course, and – well, it's a lucky thing for all of Costello bashed me when he did."

De Grandin's little, round blue eyes were alight with excitement and appreciation. "And how did you escape, *Monsieur?*" he asked.

The Englishman laughed shortly. "Got a pair of handcuffs?" he demanded.

"I have," supplied Renouard.

"Lock 'em on me."

The manacles clicked round his wrists and he turned to us with a grin. "Absolutely no deception, gentlemen, nothing concealed in the hands, nothing up the sleeves," he announced in a droning sing-song, then, as easily as though slipping them through his shirt sleeves, drew his hands through the iron bracelets. "Just a matter of small bones and limber muscles," he added with another smile. "Being double-jointed helps some, too. It was no trick at all to slip the darbies off when the constables joined Costello for the raid. I put the irons on the other person – locked 'em on his ankles – so the boys would find 'em when they came back to the motor."

"But–" Renouard began, only to pause with the next word half uttered. From upstairs came a quavering little frightened cry, like the tremulous call of a screech-owl or of a child in mortal terror.

"No noise!" de Grandin warned as he leaped from his seat and bounded up the stairway three steps at a time, Renouard and Ingraham close behind him.

We raced on tiptoe down the upper hall and paused a second by the bedroom door; then de Grandin kicked it open.

Alice crouched upon the bed, half raised upon one elbow, her other arm bent guardingly across her face. The red robe we had put upon her when we fled the Devil's temple had fallen back, revealing her white throat and whiter breast, her loosened hair fell across her shoulders.

Close by the open window, like a beast about to spring, crouched a man. Despite his changed apparel, his heavy coat and tall, peaked cap of astrakhan, we recognized him in a breath. Those big, sad eyes fixed on the horror-stricken girl, that old and wrinkle-bitten face, could be none other's than the red priest's. His slender, almost womanish hands were clenched to talons, every muscle of his little, spare frame was taut-stretched harp-string tight for the leap he poised to make. Yet there was no malignancy – hardly any interest – in his old, close-wrinkled face. Rather, it seemed to me, he looked at her a gaze of brooding speculation.

"*Parbleu, Monsieur du Diable*, you honor us too much; this call was wholly unexpected!" de Grandin said, as he stepped quickly forward.

Quick as he was, the other man was quicker. One glance – one murderous glance which seemed to focus all the hate and fury of a thwarted soul – he cast upon the Frenchman, then leaped back through the window.

*Crash!* de Grandin's pistol-shot seemed like a clap of thunder in the room as he fired at the retreating form, and a second shot sped through the window as the intruder landed on the snow below and staggered toward the street.

"Winged him, by Jove!" the Englishman cried exultantly. "Nice shooting, Frenchy!"

"Nice be damned and roasted on the grates of hell–" de Grandin answered furiously. "Is he not free?"

They charged downstairs, leaving me to comfort Alice, and I heard their voices as they searched the yard. Ten minutes later they returned, breathing heavily from their efforts, but empty-handed.

"Slipped through us like an eel!" the Englishman exclaimed. "Must have had a motor waiting at the curb, and–"

"*Sacre nom d'un nom d'un nom*!" de Grandin stormed. "What are they thinking of, those stupid-heads? Is not he charged with murder? Yes, *pardieu*, yet they let him roam about at will, and – it is monstrous; it is vile; it is not to be endured!"

Snatching up the telephone he called police headquarters, then: "What means this, Sergeant?" he demanded when Costello answered. "We sit here like four *sacre* fools and think ourselves secure, and that one – that so vile murderer – comes breaking in the house and – what? *Pas possible*!"

"It is, sor," we heard Costello's answer as de Grandin held the receiver from his ear. "That bur-rd ye handed me is in is cell this minute, an' furthermore, he's been there every second since we locked 'im up!"

## 18. REUNION

Looking very charming and demure in a suit of Jules de Grandin's lavender pajamas and his violet silk dressing-gown, Alice Hume lay upon the chaise-lounge in the bedroom, toying with a grapefruit and poached egg. "If you'd send for Mother, please," she told us. "I'd feel so much better. You see" – her voice shook slightly and a look of horror flickered in her eyes – "you see there are some things I want to tell her – some advice I'd like to get before you let John see me, and – why, what's the matter?" She put the breakfast tray upon the tabouret and looked at us in quick concern. "Mother – there's nothing wrong, is there? She's not ill? Oh–"

"My child," de Grandin answered softly, "your dear mother never will again be ill. You shall see her, certainly; but not until God's great tomorrow dawns. She is–"

"Not – dead?" the word was formed rather than spoken, by the girl's pale lips.

The little Frenchman nodded slowly.

"When? How?"

"The night you – you went away, *ma pauvre*. It was murder."

"Murder?" slowly, unbelievingly, she repeated. "But that *can't* be! Who'd want to murder my poor mother?"

De Grandin's voice was level, almost toneless. "The same unconscionable knaves who stole you from the marriage altar," he returned. "They either feared she knew too much of family history – knew something of the origin of David Hume – or else they wished all earthly ties you had with home and kindred to be severed. At any rate, they killed her. They did it subtly, in such a manner that it was thought suicide, but it was murder, none the less."

"O-oh!" The girl's faint moan was pitiful, hopeless. "Then I'm all alone, all, all alone – I've no one in the world to–"

"You have your fiancé, the good young *Monsieur Jean*," the Frenchman told her softly. "You also have Friend Trowbridge, as good and staunch a friend as ever was, then there is Jules de Grandin. We shall not fall you in your need, my small one."

For a moment she regarded us distractedly, then suddenly put forth her hands, one to Jules de Grandin, one to me. "Oh, good, kind friends," she whispered. "please help me, if you can. God knows I am in need of help, if ever woman was, for I'm as foul a murderess as ever suffered death. I was accessory to those little children's murders – I was – oh-what was it that the lepers used to cry? 'Unclean'? Oh, God, I am unclean, unclean – not fit to breathe the air with decent men! Not fit to marry John! How could I bring children into the world? I who have been accessory to the murder of those little innocents?" She clenched her little hands to fists and beat them on her breast, her tear-filled eyes turned upward as though petitioning pardon for unpardonable sin. "Unclean, unclean!" she wailed. Her breath came slowly, like that of a dumb animal which resents the senseless persistency of pain.

"What is that you say? A murderess – you?" de Grandin shot back shortly.

"Yes – I. I lay there on their altar while they brought those little boys and cut their – oh, I didn't want to do it, I didn't want them to be killed; but I lay there just the same and let them do it – I never raised a finger to prevent it!"

De Grandin took a deep breath. "You are mistaken, *Mademoiselle*," he answered softly. "You were in a drugged condition; the victim of a vicious Oriental drug. In that all-helpless state one sees visions, unpleasant visions, like the figments of a naughty dream. There were no little boys; no murders were committed while you lay thus upon the Devil's altar. It was a seeming, an illusion, staged for the edification of those wicked men and women who made their prayer to Satan. In the olden days, when such things were, they sacrificed small boys upon the altar of the Devil, but this is now; even those who are far gone in sin would halt at such abominations. They were but waxen simulacra, mute, senseless reproductions of small boys, and though they went through all the horrid rite of murder, they let no blood, they did perform no killings. No; certainly not." Jules de Grandin, physician, soldier and policeman, was lying like the gallant gentleman he was, and lying most convincingly.

"But I heard their screams – I heard them call for help, then strangle in their blood!" the girl protested.

"All an illusion, *ma chere*," the little Frenchman answered. "It was a ventriloquial trick. At the conclusion of the ceremony the good Trowbridge and I would have sworn we heard a terrible, thick voice conversing with the priest upon the altar; that also was a juggler's trick, intended to impress the congregation. *Non, ma chere*, your conscience need not trouble you at all; you are no accessory to a murder. As to the rest, it was no fault of yours; you were their prisoner and the helpless slave of wicked drugs; what you did was done with the body, not the soul. There is no reason why you should not wed. I tell you."

She looked at him with tear-dimmed eyes. Though she had mastered her first excess of emotion, her slender fingers clasped and unclasped nervously and she returned his steady gaze with something of the vague, half-believing apprehension of a child. "You're sure?" she asked.

"Sure?" he echoed. "To be sure I am sure, *Mademoiselle*. Remember, if you please, I am Jules de Grandin; I do not make mistakes.

"Come, calm yourself. *Monsieur Jean* will be here at any moment;

then–"

He broke off, closing his eyes and standing in complete silence. Then he put his fingers to his pursed lips and from them plucked a kiss and tossed it upward toward the ceiling. "*Mon dieu*," he murmured rapturously, "*la passion delicieuse*, is it not magnificent?"

"Alice! Alice, beloved–" Young Davisson's voice faltered as he rushed into the room and took the girl into his arms. "When they told me that they'd found you at last, I could hardly believe – I knew they were doing everything but–" Again his speech halted for very pressure of emotion.

"Oh, my dear!" Alice took his face between her palms and looked into his worshipping eyes. "My dear, you've come to me again, but–" She turned from him, and fresh, hot tears lay upon her lashes.

"No buts, *Mademoiselle*!" de Grandin almost shouted. "Remember what I said. Take Love when he comes to you, my little friends; oh, do not make excuses to turn him out of doors – hell waits for those who do so! There is no obstacle to your union, believe me when I say so. Take my advice and have the good *curé* come here this very day, I beg you!"

Both Davisson and Alice looked at him amazed, for he was fairly shaking with emotion. He waved a hand impatiently. "Do not look so, make no account of doubts or fears or feelings of unworthiness!" he almost raged. "Behold me, if you please; an empty shell, a soulless shadow of a man, a being with no aim in life, no home nor fireside to bid him welcome when he has returned from duty! Is that the way to live? *Mille fois non*, I shall say not, but–

"I let Love pass me by, my friends, and have regretted it but once, and that once all my aimless, empty life. *Ecoutez-moi*! In the springtime, of our youth we met, sweet Heloise and I, beside the River Loire. I was a student at the Sorbonne, my military service yet to come; she, *cher Dieu*, was an angel out of Paradise!

"Beside the silver stream we played together; we lay beneath the poplar trees, we rowed upon the river; we waded barefoot in the shallows. Yes, and when we finished wading she plucked cherries, red ripe cherries from the trees, and twined their stems about her toes, and gave me her white feet to kiss. I ate the cherries from her feet and kissed her toes, one kiss for every cherry, one cherry for each kiss. And when we said *bonne nuit – mon Dieu*, to kiss and cling and shudder in such ecstasy once more!

"Alas, my several times great grandsire, he whose honored name I bore, had cut and hacked his way through raging Paris on the night of August 24 in 1572 – how long his bones have turned to ashes in the family tomb – while her ancestors had worn the white brassard and cross, crying 'Messe ou mort! A bas les Huguenots!'"

He paused a moment and raised his shoulders in shrug of resignation. "It might not be," he ended sadly. "Her father would have none of me, my family forbade the thought of marriage. I might have joined her in her faith, but I was filled with scientific nonsense which derided old beliefs; she might have left the teachings her forebears and accepted my ideas, but twenty generations of belief weigh heavily upon the shoulders of a single fragile girl. To save my soul she forfeited all claim upon my body; if she might not have me for husband she'd have no mortal man, so she professed religion. She joined the silent Carmelites, the Carmelites who never speak except in prayer, and the last fond word I had from her was that she would pray ceaselessly for my salvation.

"*Helas*, those little feet so much adored – how many weary steps of needless penance have they taken since that day so long ago! How fruitless life has been to me since my stubbornness closed the door on happiness! Oh, do not wait, my friends! Take the Love the good God gives, and hold it tight against your hearts – it will not come a second time!

"Come, Friend Trowbridge," he commanded me, "let us leave them in their happiness. What have we, who clasped Love's hand in ours long years ago, and saw the purple shadow of his smile grow black with dull futility, to do with them? Nothing, *pardieu*! Come, let us take a drink."

We poured cherry brandy into wide-mouthed goblets, for de Grandin liked to scent its rich bouquet before he drank. I studied him covertly as he raised his glass. Somehow, the confession he had made seemed strangely pitiful. I'd known him for five years, nearly always gay, always nonchalant, boastfully self-confident, quick, brave and reckless, ever a favorite with women, always studiously gallant but ever holding himself aloof, though more than one fair charmer had deliberately paid court to him. Suddenly I remembered our adventure of the "Ancient Fires"; he had said something then about a love that had been lost. But now, at last I understood Jules de Grandin – or thought I did.

"To you, my friend," he pledged me. "To you, and friendship, and brave deeds of adventure, and last of all to Death, the last sweet friend who flings the door back from our prison, for–"

The clamoring telephone cut short his toast.

"Mercy Hospital," a crisp feminine voice announced I picked up the instrument. "Will you and Doctor Grandin come at once? Detective Sergeant Costello wants to see you just as soon as – oh, wait a minute, they plugged a phone through from his room."

"Hullo. Doctor Trowbridge, sor," Costello's salutation came across the wire a moment later. "They like to got me, sor – in broad daylight, too."

"Eh? What the deuce?" I shot back. "What's the trouble,

Sergeant?"

"A chopper, sor."

"A *what*?"

"Machine-gun, sor. Hornsby an' me wuz standin' be th' corner o' 34th an' Tunlaw Streets half an hour back, when a car comes past like th' hammers o' hell, an' they let us have a dose o' bullets as they passed. Pore Hornsby got 'is first off – went down full o' lead as a Christmas puddin' is o' plums, sor – but I'm just messed up a little. Nawthin' but a bad ar-rm an' a punctured back, praise th' Lord!"

"Good heavens!" I exclaimed. "Have you any idea who–"

"I have that, sor; I seen 'im plain as I see you – as I would be seein' ye if ye wuz here, I mean, sor, an'–"

"Yes?" I urged as he paused a moment and a swallow sounded audibly across the wire.

"Yes, sor. I seen 'im, an' there's no mistake about it. It were th' felly you an' Doctor de Grandin turned over to me to hold fer murther last night. I seen 'im plain as day; there's no mistakin' that there map o' his."

"Good Lord, then he did escape!"

"No, sir; he didn't. He's locked up tight in his cell at headquarters this minute, waitin' arraignment fer murther!"

## 19. THE LIGHTNING-BOLTS OF JUSTICE

That evening Alice suffered from severe headaches and shortly afterward with sharp abdominal pains. Though a careful examination disclosed neither enlarged tonsils nor any evidence of mechanical stoppage, the sensation of a ball rising in her throat plagued her almost ceaselessly; when she attempted to cross the room her knees buckled under her as though they had been the boneless joints of a rag-doll.

Jules de Grandin pursed his lips, shook his head and tweaked the needle-ends of his mustache disconsolately. "*L'hysterie*," he murmured. "It might have been foreseen. The emotional and moral shock the poor one has been through is enough to shatter any nerves. *Helas*, I fear the wedding may not be so soon, Friend Trowbridge. The experience of marriage is a trying one to any woman – the readjustment of her mode of life, the blending of her personality with another's – it is a strain. No, she is in no condition to essay it."

Amazingly, he brightened, his small eyes gleaming as with sudden inspiration. "*Parbleu*, I have it!" he exclaimed. "She, *Monsieur Jean* and you, *mon vieux*, shall take a trip. I would suggest the Riviera, were it not that I desire isolation for you all until – no matter. Your practise is not so pressing that it can not be assumed by your estimable colleague, Doctor Phillips; and *Mademoiselle* Alice will most certainly improve more quickly if you accompany her as personal physician. You will go? Say that you will, my friend; a very great much depends on it!"

Reluctantly, I consented, and for six weeks Alice, John Davisson and I toured the Caribbean, saw devastated Martinique, the birthplace of the Empress Josephine, drank Haitian coffee fresh from the plantation, investigated the sights and sounds and, most especially, the smells of Panama and Colon, finally passed some time at the Jockey Club and Sloppy Joe's in Habana. It was a well and sun-tanned Alice who debarked with us and caught the noon train out of Hoboken.

Arrangements for the wedding were perfected while we cruised beneath the Southern Cross. The old Hume house would be done over and serve the bride and groom for home, and in view of Alice's bereavement the formal ceremony had been canceled, a simple service in the chapel of St. Chrysostom's being substituted. Pending the nuptials Alice took up residence at the Hotel Carteret, declaring that she could not think of lodging at my house, warm as was my invitation.

"All has been finished," de Grandin told me jubilantly as he, Renouard and Ingraham accompanied me from the station. "The justice of New Jersey, of which you speak so proudly; she has more than justified herself. Oh yes."

"Eh?" I demanded.

Renouard and Ingraham chuckled.

"They gave it to him," the Englishman explained.

"In the throat – the neck, I should remark," Renouard supplied, wrestling bravely with the idiom.

"The party will be held tomorrow night," de Grandin finished.

"Who – what – whatever are you fellows saying?" I queried. "What party d'ye mean, and–"

"Grigor Bazarov," de Grandin answered with another laugh, "the youthful-bodied one with the aged, evil face; the wicked one who celebrated the Black Mass. He is to die tomorrow night. Yes, *parbleu*, he dies for murder!"

"But–"

"Patience, *mon vieux*, and I shall tell you all. You do recall how we – Monsieur Hiji, Renouard and I – did apprehend him on the night we rescued *Mademoiselle* Alice? Of course. Very well.

"You know how we conspired that he should be tried for a murder which he did not perpetrate, because we could not charge him with his many other crimes? Very good. So it was.

"When we had packed you off with *Monsieur Jean* an his so charming fiancée, your testimony could not serve to save him. No, we had the game all to ourselves, and how nobly we did swear his life away! *Mordieu*, when they heard how artistically we committed perjury, I damn think Ananias and Sapphira hung their heads and curled up like two anchovies for very jealousy! The jury almost wept when we described his shameful crime. It took them only twenty minutes to decide his fate. And so tomorrow night he gives his life in expiation for those little boys he sacrificed upon the Devil's altar and for the dreadful death he brought upon poor Abigail.

"Me, I am clever, my friend. I have drawn upon the wires of political influence, and we shall all have seats within the death house when be goes to meet the lightning bolt of Jersey justice. Yes, certainly, of course."

"You mean we're to witness the execution?"

"*Mais oui; et puis*. Did I not swear he should pay through the nose when he slew that little helpless lad upon the Devil's altar? But certainly. And now, by damn, he shall learn that Jules de Grandin does not swear untruly – unless he wishes to. Unquestionably."

\* \* \* \*

Deftly, like men accustomed to their task, the state policemen patted all our pockets. The pistols my companions wore were passed unquestioned, for only cameras were taboo within the execution chamber.

"All right, you can go in," the sergeant told us when the troopers had completed their examination, and we filed down a dimly lighted corridor behind the prison guard.

The death room was as bright as any clinic's surgery, immaculate white tile reflecting brilliant incandescent bulbs' hard rays. Behind a barricade of white-enameled wood on benches which reminded me of pews, sat several young men whose journalistic calling was engraved indelibly upon their faces, and despite their efforts to appear at ease it took no second glance to see their nerves were taut to the snapping-point; for even seasoned journalists react to death – and here was death, stark and grim as anything to be found in the dissecting rooms.

"The chair", a heavy piece of oaken furniture, stood near the farther wall, raised one low step above the tiled floor of the chamber, a brilliant light suspended from the ceiling just above it, casting its pitiless spotlight upon the center of the tragic stage. The warden and a doctor, stethoscope swung round his neck as though it were a badge of office, stood near the chair, conversing in low tones; the lank cadaverous electrician whose duty was to send the lethal current through the condemned man's body, stood in a tiny alcove like a doorless telephone booth slightly behind and to the left of the chair. A screen obscured a doorway leading from the room, but as we took our seats in front I caught a fleeting glimpse of a white-enameled wheeled bier, a white sheet lying neatly folded on it. Beyond, I knew, the surgeon and the autopsy table were in readiness when the prison doctor had announced his verdict.

The big young Englishman went pale beneath his tropic tan as he surveyed the place; Renouard's square jaw set suddenly beneath his bristling square-cut beard; de Grandin's small, bright eyes roved quickly round the room, taking stock of the few articles of furniture; then, involuntarily his hand flew upward to tease the tightly waxed hairs of his mustache to a sharper point. These three, veterans of police routine, all more than once participants in executions, were fidgeting beneath the strain of waiting.

As for me – if I came through without the aid of smelling-salts, I felt I should be lucky.

A light tap sounded on the varnished door communicating with the death cells. A soft, half-timid sort of tap it was, such as that a person unaccustomed to commercial life might give before attempting to enter an office.

The tap was not repeated. Silently, on well-oiled hinges, the door swung back, and a quartet halted on the threshold. To right and left were prison guards; between them stood the Red Priest arrayed in open shirt and loose black trousers, list slippers on his feet. As he came to halt I saw that the right leg of the trousers had been slit up to the knee and flapped grotesquely round his ankle. The guards beside him held his elbows lightly, and another guard brought up the rear.

Pale, calm, erect, the condemned man betrayed no agitation, save by a sudden violent quivering of the eyelids, this perhaps being due to the sudden flood of light in which he found himself. His great, sad eyes roved quickly round the room, not timorously, but curiously, finally coming to rest upon de Grandin. Then for an instant a flash showed in them, a lambent flash which died as quickly as it came.

Quickly the short march to the chair began. Abreast of us, the prisoner wrenched from his escorts, cleared the space between de Grandin and himself in one long leap, bent forward and spat into the little Frenchman's face.

Without a word or cry of protest the prison guards leaped on him, pinioned his elbows to his sides and rushed him at a staggering run across the short space to the chair.

De Grandin drew a linen kerchief from his cuff and calmly wiped the spittle from his cheek. "*Eh bien*," he murmured, "it seems the snake can spit, though justice has withdrawn his fangs, *n'est-ce-pas?*"

The prison warders knew their work. Straps were buckled round the prisoner's wrists, his ankles, waist. A leather helmet like a football player's was clamped upon his head, almost totally obscuring his pale, deep-wrinkled face.

There was no clergyman attending. Grigor Bazarov was faithful to his compact with the Devil, even unto death. His pale lips moved: "God is tyranny and misery. God is evil. To me, then, Lucifer!" he murmured in a sing-song chant.

The prison doctor stood before the chair, notebook in hand, pencil poised. The prisoner was breathing quickly, his shoulders fluttering with forced respiration. A deep, inhaling gulp, a quick, exhaling gasp – the shoulders slanted forward.

So did the doctor's pencil, as though he wrote. The thin-faced executioner, his quiet eyes upon the doctor's hands, reached upward. There was a crunching of levers, a sudden whir, a whine, and the criminal's body started forward, lurching upward as though he sought to rise and burst from the restraining straps. As much as we could see of his pale face grew crimson, like the face of one who holds his breath too long. The bony, claw-like hands were taut upon the chair arms, like those of a patient in the dentist's chair when the drill bites deeply.

A long, eternal moment of this posture, then the sound of grating metal as the switches were withdrawn, and the straining body in the chair sank limply back, as though in muscular reaction to fatigue.

Once more the doctor's pencil tilted forward, again the whirring whine. Again the body started up, tense, strained, all but bursting through the broad, strong straps which bound it to the chair. The right hand writhed and turned, thumb and forefinger meeting tip to tip, as though to take a pinch of snuff. Then absolute flaccidity as the current was shut off.

The prison doctor put his book aside and stepped up to the chair. For something like a minute the main tube of his questing stethoscope explored the reddened chest exposed as he put back the prisoner's open shirt; then, "I pronounce this man dead."

"*Mon dieu*," exclaimed Renouard.

"For God's sake!" Ingraham muttered thickly.

I remained silent as the white-garbed orderlies took the limp form from the chair, wrapped it quickly in a sheet and trundled it away on the wheeled bier to the waiting autopsy table.

"I say," suggested Ingraham shakily, "suppose he ain't quite dead? It didn't seem to me–"

"*Tiens*, he will be thoroughly defunct when the surgeon's work is done," de Grandin told him calmly. "It was most interesting, was it not?"

His small eyes hardened as he saw the sick look on our faces. "Ah bah, you have the sympathy for him?" he asked almost accusingly. "For why? Were they not more merciful to him than he was to those helpless little boys he killed, those little boys whose throats he slit – or that poor woman whom he crucified? I damn think yes!"

## 20. THE WOLF-MASTER

"*Tiens*, my friends, I damn think there is devilment afoot!" de Grandin told us as we were indulging in a final cup of coffee in the breakfast room some mornings later.

"But no!" Renouard expostulated

"But yes!" his *confrère* insisted.

"Read it, my friend," he commanded, passing a folded copy of *The Journal* across the table to me. To Ingraham and Renouard he ordered: "Listen; listen and become astonished!"

MAGNATE'S MENAGERIE ON RAMPAGE
*Beasts on Karmany Estate Break Cages and Pursue Intruder – Animals' Disappearance a Mystery.*

I read aloud at his request.

"*Early this morning keepers at the private zoo maintained by Winthrop Karmany, well known retired Wall Street operator, at his palatial estate near Raritan, were aroused by a disturbance among the animals. Karmany is said to have the finest, as well as what is probably the largest, collection of Siberian white wolves in captivity, and it was among these beasts the disturbance occurred.*

"*John Noles, 45, and Edgar Black, 30, caretakers on the Karmany estate, hastily left their quarters to ascertain the cause of the noise which they heard coming from the wolves' dens about 3:30 a.m. Running through the dark to the dens, they were in time to see what they took to be a man enveloped in a long, dark cloak, running at great speed toward the brick wall surrounding the animals' enclosure. They also noticed several wolves in hot pursuit of the intruder. Both declare that though the wolves had been howling and baying noisily a few minutes before, they ran without so much as a growl as they pursued the mysterious visitor.*

"*Arriving at the den the men were amazed to find the cage doors swinging open, their heavy locks evidently forced with a crowbar, and all but three of the savage animals at large.*

"*The strange intruder, with the wolves in close pursuit, was seen by Noles and Black to vault the surrounding wall, but all had disappeared in the darkness when the keepers reached the barrier. Citizens in the vicinity of the Karmany estate are warned to be on the lookout for the beasts, for though they had been in confinement several years and consequently have lost much of their native savagery, it is feared that unless they are speedily recaptured or voluntarily find their way back to* their dens, they may revert to their original ferocity when they become hungry. Livestock may suffer from their depredations, and if they keep together and hunt in a pack even human beings are in danger, for all the beasts are unusually large and would make dangerous antagonists.

"This morning at daylight a posse of farmers, headed by members of the state constabulary, was combing the woods and fields in search of the missing animals, but though every spot where wolves might be likely to congregate was visited, no trace of them was found. No one can be found who admits seeing any sign of the runaway wolves, nor have any losses of domestic animals been reported to the authorities.

"The manner in which the wolf pack seems to have vanished completely, as well as the identity of the man in black seen by the two keepers, and the reason which may have actuated him in visiting the Karmany menagerie are puzzling both the keepers and authorities. It has been intimated that the breaking of the cages may have been the vagary of a disordered mind. Certain insane persons have an almost uncontrollable aversion to the sight of caged animals, and it is suggested an escaped lunatic may have blundered into the Karmany zoo as he fled from confinement. If this is so it is quite possible that, seeing the confined beasts, he was suddenly seized with an insane desire to liberate them, and consequently forced the locks of their cages. The released animals seem to have been ungrateful, however, for both Noles and Black declare the mysterious man was obviously running for his life while the wolves pursued him in silent and ferocious determination. However, since no trace of the body has been found, nor any report of a man badly mauled by wolves made in the locality, it is supposed the unidentified man managed to escape. Meanwhile, the whereabouts of the wolf pack is causing much concern about the countryside.

"Karmany is at present occupying his southern palace at Winter Haven, Fla., and all attempts to reach him have been unsuccessful at the time this issue goes to press."

"H'm, it's possible," I murmured as I put the paper down.

"Absolutely," Ingraham agreed.

"Of course; certainly," de Grandin nodded, then, abruptly: "What is?"

"Why – er – a lunatic *might* have done it," I returned. "Cases of zoophilia–"

"And of zoofiddlesticks!" the little Frenchman interrupted. "This was no insanatic's vagary, my friends; this business was well planned beforehand, though why it should be so we can not say. Still–"

"I don't care if he is at breakfast, I've got to see him!" a hysterically shrill voice came stridently from the hallway, and John

Davisson strode into the breakfast room, pushing the protesting Nora McGinnis from his path. "Doctor de Grandin – Doctor Trowbridge – she's gone!" he sobbed as he half fell across the threshold.

"*Mon Dieu*, so soon?" de Grandin cried. "How was it, *mon pauvre?*"

Davisson stared glassy-eyed from one of us to the other, his face working spasmodically, his hands clenched till it seemed the bones must surely crush.

"He stole her – he and his damned wolves!"

"Wolves? I say!" barked Ingraham.

"*Grand Dieu* – wolves!" Renouard exclaimed.

"*A-a-ah* – wolves? I begin to see the outlines of the scheme," de Grandin answered calmly. "I might have feared as much.

"Begin at the beginning, if you please, Monsieur, and tell us everything that happened. Do not leave out an incident, however trivial it may seem; in cases such as this there are no trifles. Begin, commence; we listen."

Young Davisson exhaled a deep, half-sobbing breath and turned his pale face from de Grandin to Renouard, then back again.

"We – Alice and I – went riding this morning as we always do," he answered. "The horses were brought round at half-past six, and we rode out the Albermarle Pike toward Boonesburg. We must have gone about ten miles when we turned off the highway into a dirt road. It's easier on the horses, and the riders, too, you know.

"We'd ridden on a mile or so, through quite a grove of pines, when it began to snow and the wind rose so sharply it cut through our jackets as if they had been summerweight. I'd just turned round to lead the way to town when I heard Alice scream. She'd ridden fifty feet or so ahead of me, so she was that much behind when we turned.

"I wheeled my horse around, and there, converging on her from both sides of the road, were half a dozen great white wolves!

"I couldn't believe my eyes at first. The brutes were larger than any I'd ever seen, and though they didn't growl or make the slightest sound I could see their awful purpose in their gleaming eyes and flashing fangs. They hemmed my poor girl in on every side, and as I turned ride to her, they gathered closer, crouching till their bellies almost touched the ground, and seemed to stop abruptly, frozen, waiting for some signal from the leader of the pack.

"I drove the spurs into my mare and laid the whip on her with all my might, but she balked and shied and reared, and all my urging couldn't force her on a foot.

"Then, apparently from nowhere, two more beasts came charging through the woods and leaped at my mount's head. The poor brute gave a screaming whinny and bolted.

"I tugged at the bridle and sawed at her mouth, but might have been a baby for all the effect my efforts had. Twice I tried to roll out of the saddle, but she was fair flying, and try as I would I didn't seem able to disengage myself. We'd reached the Pike and traveled half a mile so toward town before I finally brought her to a halt.

"Then I turned back, but at the entrance to the lane she balked again, and nothing I could do would make her leave the highway. I dismounted and hurried down the lane on foot, but it was snowing pretty hard by then, and I couldn't even be sure when I'd reached the place when Alice, was attacked. At any rate, I couldn't find a trace of her or of her horse."

He paused a moment breathlessly, and de Grandin prompted softly: "And this 'he' to whom you referred when you first came in, *Monsieur?*"

"Grigor Bazarov!" the young man answered, and his features quivered in a nervous tic. "I recognized him instantly!

"As I rushed down that lane at break-neck speed on my ungovernable horse I saw – distinctly, gentlemen – a human figure standing back among the pines. It was Grigor Bazarov, and he stood between the trees, waving his hands like a conductor leading an orchestra. Without a spoken syllable *he was directing that pack of wolves*. He set them after Alice and ordered them to stop when they'd surrounded her. He set them on me, and made them leap at my horse's head without actually fleshing their teeth in her and without attempting to drag me from the saddle – which they could easily have done. Then, when he'd worked his plan and made my mare bolt, he called them back into the woods. It was Alice he was after, and he took her as easily as a shepherd cuts a wether from the flock with trained sheep-dogs!"

"How is this?" de Grandin questioned sharply. "You say it was Grigor Bazarov. How could you tell? You never saw him."

"No, but I've heard you tell of him, and Alice had described him, too. I recognized those great, sad eyes of his, and his mummy-wrinkled face. I tell you–"

"But Bazarov is dead," I interrupted. "We saw him die last week – all of us. They electrocuted him in the penitentiary at Trenton, and–"

"And while he was all safely lodged in jail he broke into this house and all but made away with *Mademoiselle* Alice," de Grandin cut in sharply. "You saw him with your own two eyes, my Trowbridge. So did Renouard and Monsieur Hiji. Again, while still in jail he murdered the poor Hornsby, and all but killed the good Costello. The evidence is undisputed, and–"

"I know, but he's dead, now!" I insisted.

"There is a way to tell," de Grandin answered. "Come, let us go."

"Go? Where?"

"To the cemetery, of course. I would look in the grave of this one who can be in jail and in your house at the same time, and kill a *gendarme* in the street while safely under lock and key. Come, we waste our time, my friends."

We drove to the county court house, and de Grandin was closeted with the Recorder Glassford in his chambers for a few minutes. "*Tres bon*," he told us as he reappeared. "I have the order for the exhumation. Let us make haste."

The early morning snow had stopped, but a thin veneer of leaden clouds obscured the sky, and the winter sun shone through them with a pale, half-hearted glow as we wheeled along the highway toward the graveyard. Only people of the poorer class buried their dead in Willow Hills; only funeral directors of the less exclusive sort sold lots or grave-space there. Bazarov's unmarked grave was in the least expensive section of the poverty-stricken burying-ground, one short step higher than the Potter's Field.

The superintendent and two overalled workmen waited at the graveside, for de Grandin had telephoned the cemetery office as soon as he obtained the order for the exhumation. Glancing perfunctorily at the little Frenchman's papers, the superintendent nodded to the Polish laborers. "Git goin'," he commanded tersely, "an' make it snappy."

It was dismal work watching them heave lumps of frosty clay from the grave. The earth was frozen almost stony-hard, and the picks struck on it with a hard, metallic sound. At length, however, the dull, reverberant thud of steel on wood warned us that the task was drawing to a close. A pair of strong web straps were lowered, made fast to the rough box enclosing the casket, and at a word from the superintendent the men strained at the thongs, dragging their weird burden to the surface. A pair of pick-handles were laid across the open grave and the rough box rested on them. Callously, as one who doe such duties every day, the superintendent wrenched the box-lid off, and the laborers laid it by the grave. Inside lay the casket, a cheap affair of chestnut covered with shoddy broadcloth, the tinny, imitation-silver nameplate on its lid already showing a dull, brown-blue discoloration.

*Snap!* The fastenings which secured the casket lid were thrown back; the superintendent lifted the panel and tossed it to the frozen ground.

Head resting on the sateen rayon pillow, hands fold on his breast, Grigor Bazarov lay before us and gave us stare for stare. The mortuarian who attended him had lacked the skill or inclination to do a thorough job, and despite the intense cold of the weather putrefaction had made progress. The dead man's mouth was slightly open, a quarter-inch or so of purple, blood-gorged tongue protruding from his lips as though in low derision; the lids were partly raised from his great eyes, and though these had the sightless glaze of death, it seemed to me some subtle mockery lay in them.

I shuddered at the sight despite myself, but I could not forbear the gibe: "Well, is he dead?" I asked de Grandin.

"*Comme un mouton*," he answered, in nowise disconcerted.

"Restore him to his bed, if you will be so good, *Monsieur*," he added to the superintendent, "and should you care to smoke–" A flash of green showed momentarily as a treasury note changed hands, and the cemetery overseer grinned.

"Thanks," he acknowledged. "Next time you want to look at one of 'em, don't forget we're always willing to oblige."

"Yes, he is dead," the Frenchman murmured thoughtfully as we walked slowly toward the cemetery gate, "dead like a herring, yet–"

"Dead or not," John Davisson broke in, and his words were syncopated by the chattering of his teeth, "dead or not, sir, the man we just saw in that coffin was the man I saw beside the lane this morning. No one could fail to recognize that face!"

## 21. WHITE HORROR

"Here's a special delivery letter for Misther Davisson, come whilst yez wuz out, sor," Nora McGinnis announced as we entered the house. "Will ye be afther havin' the tur-key or th' roast fer dinner tonight, an' shall I make th' salad wid tomatoes or asparagus?"

"Turkey, by all means, he is a noble bird," de Grandin answered for me, and tomatoes with the salad, if you please, *ma petite*."

The big Irishwoman favored him with an affectionate smile as she retired kitchenward, and young Davisson slit the envelope of the missive she had handed him.

For a moment he perused t with wide-set, unbelieving eyes, then handed it to me, his features quivering once again with nervous tic.

*John Darling:*
*When you get this I shall be on my way to fulfil the destiny prepared for me from the beginning of the world. Do not seek to follow me, nor think of me, save as you might think kindly of one who died, for I am dead to you. I have forever given up the thought of marriage to you or any man, and I release you from your engagement. Your ring will be delivered to you, and that you may some day put it on the finger of a girl who can return the love you give is the hope of ALICE.*

"*I can't – I won't believe* she means it!" the young man cried. "Why, Alice and I have known each other since we were little kids; we've been in love since she first put her hair up, and–"

"*Tiens*, my friend," de Grandin interrupted as he gazed at the message, "have you by chance spent some time out in the country?"

"Eh?" answered Davisson, amazed at the irrelevant question.

"Your hearing is quite excellent, I think. Will you not answer me?"

"Why – er – yes, of course, I've been in the country – I spent practically all my summers on a farm when I was a lad, but–"

"*Tres bon*," the little Frenchman laughed. "Consider: did not you see the wicked Bazarov urge on his wolves to take possession of your sweetheart? But certainly. And did he not forbear to harm you, being satisfied to drive you from the scene while he kidnapped *Mademoiselle* Alice? Of course. And could he not easily have had his wolf-pack drag you from your horse and slay you? You have said as much yourself. Very well, then; recall your rural recollections, if you will:

"You have observed the farmer as he takes his cattle to the butcher. Does he take the trouble to place his cow in leading strings? By no means. He puts the little, so weak calf, all destined to be veal upon the table in a little while, into a wagon, and drives away to market. And she, the poor, distracted mother-beast, she trots along behind, asking nothing but to keep her little baby-calf in sight. Lead her? *Parbleu*, ropes of iron could not drag her from behind the tumbril in which her offspring rides to execution! Is it not likely so in this case also? I damn think yes.

"This never-to-be-sufficiently-anathematized stealer of women holds poor *Mademoiselle* Alice in his clutch. He spares her *fiancé*. Perhaps he spares him only as the cruel, playful pussy-cat forbears to kill the mouse outright; at any rate, he spares him. For why? *Pardieu*, because by leaving *Monsieur Jean* free he still allows poor *Mademoiselle* Alice one little, tiny ray of hope; with such vile subtlety as only his base wickedness can plan, he holds her back from black despair and suicide that he may force her to his will by threats against the man she loves. *Sacre nom d'un artichaut*, I shall say yes! Certainly, of course."

"You mean – he'll make her go with him – leave me – by threats against my life?" young Davisson faltered.

"*Precisement, mon vieux*. He has no need to drug her now with *scopolamin apomophia*; he holds her in a stronger thrall. Yes, it is entirely likely."

He folded the girl's note between his slim, white hands, regarding it idly for a moment; then, excitedly: "Tell me, *Monsieur Jean*, did *Mademoiselle* Alice, by any chance, know something of telegraphy?"

"Eh? Why, yes. When we were kids we had a craze for it – had wires strung between our houses with senders and receivers at each end, and used to rouse each other at all sorts of hours to tap a message–"

"*Hourra*, the Evil One is circumvented! *Regardez-vous*."

Holding the letter to the study desk-lamp, he tapped its bottom margin with his finger. Invisible except against the light, a series of light scratches, as though from a pin-point or dry pen, showed on the paper:

– –. .. –.. ... – – .. – –

"You can read him?" he asked anxiously. "Me, I understand the international, but this is in American Morse, and–"

"Of course I can," young Davisson broke in. "'Jones' Mill', it says. Good Lord, why didn't I think of that?"

"Ah? And this mill of *Monsieur* Jones–"

"Is an old ruin several miles from Boonesburg. No one's occupied it since I can remember, but it can't be more then three miles from the place where we met the wolves, and–"

"*Eh bien*, if that be so, why do we sit here like five sculptured figures on the Arc de Triomphe? Come, let us go at once, my friends. Trowbridge, Renouard, Friend Hiji, and you, Friend *Jean*, prepare yourselves for service in the cold. Me, I shall telephone the good Costello for the necessary implements.

"*Oui-da, Messieurs les Loups*, I think that we shall give you the party of surprise – we shall feed you that which will make your bellies ache most villainously!"

It was something like a half-hour later when the police car halted at the door. "It's kind o' irreg'lar, sor," Sergeant Costello announced as he lugged several heavy satchels up the steps with the aid of two patrolmen, "but I got permission fer th' loan. Seems like you got a good stand-in down to headquarters."

The valises opened, he drew forth three sub-machine guns, each with an extra drum of cartridges, and two riot guns, weapons similar to the automatic shotgun, but heavier in construction and firing shells loaded with much heavier shot.

"You and Friend *Jean* will use the shotguns, Friend Trowbridge," de Grandin told me. "Renouard, Ingraham and I will handle the quickfirers. Come, prepare yourselves at once. Heavy clothing, but no long coats; we shall need leg-room before the evening ends."

I fished a set of ancient hunting-togs out of my wardrobe – thick trousers of stout corduroy, a pair of high lace boots, a heavy sweater and suede jerkin, finally a leather cap with folds that buckled underneath the chin. A few minutes' search unearthed another set for Davisson, and we joined the others in the hallway. De Grandin was resplendent in a leather aviation suit; Renouard had slipped three sweaters on above his waistcoat and bound the bottoms of his trousers tight about his ankles with stout linen twine; Ingraham was arrayed in a suit of corduroys which had seen much better days, though not recently.

"Are we prepared?" de Grandin asked. "*Tres bon*, Let us go."

The bitter cold of the afternoon had given way to slightly warmer weather, but before we had traversed half a mile the big, full, yellow moon was totally obscured by clouds, and shortly afterward the air was filled with flying snowflakes and tiny, cutting grains of hail which rattled on the windshield and stung like whips when they blew into our faces.

About three-quarters of a mile from the old mill I had to stop my motor, for the road was heavy with new-fallen snow and several ancient trees had blown across the trail, making further progress impossible.

"*Eh bien*, it must be on foot from now on, it seems," de Grandin murmured as he clambered from the car. "Very well; one consents when one must. Let us go; there is no time to lose."

The road wound on, growing narrower and more uneven with each step. Thick ranks of waving, black-boughed pines marched right to the border of the trail on either side, and through their swaying limbs the storm-wind soughed eerily, while the very air seemed colder with a sharper, harder chill, and the wan and ghastly light which sometimes shines on moonless, snow-filled winter nights, seemed filled with creeping, shifting phantom-shapes which stalked us as a wolf-pack stalks a stag.

"*Morbleu*, I so not like this place, me," Renouard declared. "It has an evil smell."

"I think so, too, *mon vieux*," de Grandin answered, "three times already I have all but fired at nothing. My nerves are not so steady as I thought."

"Oh, keep your tails up," Ingraham comforted. "It's creepy as a Scottish funeral here, but I don't see anything–"

"*Ha*, do you say it? Then look yonder, if you will, and tell me what it is you do not see, my friend," de Grandin interrupted.

Loping silently across the snow, themselves a mere shade darker than the fleecy covering of the ground, came a pack of great, white wolves, green-yellow eyes a-glint with savagery, red tongues lolling from their mouths as they drew nearer through the pines, then suddenly deployed like soldiers at command, and, their cordon formed, sank to the snow and sat there motionless.

"*Cher Dieu*," Renouard said softly. "It is the pack of beasts which made away with *Mademoiselle* Alice, and–"

A movement stirred within the pack. A brute rose from its haunches, took a tentative step forward, then sank down again, belly to the snow, and lay there panting, its glaring eyes fixed hungrily upon us.

And as the leader moved, so moved the pack. A score of wolves were three feet nearer us, for every member of the deadly circle had advanced in concert with the leader.

I stole a quick glance at de Grandin. His little round blue eyes were glaring fiercely at those of any of the wolves; beneath his little blond mustache his lips were drawn back savagely, showing his small, white, even teeth in a snarl of hate and fury.

Another rippling movement in the wolf-pack, and now the silence crashed, and from the circle there went up such pandemonium of hellish howls as I had never heard; not even in the worst of nightmares. I had a momentary vision of red mouths and gleaming teeth and shaggy, gray-white fur advancing toward me in a whirlwind rush, then:

"Give fire!" de Grandin shouted.

And now the wolf-pack's savage battle-cry was drowned out by another roar as de Grandin, Ingraham and Renouard, back touching back, turned loose the venom of their sub-machine guns. Young Davisson and I, too, opened fire with our shotguns, not taking aim, but pumping the mechanisms frenziedly and firing point-blank into the faces of the charging wolves.

How long the battle lasted I have no idea, but I remember that at last I felt de Grandin's hand upon my arm and heard him shouting in my ear: "Cease firing, Friend Trowbridge, there is no longer anything to shoot. *Parbleu*, if wolves have souls, I damn think hell is full with them tonight!"

## 22. THE CRIMSON CLUE

He turned abruptly to Renouard: "*Allez au feu, mon brave*," he cried, "*pour la partie!*"

We charged across the intervening patch of snow-filled clearing, and more than once de Grandin or Renouard or Ingraham paused in his stride to spray the windows of the tumble-down old house with a stream of lead. But no shot replied, nor was there any sign of life as we approached the doorless doorway.

"Easy on," Ingraham counseled. "They may be lyin' doggo, waitin' for a change–"

"But no," de Grandin interrupted. "Had that been so, they surely would not have missed the chance to shoot us to death a moment ago – we were a perfectly defined target against the snow, and they had the advantage of cover. Still, a milligram of caution is worth a double quintal of remorse; so let us step warily.

"Renouard and I will take the lead. Friend Trowbridge, you and Friend *Jean* walk behind us and flash your search-lights forward, and well above our heads. That way, if we are ambushed, they will shoot high and give us opportunity to return their fire. Friend Hiji, do you bring up the rear and keep your eyes upon the ground which we have traversed. Should you see aught which looks suspicious, shoot first and make investigation afterward, I do not wish that we should die tonight."

Accordingly, in this close formation, we searched the old house from its musty cellar to its drafty attic, but nowhere was there any hint of life or recent occupancy until, as we forced back the sagging door which barred the entrance to the old grainbins, we noted the faint, half-tangible aroma of *narcisse noir*.

"Alice!" John Davisson exclaimed. "She's been here – I recognize the scent!"

"U'm?" de Grandin murmured thoughtfully. "Advance your light a trifle nearer, if you please, Friend Trowbridge."

I played the flashlight on the age-bleached casing of the door. There, fresh against the wood's flat surface were three small pits, arranged triangularly. A second group of holes, similarly spaced, were in the hand-hewn planking of the door, exactly opposite those which scarred the jamb.

"Screw-holes," de Grandin commented, "and on the outer side. You were correct, Friend *Jean*; your nose and heart spoke truly. This place has been the prison of your love – here are the marks where they made fast the lock and hasp to hold her prisoner – but *helas*, the bird is flown; the cage deserted."

Painstakingly as a paleographer might scan a palimpsest, he searched the little, wood-walled cubicle, flashing his search-light's darting ray on each square inch of aged planking. "*Ah-ha?*" he asked of no one in particular as the flashlight struck into a corner, revealing several tiny smears of scarlet on the floor.

"*Morbleu!* Blood?" Renouard exclaimed. "Can it be that–"

De Grandin threw himself full length upon the floor, his little, round blue eyes a scant three inches from the row of crimson stains. "Blood? *Non!*" he answered as he finished his examination. "It is the mark of *pamade pour les levres*, and unless I do mistake–"

"You mean lipstick?" I interrupted. "What in the world–"

"*Zut!*" he cut me short. "You speak too much my friend." To Davisson:

"See here, Friend *Jean*, is not some system of design in this? Is it not–"

"Of course it is!" the young man answered sharply. "It's another telegraphic message, like the one she sent in the letter. Can't you see? Dash, dash; dot, dash; dot, dot; dot, dash; dash, dot–" He read the code through quickly.

De Grandin looked at him with upraised brows. "*Exactement,*" he nodded, "and that means–"

"*M-a-c-a-n-d-r-e-w-s s-i-e–*" Davisson spelled the message out, then paused, shook his head in puzzlement and once again essayed the task.

"I can't get any sense from it," he finally confessed. "That's what it spells, no doubt of it, but what the devil–"

"I say, old chap, go over it once more," asked Ingraham. "I may be blotto, but–"

*Crash!* The thunderous detonation shook the floor beneath us and a heavy beam came hurtling from the ceiling followed by a cataract of splintered planks and rubble.

*Crash!* A second fulmination smashed the wooded wall upon our right and a mass of shattered brick and timber poured into the room.

"*Bombes d'air!*" Renouard cried wildly. "Down – down, my friends; it is the only way to–" His warning ended in a choking grunt as a third explosion ripped the cover off our hiding place and a blinding pom-pom of live flame flashed in our eyes.

I felt myself hurled bodily against the farther wall, felt the crushing impact as I struck the mortised planks, and then I felt no more.

"Trowbridge, my friend, my good, brave comrade; do you survive, have you been killed to death? *Mordieu*, say that you live, my old one!" I heard de Grandin's voice calling from immeasurable distance, and slowly realized he held my head upon his shoulder while with frantic hands he rubbed snow on my brow.

"Oh, I'm all right, I guess," I answered weakly, then sank again in comforting oblivion.

When next I struggled back to consciousness, I found myself on my own surgery table, de Grandin busy with a phial of smelling salts, a glass of aromatic spirit on the table, and a half-filled tumbler of cognac next to it. "Thanks be to God you are yourself once more!" he exclaimed fervently, handed me the water and ammonia and drained the brandy glass himself. "*Pardieu*, my friend, I thought that we should surely lose you!" he continued as he helped me to a chair.

"You had a close squeak, no doubt of it," Ingraham agreed.

"What happened?" I demanded weakly.

De Grandin fairly ground his teeth in rage. "They made a foolishness of us," he told me. "While we were busy with their *sacre* wolves they must have been escaping, and the thunder of our guns drowned out the whirring of their motors. Then, when we were all safe and helpless in the house, they circled back and dropped the hand grenades upon us. Luckily for us they had no aerial torpedoes, or we should now be practising upon the harp. As it is–" he raised his shoulders in a shrug.

"B-but, you mean they had a *plane*?" I asked amazed.

"*Ha*, I shall say as much!" he answered. "Nor did they stop to say a 'by-your-leave' when they obtained it. This very night, an hour or so before we journeyed to that thirty-thousand-times-accursed mill of *Monsieur* Jones, two men descended suddenly upon the hangars at New Bristol. A splendid new amphibian lay in the bay, all ready to be drawn into her shed. The people at the airport are much surprised to see her suddenly take flight, but – aviators are all crazy, else they would remain on land, and who shall say what form their latest madness takes? It was some little time before the truth was learned. Then it was too late.

"Stretched cold upon the runway of the hangar they found the pilot and his mechanician. Both were shot dead, yet not a shot was heard. The miscreants had used silencers upon their guns, no doubt.

"*Tiens*, at any rate, they had not stopped at murder and they had made off with the plane, had landed it upon the frozen millpond, then sailed away, almost – but not quite, thank God! – leaving us as dead as we had left the guardian wolves."

"*Helas*, and we shall never overtake them!" Renouard said mournfully. "It is too obvious. They chose the amphibian plane that they might put to sea and be picked up by some ship which waited; and where they may be gone we can not say. There is no way of telling, for–"

"Hold hard, old thing; I think perhaps there is!" the Englishman broke in. "When Trowbridge toppled over it knocked the thought out of my head, but I've an idea we may trace 'em. I'll pop off to the cable office and send a little tracer out. We ought to get some solid information by tomorrow."

We were still at breakfast the next morning when the young man from the cable office came. "Mr. In-gra-ham here?" he asked.

"Don't say it like that, young feller, me lad, it's Ingraham – 'in' as in 'inside,' and 'graham' as in biscuit, yer know," returned the Englishman with a grin as he held out his hand for the message.

Hastily he read it to himself, then aloud to us:

*No strangers seeking access to the bush through here but French report a hundred turned back from Konakri stop unprecedented number of arrivals at Monrovia stop investigation underway*
SYMMES, Supt.

"*Tres bon*," de Grandin nodded. "Now, if you will have the goodness to translate–" he paused with brows raised interrogatively.

"Nothin' simpler, old thing," the Englishman responded. "You see, it was like this:

"'Way up in the back country of Sierra Leone, so near the boundary line of French Guinea that the French think it's British territory and the British think it's French, an old goop named MacAndrews got permission to go diggin' some twenty years ago. He was a dour old Scotsman, mad as a dingo dog, they say, but a first-rate archeologist. There were some old Roman ruins near the border, and this Johnny had the idea he'd turn up something never in the books if he kept at it long enough. So he built a pukka camp and settled down to clear the jungle off; but fever beat his schedule and they planted the old cove in one of his own trenches.

"That ended old Mac's diggin', but his camp's still there. I passed it less than five years ago, and stopped there overnight. The natives say the old man's ghost hangs around the place, and shun it like 'the plague – haven't even stolen anything."

"Ah?" de Grandin murmured. "And–"

"Oh, quite, old dear. A big 'and'. That's what got the massive intellect workin', don't you know. There's a big natural clearin' near MacAndrews' and a pretty fair-sized river. The place is so far inland nobody ever goes there unless he has to, and news – white man's news, I mean – is blessed slow gettin' to the coast. Could anything be sweeter for our Russian friends' jamboree?

"Irak is under British rule today, and any nonsense in that neighborhood would bring the police sniffin' round. The Frenchmen in Arabia don't stand much foolishness, so any convocation of the Devil-Worshippers is vetoed in advance so far as that locality's concerned. But *what about MacAndrews'*? They could plant and harvest the finest crop of merry young hell you ever saw out there and no one be the wiser. But they've got to get there. That's the blighted difficulty, me lad. Look here–"

He drew a pencil and notebook from his pocket and blocked out a rough map: "Here's Sierra Leone; here's French Guinea; here's Liberia. Get it? Our people in Freetown have to be convinced there's some good reason why before they'll pass a stranger to the bush country; so do the French. But Liberia – any man, black, white, yellow or mixed, who lands there with real money in his hand can get unlimited concessions to go hunting in the back country, and no questions asked.

"There you are, old bean. When Davisson decoded the message on the floor last night it hit me like a brick. The gal had told us where she was in the letter; now, she takes a chance we'll go to Jones' Mill and starts to write a message on the floor. They've talked before her, and she takes her lipstick and starts to write her destination down – 'MacAndrews, Sierra Leone' – but only gets 'MacAndrews' and the first three letters of 'Sierra' down when they come for her and she has to stop. That's the way I figured it – it's great to have a brain like mine!

"Now, if they've really picked MacAndrews' old camp for their party, there'll be a gatherin' of the clans out there. And the visitors will have to come overland or enter through Freetown, one of the French ports or Liberia. That's reasonin', old top.

"So I cabled Freetown to see if any one's been tryin' to bootleg himself through the lines, or if there'd been much sudden immigration through the French ports. You have the answer. All these coves will have to do is strike cross-country through the bush and–"

"And we shall apprehend them!" Renouard exclaimed delightedly.

"Right-o, dear sir and fellow policeman," the Englishman returned. "I'm bookin' passage for West Africa this mornin', and–"

"Book two," Renouard cut in. "This excavation *Monsieur* MacAndrews, it is near the border; me, I shall be present with a company of Senegalese *gendarmes* and–"

"And with me, *pardieu*! Am I to have no pleasure?" broke in Jules de Grandin.

"Me, too," John Davisson asserted. "If they've got Alice, I must be there too."

"You might as well book passage for five," I finished. "I've been with you so far, and I'd like to see the finish of this business. Besides, I owe 'em something for that bomb they dropped on me last might."

## 23. PURSUIT

There was no scarcity of offered labor when we debarked at Monrovia. A shouting, sweating, jostling throng of black boys crowded round us, each member of the crowd urging his own peculiar excellence as a baggage-carrier in no uncertain terms, Foremost – and most vocal – was a young man in long and much soiled nightgown, red slippers and very greasy tarboosh. "Carry luggage, sar? Carry him good; not trust dam' bush nigger!" he asseverated, worming with serpentine agility through the pressing crowd of volunteers and plucking Ingraham's sleeve solicituously.

"Right; carry on, young feller," the Englishman turned, kicking his kit toward the candidate for portership.

"Hi-yar, this way – grab marster's duffle!" the favored one called out, and from the crowd some half-dozen nondescript individuals sprang forward, shouldered our gear and, led by the man Ingraham had engaged, preceded us at a shuffling jog-trot up the winding street toward the apology for a hotel.

Evidently Ingraham was familiar with conventions, for when we had arrived at our hotel he made no effort to distribute largesse among the porters, but beckoned to the head man to remain in our room while the remainder of the gang dispersed themselves in such shade as offered in the street outside, awaiting the emergence of their leader.

The moment the door closed a startling transformation came over our chief porter. The stooping, careless bearing which marked his every movement fell from him like a cloak, his shoulders straightened back, his chin went up, and heels clicked together, he stood erectly at attention before Ingraham. "Sergeant Bendigo reporting, sar" he announced.

"At ease," commanded Ingraham. Then: "Did you go out there?"

"Yes, O Hiji, even as you ordered, so I did. Up to the place where all of the great waters break in little streams I went, and there at the old camp where ghosts and djinn and devils haunt the night I found the tribesmen making *poro*. Also, O Hiji, I think the little leopards are at large again, for in the night I heard their drums, and once I saw them dancing round a fire while something – *wah*, an unclean thing, I think – stewed within their pots. Also, I heard the leopard scream, but when I looked I saw no beast, only three black feller walking through a jungle path."

"U'm? Any white men there?" demanded Ingraham.

"Plenty lot, sar. No jolly end. Plenty much white feller, also other feller with dark skin, not white like Englishman or French, not black like bush boy or brown like Leoni, but funny-lookin' feller, some yeller, some brown, some white, but dark and big-nosed, like Jewish trading man. Some, I think, are Hindoos, like I see sometime in Freetown. They come trekking long time through the jungle from Monrovia, ten, twenty, maybe thirty at once, with Liberian bush boys for guide, and–"

"All right, get on with it," Ingraham prompted sharply.

"Then make killing palaver, Hiji," the young man told him earnestly. "Those bush boys come as guides; but *they not return*. They start for home, but something happen – I saw one speared from ambush. I think those white men put bad thoughts in bush men's heads. Very, very bad palaver, sar."

"What's doing up at MacAndrews'?"

"*Hou*! Bush nigger from all parts of the forest work like slaves; all time they dig and chop. Clear off the jungle, dig up old stones where ghosts are buried. I think there will be trouble there."

"No doubt of it," the Englishman concurred.

"Tell me, O sergeant man, was there among these strangers some one woman of uncommon beauty whom they guarded carefully, as though a prisoner, yet with reverence, as though a queen?"

"Allah!" exclaimed the sergeant, rolling up his eyes ecstatically.

"Never mind the religious exercises. Did you see the woman?"

"*Wah*, a woman, truly, Hiji, but a woman surely such as never was before. Her face is like the moon at evening, her walk like that of the gazelle, and from her lips drips almond-honey. Her voice is like the dripping of the rain in thirsty places, and her eyes – *bismillah*, when she weeps the tears are sapphires. She has the first-bloom of the lotus on her cheek, and–"

"Give over, you've been reading Hafiz or Elinor Glya, young feller. Who's the leader of this mob?"

"*Wallah*!" – Sergeant Bendigo passed his fingers vertically across his lips and spat upon the floor – "he is called Bazarri, Hiji, and verily he is the twin of Satan, the stoned and the rejected. A face of which the old and wrinkled monkey well might be ashamed is his, with great sad eyes that never change their look, whatever they behold. *Wah*, in Allah's glorious name I take refuge from the rejected one–"

"All right; all right, take refuge all you please, but get on with your report," Ingraham cut in testily. "You say he has the natives organized?"

"Like the blades of grass that come forth in the early rains, O Hiji. Their spears are numerous as the great trees of the forest, and everywhere they range the woods lest strangers come upon them. They killed two members of the Mendi who came upon them unawares, and I was forced to sleep in trees like any of the monkey people; for to be caught near MacAndrews' is to enter into Paradise – and the cooking-pot."

"Eh? The devil! They're practising cannibalism?"

"Thou sayest."

"Who–"

"The white man of the evil, wrinkled face; he whom they call Bazarri; he has appointed it. Also he gives them much trade gin. I think there will be shooting before long; spears will fly as thick as gnats about the carcass – *hai*, and bullets, too. The little guns which stutter will laugh the laugh of death, and the bayonets will go *bang!* as we drive them home to make those dam' bush feller know our lord the Emperor-King is master still."

"Right you are," the Englishman returned, and there was something far from pleasant at the corners of his mouth as he smiled at Sergeant Bendigo.

"Gentlemen" – he turned to us – "this is my sergeant and my right-hand man. We can accept all that he tells us as the truth.

"Sergeant, these men come from far away to help us hunt this evil man of whom you tell me."

The sergeant drew himself erect again and tendered us a grave salute. His slightly flaring nostrils and smooth, brown skin announced his negroid heritage, but the thin-lipped mouth, the straight, sleek hair and finely modeled hands and feet were pure Arab, while the gleaming, piercing eyes and quick, cruel smile were equally pure devil. De Grandin knew him for a kindred spirit instantly.

"*Tiens, mon brave*, it is a fine thing you have done, this discovering of their devil's nest," he complimented as he raised his hand in answer to the sergeant's military courtesy. "You think we yet shall come to grips with them?"

Bendigo's eyes shone with anticipation and delight, his white teeth flashed between his back-drawn lips. "May Allah spare me till that day!" he answered. It was a born killer speaking, a man who took as aptly to the deadly risks of police work as ever duckling took to water.

"Very well, Sergeant," Ingraham ordered: "take the squad and hook it for Freetown as fast as you can; we be along in a few days."

Bendigo saluted again, executed a perfect about-face and marched to the door. Once in the hotel corridor he dropped his military bearing and slouched into the sunshine where his *confrères* waited.

"Stout feller, that," Ingraham remarked. "I sent him a wire to go native and pop up to MacAndrews' and nose round, then follow the trail overland to Monrovia, pickin' up what information he could *en route*. It's a holy certainty nothing happened on the way he didn't see, too."

"But isn't there a chance some of that gang he called to help him with our luggage may give the show away?" I asked. "They didn't seem any too choice a crowd to me."

Ingraham smiled a trifle bleakly. "I hardly think so,' he replied. "You see, they're all members of Bendigo platoon. He brought 'em here to help him carry on."

De Grandin and Renouard went on to Dakar, while Ingraham, John Davisson and I took packet north to Freetown.

Our expedition quickly formed. A hundred frontier policemen with guns and bayonets, five Lewis guns in charge of expert operators, with Ingraham and Bendigo in command, set out in a small wood-burning steamer toward Falaba. We halted overnight at the old fortress town, camping underneath the loop-holed walls, then struck out overland toward the French border.

The rains had not commenced, nor would they for a month or so, and the *Narmattan*, the ceaseless north west wind blowing up from the Sahara, swept across the land like a steady draft from a boiler room. The heat was bad, the humidity worse; it was like walking through a super-heated hothouse as we beat our way along the jungle trails, now marching through comparatively clear forest, now hacking at the trailing undergrowth, or pausing at the mud-bank of some sluggish stream to force a passage while our native porters beat the turbid water with sticks to keep the crocodiles at a respectful distance.

"We're almost there," Ingraham announced one evening as we sat before his tent, imbibing whisky mixed with tepid water, "and I don't like the look of things a bit."

"How's that?" I asked. "It seems extremely quiet to me; we've scarcely seen–"

"That's it! We haven't seen a bloomin' thing, or heard one, either. Normally these woods are crawlin' with natives – Timni or Sulima, even if the beastly Mendi don't show up. This trip we've scarcely seen a one. Not only that, they should be gossipin' on the *lokali* – the jungle telegraph – drum, you know – tellin' the neighbors miles away that we're headin' north by east, but – damn it; I don't *like* it!"

"Oh, you're getting nerves," Davisson told him with a laugh. "I'm going to turn in. Good-night."

Ingraham watched him moodily as he walked across the little clearing to his tent beneath an oil-palm tree. "Silly ass," he muttered. "If he knew this country as I do he'd be singin' a different sort o' shanty. Nerves – good Lord!"

He reached inside his open tunic for a tobacco pouch and pipe, but stiffened suddenly, like a pointer coming on a covey of quail. Next instant he was on his feet, the Browning flashing from the holster strapped against his leg, and a savage spurt of flame stabbed through the darkness.

Like a prolongation of the pistol's roar there came a high-pitched, screaming cry, and something big and black and bulky crashed through the palm-tree's fronds, hurtling to the earth right in Davisson's path.

We raced across the clearing, and Ingraham stooped and struck a match. "Nerves, eh?" he asked sarcastically, as the little spot of orange flame disclosed a giant native, smeared with oil and naked save for a narrow belt of leopard hide bound round his waist and another band of spotted fur wound round his temples. On each hand he wore a glove of leopard skin, and fixed to every finger was a long, hooked claw of sharpened iron. One blow from those spiked gloves and anyone sustaining it would have had the flesh ripped from his bones.

"Nerves, eh?" the Englishman repeated. "Jolly good thing for you I had 'em, young feller-me-lad, and that saw this beggar crouchin' in the tree–

"The devil! You would, eh?" The inert native, bleeding from a bullet in his thigh, had regained the breath the tumble from the tree had knocked from him, raised on his & bow and struck a slashing blow at Ingraham's legs. The Englishman swung his pistol barrel with crushing force upon the native's head; then, as Bendigo and half a dozen Houssas hurried up:

"O Sergeant Man, prepare a harness for this beast and keep him safely till his spirit has returned."

The sergeant saluted, and in a moment the prisoner was securely trussed with cords.

Some twenty minutes later Bendigo stood at Ingraham's tent, a light of pleased anticipation shining in his eyes, "Prisoner's spirit has come back, O Hiji," he reported.

"Good, bring him here.

"I see you, Leopard Man," he opened the examination when they brought the fettered captive to us.

The prisoner eyed him sullenly, but volunteered no answer.

"Who sent you through the woods to do this thing?" Ingraham pursued.

"The leopard hates and kills, he does not talk," man replied.

"*Oko!*" the Englishman returned grimly. "I think this leopard will talk, and be jolly glad to. Sergeant, build a fire!"

Sergeant Bendigo had evidently anticipated this, for dry sticks and kindling were produced with a celerity nothing short of marvelous.

"I hate to do this, Trowbridge," Ingraham told me, "but I've got to get the truth out of this blighter, and get it in a hurry. Go to your tent if you think you can't stand it."

The captive howled and beat his head against the earth and writhed as though he were an eel upon the barbs when they thrust his bare soles into the glowing embers; but not until the stench of burning flesh rose sickeningly upon the still night air did he shake his head from side to side in token of surrender.

"Now, then, who sent you?" Ingraham demanded when the

prisoner's blistered feet were thrust into a canvas bucket full of water. "Speak up, and speak the truth, or–" he nodded toward the fire which smoldered menacingly as a Houssa policeman fed it little bits of broken sticks to keep it ready for fresh service.

"You are Hiji," said the prisoner, as though announcing that the sun had ceased to shine and the rivers ceased to flow. "You are He-Who-Comes-When-No-Man-Thinks-Him-Near. They told us you were gone away across the mighty water."

"Who told you this great lie, O fool?"

"Bazarri. He came with other white men through the woods and told us you were fled and that the soldiers of the Emperor-King would trouble us no more. They said the Leopard Men should rule the land again, and no one bid us stop."

"What were you doing here, son of a fish?"

"Last moon Bazarri sent us forth in search of slaves. Much help is needed for this digging which he makes, for he prepares a mighty pit where, in a night and a night, they celebrate the marriage of a mortal woman to the King of all the Devils. My brethren took the prisoners back, but I and as many others as a man has eyes remained behind to–"

"To stage a little private cannibalism, eh?"

"They told us that the soldiers would not come this way again," the prisoner answered in excuse.

Ingraham smiled, but not pleasantly. "That's the explanation, eh?" he murmured to himself. "No wonder we haven't seen or heard anything of the villagers. These damned slavers have taken most of 'em up to MacAndrews' and those they didn't kill or capture are hidin' in the bush." To the prisoner:

"Is this Bazarri a white man with the body of a youth and the wrinkled face of an old monkey?"

"Lord, who can say how you should know this thing?"

"Does he know that I am coming with my soldiers to send him to the land of ghosts?"

"Lord, he does not know. He thinks that you have gone across the great water. If he knew you were here he would have gone against you with his Leopard Men to kill you while you slept."

"The Emperor-King's men never sleep, retorted Ingraham. To Bendigo: "A firing-party for this one, Sergeant. The palaver is over.

"We must break camp at once," he added as eight tarbooshed policemen marched smartly past, their rifles at slant arms. "You heard what he said; they're all set to celebrate that girl's marriage to the Devil in two more nights. We can just make it to MacAndrews' by a forced march."

"Can't you spare this poor fellow's life?" I pleaded. "You've gotten what you want from him, and–"

"No chance," he told me shortly. "The penalty for membership in these Leopard Societies is death; so is the punishment for slaving and cannibalism. If it ever got about that we'd caught one of the 'Little Leopards' red-handed and let him off, government authority would get an awful black eye."

He buttoned his blouse, put on his helmet and marched across the clearing. "Detail halt; front rank, kneel; ready; take aim – *fire!*" His orders rang in sharp staccato, and the prisoner toppled over with eight rifle bullets in his breast.

Calmly as though it were a bit of everyday routine, Sergeant Bendigo advanced, drew his pistol and fired a bullet in the prone man's ear. The head, still bound in its filet of leopard skin, bounced upward with the impact of the shot, then fell back flaccidly. The job was done.

"Dig a grave and pile some rocks on it, then cover it with ashes from the fire," Ingraham ordered. To me he added:

"Can't afford to have hyenas unearthin' him or vultures wheelin' round, you know. It would give the show away. If any of his little playmates found him and saw the bullet marks they might make tracks for MacAndrews' – and we want to get there first."

We broke camp in half an hour, pushed onward through the night and marched until our legs were merely so much aching muscle the next day. Six hours' rest then again the endless, hurrying march.

Twice we saw evidence of the Leopards' visits, deserted villages where blackened rings marked the site of burned huts, red stains upon the earth, vultures disputing over ghastly scraps of flesh and bone.

As we passed through the second village the scouts brought back a woman, a slender frightened girl of fifteen or so, with a face which might have been a Gorgon's and a figure fit to make a Broadway entrepreneur discharge his entire chorus in disgust.

"Thou art my father and my mother," she greeted Ingraham conventionally.

"Where are thy people?" he demanded.

"In the land of ghosts, lord," she replied. "A day and a day ago there came to us the servants of Bazarri, men of the Little Leopards, with iron claws upon their hands and white men's guns. They said to us: 'The Emperor-King is overthrown; no longer shall his soldiers bring the law to you. Come with us and serve Bazarri, who is the servant of the Great King of All Devils, and we shall make you rich.'

"'This is bad palaver, and when Hiji comes he will hang you to a tree,' my father told them.

"'Hiji is gone across the great water, and will never come here more,' they told my father. Then they killed many of my people, and some they took as slaves to serve Bazarri where the King of Devils makes a marriage with a mortal woman. Lord, hadst thou been my father had not died."

"Maiden," Ingraham answered, "go tell thy people to come again into their village and build the huts the evil men burned down. Behold, I and my soldiers travel swiftly to give punishment to these evil men. Some I shall hang and some my men will shoot; but surely I shall slay them all. Those defy the Emperor-King's commands have not long lives."

The sudden tropic dark had long since fallen, and it was almost midnight by the hands on Ingraham's luminous watch dial when we reached the edge of a large clearing with a sharply rising hill upon its farther side. From behind this elevation shone a ruddy light, as though a dozen wooden houses burned at once.

"Quiet, thirty lashes for the one who makes a sound," said Ingraham as we halted at the forest edge. "Get those Lewis guns ready; fix bayonets.

"Sergeant, take two men and go forward. If anyone accost you, shoot him down immediately. We'll charge the moment we hear a shot."

Twenty minutes, half an hour, three-quarters, passed. Still no warning shot, no sign of Sergeant Bendigo or his associates.

"By the Lord Harry, I'm half a mind to chance it!" Ingraham muttered. "They may have done Bendigo in, and–"

"No, sar, Bendigo is here," a whisper answered him, and a form rose suddenly before us. "Bendigo has drunk the broth of serpent's flesh, he can move through the dark and not be seen."

"I'll say he can," the Englishman agreed. "What's doing?"

"No end dam' swanky palaver over there," returned the sergeant. "Many people sit around like elders at the council and watch while others make some show before them. I think we better go there pretty soon."

"So do I," returned his officer.

"Attention, charge bayonets; no shooting till I give the word. Quick step, march!"

We passed across the intervening clearing, mounted the steep slope of grassy bank, and halted at the ridge. Before us, like a stage, was such a sight as I had never dreamed of, even in my wildest flights of fancy.

## 24. THE DEVIL'S BRIDE

"Great guns!" Ingraham exclaimed as we threw ourselves upon our stomachs and wriggled to the crown of the hill, "Old MacAndrews knew a thing or two, dotty as he was! Look at that masonry – perfect as it was when Augustus Caesar ruled the world! The old Scotsman would have had the laugh on all of 'em, if he'd only lived."

What I had thought a long, steep-sided natural hill was really the nearer of two parallel earthen ramparts, and between these, roughly oval in form, a deep excavation had been made, disclosing tier on tier of ancient stone benches rising terrace-like about an amphitheater. Behind these were retaining walls of mortised stone – obviously the well-preserved remains of a Roman circus.

The arena between the curving ranks of benches was paved with shining sand, washed and rewashed until it shone with almost dazzling whiteness, and the whole enclosure was aglow with ruddy light, for stretching in an oval round the sanded floor was set a line of oil-palms, each blazing furiously, throwing tongues of orange flame high in the air and making every object in the excavation visible as though illumined by the midday sun.

The leaping, crackling flames disclosed the tenants of the benches, row after row of red-robed figures, hoods drawn well forward on their faces, hands hidden in the loose sleeves of their gown, but every one intent upon the spectacle below, heads bent, each line of their voluminously-robed bodies instinct with eagerness and gloating, half-restrained anticipation.

The circus proper was some hundred yards in length by half as many wide. Almost beneath us crouched a group of black musicians who, even as we looked, began a thumping monody on their double-headed drums, beating a sort of slow adagio with one hand, a fierce, staccato syncopation with the other. The double-timed insistence of it mounted to my head like some accursed drug. Despite myself I felt my hands and feet twitching to the rhythm of those drums, a sort of tingling racing up my spine. The red-robed figures on the benches were responding, too, heads swaying, hands no longer hidden in their sleeves, but striking together softly, as if in acclamation of the drummers' skill.

At the arena's farther end, where the double line of benches broke, was hung a long red curtain blazoned with the silver image of the strutting peacock, and from behind the folds of the thick drapery we saw that some activity was toward, for the carmine cloth would swing in rippling folds from time to time as though invisible hands were clutching it.

"Now, I wonder what the deuce–" Ingraham began, but stopped

abruptly as the curtain slowly parted and into the firelight marched a figure. From neck to heels he was enveloped in a robe of shimmering scarlet silk, thicksewn with glistening gems worked in the image of a peacock. Upon his head he wore a beehive-shaped turban of red silk set off with a great medallion of emeralds.

One look identified him. Though we had seen him suffer death in the electric chair and later looked upon him lying in his casket, there was no doubt in either of our minds. The Oriental potentate who paced the shining sands before us was Grigor Bazarov, the Red Priest who officiated at the Mass of St. Secaire.

Beside him, to his right and left, and slightly to the rear, marched the men who acted as deacon and sub-deacon when he served the altar of the Devil, but now they were arrayed in costumes almost as gorgeous as their chief's, turbans of mixed red and black upon their heads, broaches of red stones adorning them, curved swords flashing in jeweled scabbards at their waists.

Attended by his satellites the Red Priest made the circuit of the colosseum, and as he passed, the red-robed figures on the benches arose and did him reverence.

Now he and his attendants took station before the squatting drummers, and as he raised his hand in signal the curtains at the arena's farther end were parted once again and from them came a woman, tall, fair-haired, purple-eyed, enveloped in a loose-draped cloak of gleaming cloth of gold. A moment she paused breathlessly upon the margin of the shining sand,. and as she waited two tall black women, stark naked save for gold bands about their wrists and ankles, stepped quickly forward from the curtain's shrouding folds, grasped the golden cloak which clothed her and lifted it away, so that she stood revealed as nude as her two serving-maids, her white and lissom body gleaming in sharp contrast to their black forms as an ivory figurine might shine beside two statuettes of ebony.

A single quick glance told us she was crazed with aphrodisiacs and the never-pausing rhythm of the drums. With a wild, abandoned gesture she threw back her mop of yellow hair, tossed her arms above her head and, bending nearly double, raced across the sands until she paused a moment by the drummers, her body stretched as though upon a rack as she rose on tiptoe and reached her hands up to the moonless sky.

Then the dance. As as thin as nearly fleshless bones could make her, her figure still was slight, rather than emaciated, and as she bent and twisted, writhed and whirled, then stood stock-still and rolled her narrow hips and straight, flat abdomen, I felt the hot blood mounting in my cheeks and the pulses beating in my temples in time with the insistent throbbing of the drums. Pose after pose instinct with lecherous promise melted into still more lustful postures as patterns change their forms upon the lens of a kaleidoscope.

Now a vocal chorus seconded the music of the tom-toms:
"*Ho, ho!, hola,*
"*Ho, ho!, hold,*
"*Tou bonia berbe Azid!*"

The Red Priest and the congregation repeated the lines endlessly, striking their hands together at the ending of each stanza.

"Good God!" Ingraham muttered in my ear. "D'ye get it Trowbridge?"

"No," I whispered back. "What is it?"

"'*Tou bonia berbe Azid*' means 'thou has become a lamb of the Devil!' It's the invocation which precedes a human sacrifice!"

"B-but–" I faltered, only to have the words die upon my tongue, for the Red Priest stepped forward, unsheathing the scimitar from the jeweled scabbard at his waist. He tendered it to her, blade foremost, and I winced involuntarily as I saw her take the steel in her bare hand and saw the blood spurt like a ruby dye between her fingers as the razor-edge bit through the soft flesh to the bone.

But in her wild delirium she was insensible to pain. The curved sword whirled like darting lightning round her head, circling and flashing in the burning palm-trees' light till it made a silver halo for her golden hair. Then it all occurred so quickly that I scarcely knew what happened till the act was done. The wildly whirling blade reversed its course, struck inward suddenly and passed across her slender throat, its superfine edge propelled so fiercely by her maddened hand that she was virtually decapitated.

The rhythm of the drums increased, the flying fingers of the drummers increased, the flying fingers of the drummers beating a continuous roar which filled the sultry night like thunder, and the red-robed congregation rose like one individual, bellowing wild approval at the suicide. The dancer tripped and stumbled in her corybantic measure, a spate of ruby life-blood cataracting down her snow bosom; wheeled round upon her toes a turn or two, then toppled to the sand, her hands and feet and body twitching with a tremor like the jerking of a victim of St. Vitus dance. She raised herself upon her elbows and tried to call aloud, but the gushing blood drowned out her voice. Then she fell forward on her face and lay prostrate in the sand, her dying heart still pumping spurts of blood from her severed veins and arteries.

The sharp, involuntary twitching of the victim ceased, and with it stopped the gleeful rumble of the drums. The Red Priest raised his hand as if in invocation. "That the Bride of Lucifer may tread across warm blood!" he told the congregation in a booming voice, then pointed to the crimson pool which dyed the snowy sand before the trailing scarlet curtain.

The two black women who had taken off her cloak approached the quivering body of the self-slain girl, lifted it – one by the shoulders, the other by the feet – and bore it back behind the scarlet curtain, their progress followed by a trail of ruddy drops which trickled from the dead girl's severed throat at every step they took.

Majestically the Red Priest drew his scarlet mantle round him, waved to the drummers to precede him, then followed by his acolytes, passed through the long red curtains in the wake of the victim and the bearers of the dead.

A whispering buzz, a sort of oestrus of anticipation, ran through the red-robed congregation as the arch-priest vanished, but the clanging, brazen booming of a bell cut the sibilation short.

*Clang!*

A file of naked blacks marched out in the arena, each carrying a sort of tray slung from a strap about his shoulders, odd, gourd-like pendants hanging from the board. Each held a short stave with a leather-padded head in either hand, and with a start of horror I recognized the things – trust a physician of forty years' experience to know a human thigh-bone when he sees it!

*Clang!*

The black men squatted on the glittering, firelit sand, and without a signal of any sort that we could see, began to hammer on the little tables resting on their knees. The things were crude marimbas, primitive xylophones with hollow gourds hung under them for resonators, and, incredible as it seemed, produced a music strangely like the reeding of an organ. A long, resounding chord, so cleverly sustained that it simulated the great swelling of a bank of pipes; then, slowly, majestically, there boomed forth within that ancient Roman amphitheater the Bridal Chorus from *Lohengrin*.

*Clang!*

Unseen hands put back the scarlet curtain which had screened the Red Priest's exit. There. reared against the amphitheater's granite wall, was a cathedral altar, ablaze with glittering candles. Arranged behind the altar like a reredos, was a giant figure, an archangelic figure with great, outspread wings, but with the long, bearded face of a leering demon, goat's horns protruding from its brow. The crucifix upon the altar was reversed, and beneath its down-turned head stretched the scarlet mattress which I knew would later hold a human altar-cloth. To right and left were small side altars, like sanctuaries raised to saints in Christian churches. That to the right bore the hideous figure of a man in ancient costume with the head of a rhinoceros. I had seen its counterpart in a museum; it was the figure of the Evil One of Olden Egypt, Set, the slayer of Osiris. Upon the left was raised an altar to an obscene idol carved of some black stone, a female figure, gnarled and knotted and articulated in a manner suggesting horrible deformity. From the shoulder-sockets three arms sprang out to right and left, a sort of pointed cap adorned the head, and about the pendulous breasts serpents twined and writhed, while a girdle of gleaming skulls, carved of white bone, encircled the waist. Otherwise it was nude, with a nakedness which seemed obscene even to me, a medical practitioner for whom the human body held no secrets. Kali, "the Six-Armed One of Horrid Form", goddess of the murderous *Thags* of India, I knew the thing to be.

*Clang!*

The bell beat out its twelfth and final stroke, and from an opening in the wall directly under us a slow procession came. First walked the crucifer, the corpus of his cross head-downward, a peacock's effigy perched atop the rood, then, two by two, ten acolytes with swinging censers, the fumes of which swirled slowly through the air in writhing clouds of heady, maddening perfume. Next marched robed and surpliced man who swung a tinkling sacring bell, and then, beneath a canopy of scarlet silk embossed with gold, the Red Priest came, arrayed in full ecclesiastical regalia. Close in his footsteps marched his servers, vested as deacon and sub-deacon, and after them a double file of women votaries arrayed in red, long veils of crimson net upon their heads, hands crossed demurely on their bosoms.

Slowly the procession passed between the rows of blazing palm-trees, deployed before the altar and formed in crescent shape, the Red Priest and his acolytes in the center.

A moment's pause in the marimba music; then the Red Priest raised his hand, palm forward, as if in salutation, and chanted solemnly:

"To the Gods of Egypt who are Devils,
"To the Gods of Babylon in Nether Darkness,
"To all the Gods of all Forgotten Peoples,
"Who rest not, but lust eternally – Hail!"

Turning to the rhinoceros-headed monster on the right he bowed respectfully and called:

"Hail Thee who are Doubly Evil,
"Who comest forth from Ali,
"Who proceedest from the Lake of Nefer,
"Who comest from the Courts of Sechet – Hail!"

To the left he turned and invoked the female horror:

"Hail, Kali, Daughter of Himavat,
'Hail, Thou about whose waist hang human skulls,
"Hail, Devil of Horrid Form,
"Malign Image of Destructiveness,
"Eater-up of all that it good,

"*Disseminater of all which is wicked – Hail!*"

Finally, looking straight before him, he raised both hands above his head and fairly screamed:

"And Thou, Great Barran-Sathanas,
"Azid, Beelzebub, Lucifer, Asmodeum,
"Or whatever name Thou wishest to be known by,
"Lucifer, Mighty Lord of Earth,
"Prince of the Powers of the Air;
"We give Thee praise and adoration,
"Now and ever, Mighty Master,
"Hail all hail, Great Lucifer. Hail, all hail!"

"All hail!" responded the red congregation.

Slowly the Red Priest mounted to the sanctuary. A red nun tore away her habit, rending scarlet silk and cloth as though in very ecstasy of haste, and nude and gleaming-white, climbed quickly up and laid herself upon the scarlet cushion. They set the chalice and the paten on her branded breast and the Red Priest genuflected low before the living altar, then turned and, kneeling with his back presented to the sanctuary, crossed himself in reverse with his left hand and, rising once again, his left hand raised, bestowed a mimic blessing on the congregation.

A long and death-still silence followed, a silence so intense that we could hear the hissing of the resin as the palm-trees burned, and when a soldier moved uneasily beside me in the grass the rasping of his tunic buttons on the earth came shrilly to my ears.

"Now, what the deuce–" Ingraham began, but checked himself and craned his neck to catch a glimpse of what was toward in the arena under us; for, as one man, the red-robed congregation had turned to face the tunnel entrance leading to the amphitheater opposite the altar, and a sigh that sounded like the rustling of the autumn wind among the leaves made the circuit of the benches.

I could not see the entrance, for the steep sides of the excavation hid it from my view, but in a moment I descried a double row of iridescent peacocks strutting forward, their shining tails erected, their glistening wings lowered till the quills cut little furrows in the sand. Slowly. pridefully, as though they were aware of their magnificence, the jeweled birds marched across the hippodrome, and in their wake–

"For God's sake!" exclaimed Ingraham.

"Good heavens!" I ejaculated.

"Alice!" John Davisson's low cry was freighted with stark horror and despairing recognition.

It *was* Alice; unquestionably it was she; but how completely metamorphosed! A diadem of beaten gold, thickset with flashing jewels, was clasped about her head. Above the circlet, where dark hair and white skin met at the temples, there grew a pair of horns! They grew, there was no doubt of it, for even at that distance I could see the skin fold forward round the bony base of the protuberances; no skilful make-up artist could have glued them to her flesh in such a way. Incredible – impossible – as I knew it was, it could not be denied. A pair of curving goat-horns grew from the girl's head and reared upward exactly like the horns on carved or painted figures of the Devil!

A collar of gold workmanship, so wide its outer edges rested on her shoulders, was round her neck, and below the gleaming gorget her white flesh shone like ivory; for back, abdomen and bosom were unclothed and the nipples of her highset, virgin breasts were stained a brilliant red with henna. About her waist was locked the silver marriage girdle of the Yezidees, the girdle she had worn so laughingly that winter evening long ago when we assembled at St. Chrysostom's to rehearse her wedding to John Davisson. Below the girdle – possibly supported by it – hung a skirt of iridescent sequins, so long that it barely cleared her ankles, so tight that it gave her only four or five scant inches for each pace, so that she walked with slow, painstaking care lest the fetter of the garment's hem should trip her as she stepped. The skirt trailed backward in a point a foot or so behind her, leaving a little track in the soft sand, as though a serpent had crawled there and, curiously, giving an oddly serpentine appearance from the rear.

Bizarre and sinister as her costume was, the transformation of her face was more so. The slow, half-scornful, half-mocking smile upon her painted mouth, the beckoning, alluring glance which looked out from between her kohl-stained eyelids, the whole provocative expression of her countenance was strange to Alice Hume. This was no woman we had ever known, this horned, barbaric figure was some wanton, cruel she-devil who held possession of the body we had known as hers.

And so she trod across the shining sand on naked, milk-white feet, the serpent-track left by her trailing gown winding behind her like an accusation. And as she walked she waved her jewel-encrusted hands before her, weaving fantastic arabesques in empty air as Eastern fakirs do when they would lay a charm on the beholder.

"Hail, Bride of Night
"Hail, horned Bride of Mighty Lucifer;
"Hail, thou who comest from the depths far Abaddon;
"Hail and thrice hail to her who passes blood and fire
"That she may greet her Bridegroom!
"Hail, all hail!"

cried the Red Priest, and as he finished speaking, from each side of the altar rushed a line of red-veiled women, each bearing in her hands a pair of wooden pincers between the prongs of which there glowed and smoldered a small square of super-heated stone. That the rocks were red-hot could not be denied, for we could see the curling smoke and even little licking tongues of flame as the wooden tongs took fire from them.

The women laid their fiery burdens down upon the sand, making an incandescent path of glowing stepping-stones some ten feet long, leading directly to the altar's lowest step.

And now the strange, barbaric figure with its horn-crowned head had reached the ruddy stain upon the sand where the dancing suicide had bled her life away, and now her snowy feet were stained a horrid scarlet, but never did she pause in her slithering step. Now she reached the path of burning stones, and now her tender feet were pressed against them, but she neither hastened or retreated in her march – to blood and fire alike she seemed indifferent.

Now she reached the altar's bottom step and paused a moment, not in doubt or fear, but rather seeming to debate the easiest way to mount the step's low lift and yet not trip against the binding hobble of her skirt's tight hem.

At length, when one or two false trials had been made, she managed to get up the step by turning sidewise and raising her nearer foot with slow care, transferring her weight to it, then mounting with a sudden hopping jump.

Three steps she had negotiated in this slow, awkward fashion, when:

"For God's sake, aren't you going to do anything?" John Davisson hissed in Ingraham's ear. "She's almost up – are you going to let 'em go through with–"

"Sergeant," Ingraham turned to Bendigo, ignoring John completely, "are the guns in place?"

"Yas, sar, everything dam' top-hole" the sergeant answered with a grin.

"Very well, then, a hundred yards will be about the proper range. Ready–"

The order died upon his lips, and he and I and all of us sat forward, staring in hang-jawed amazement.

From the tunnel leading to the ancient dungeons at the back of the arena, a slender figure came, paused a moment at the altar steps, then mounted them in three quick strides.

It was Jules de Grandin.

He was in spotless khaki, immaculate from linen-covered sun-hat to freshly polished boots; his canvas jacket and abbreviated cotton shorts might just have left the laundress' hands, and from the way he bore his slender silver-headed cane beneath his left elbow one might have thought that he was ready for a promenade instead of risking almost sure and dreadful death.

"*Pardonnez moi. Messieurs-Mesdames,*" he bowed politely to the company of priests and women at the altar, "but this wedding, he can not go on. No, he must be stopped – right away; at once."

The look upon the Red Priest's face was almost comical. His big, sad eyes were opened till it seemed that they were lidless, and a corpse-gray pallor overspread his wrinkled countenance.

"Who dares forbid the banns?" he asked, recovering his aplomb with difficulty.

"*Parbleu,*" the little Frenchman answered with a smile, "the British Empire and the French Republic for two formidable objectors; and last, although by no means least Monsieur, no less a one than Jules de Grandin."

"Audacious fool!" the Red Priest almost howled.

"But certainly," de Grandin bowed, as though acknowledging a compliment, "*l'audace, encore de l'audace, toujours de l'audace*; it is I."

The Devil's Bride had reached the topmost step while this colloquy was toward. Absorbed in working herself up to the altar, she had not realized the visitor's identity. Now, standing at the altar, she recognized de Grandin, and her pose of evil provocation dropped from her as if it were a cast-off garment.

"Doctor – Doctor de Grandin!" she gasped unbelievingly, and with a futile, piteous gesture she clasped her hands across her naked bosom as though to draw a cloak around herself.

"*Precisement, ma pauvre*, and I am here to take you home," the little Frenchman answered, and though he looked at her and smiled, his little sharp blue eyes were alert to note the smallest movement of the men about the altar.

The Red Priest's voice broke in on them. "Wretch meddler, do you imagine that your God can save you now?" he asked.

"He has been known to work much greater miracles," de Grandin answered mildly. "Meantime, if you will kindly stand aside–"

The Red Priest interrupted in a low-pitched, deadly voice: "Before tomorrow's sun has risen we'll crucify you on on that altar, as–"

"As you did crucify the poor young woman in America?" de Grandin broke in coldly. "I do not think you will, my friend."

"No? Dmitri, Kasimir – seize this cursed dog!"

The deacon and sub-deacon, who had been edging closer all the while, leaped forward at their master's bidding, but the deacon halted suddenly, as though colliding with an unseen barrier, and the savage snarl upon his gipsy features gave way to a puzzled look – a look of almost comic pained surprise. Then we saw spreading on his face a widening smear of red – red blood which ran into his eyes and dripped down on his parted lips before he tumbled headlong to the crimson carpet spread before the altar.

The other man had raised his hands, intent on bringing them down on de Grandin's shoulders with a crushing blow. Now, suddenly, the raised hands shook and quivered in the air, then clutched spasmodically at nothing, while a look of agony spread across his face. He hiccupped once and toppled forward, a spate of ruby blood pouring from his mouth and drowning out his death cry.

"And still you would deny me one poor miracle, *Monsieur?*" de Grandin asked the Red Priest in a level, almost toneless voice.

Indeed, it seemed miraculous. Two men had died from gunshot wounds, by all appearances – yet we had heard no shot. But:

"Nice work, Frenchy!" Ingraham whispered approvingly. "They have some sharpshooters with silencers on their guns up there," he told me. "I saw the flashes when those two coves got it in the neck. Slick work, eh, what? He'll have those fellers groggy in a minute, and—"

The Red Priest launched himself directly at de Grandin with a roar of bestial fury. The little Frenchman sidestepped neatly, grasped the silver handle of his cane where it projected from his left elbow, and drew the gleaming sword blade from the stick.

"*Ah-ha?*" he chuckled, "*Ah-ha-ha, Monsieur Diablotin*, you did not bargain for this, *hein?*" He swung the needle-like rapier before him in a flashing circle, then, swiftly as a cobra strikes, thrust forward, "That one for the poor girl whom you crucified!" he cried, and the Red Priest staggered back a step, his hand raised to his face. The Frenchman's blade had pierced his left eyeball.

"And take this for the poor one whom you blinded!' de Grandin told him as he thrust a second time, driving the rapier point full in the other eye.

The Red Priest tottered drunkenly, his hands before his blinded eyes, but de Grandin knew no mercy. "And you may have this for the honest *gendarme* whom you shot," he added, lashing the blind man's wrinkled cheeks with the flat of his blade, "and last of all, take this for those so helpless little lads who died upon your cursed altar!" He sank backward on one foot, then straightened suddenly forward, stiffening his sword-arm and plunging his point directly in the Red Priest's opened mouth.

A scream of agonizing pain rang out with almost deafening shrillness, and the blind man partly turned, as though upon an unseen pivot, clawed with horrid impotence at the wire-fine blade of the little Frenchman's rapier, than sank slowly to the altar, his death-scream stifled to a sickening gurgle as his mouth filled up with blood.

"*Fini!*" de Grandin cried, then: "If you are ready, Mademoiselle, we shall depart." He bowed to Alice, and:

"*Holé – la corde!*" he cried abruptly, raising his hand in signal to someone overhead.

Like a great serpent, a thick hemp hawser twisted down against the amphitheater's wall, and in the fading light shed from the burning trees we saw the gleam of blue coats and red fezzes where the native *gendarmes* stood above the excavation, their rifles at the ready.

De Grandin flung an arm around Alice, took a quick turn of the rope around his other arm, and nodded vigorously. Like the flying fairies in a pantomime they rose in the air, past the high altar, past the horned and pinioned image of the Devil, past the stone wall of the coliseum, upward to the excavation's lip where ready hands stretched out to drag them back to safety.

Now the red congregation was in tumult. While de Grandin parleyed with the Red Priest, even while he slew him with his sword, they had sat fixed in stupor, but as they saw the Frenchman and the girl hauled up to safety, a howl like the war-cry of the gathered demons of the pit rose from their throats – a cry of burning rage and thwarted lust and bitter, mordant disappointment. "Kill him! – after him! – crucify him! – burn him!" came the shouted admonition, and more than one cowled member of the mob drew out a pistol and fired it at the light patch which de Grandin's spotless costume made against the shadow.

"Fire!" roared Ingraham to his soldiers, and the crashing detonation of a rifle volley echoed through the night, and after it came the deadly *clack-clack-clatter* of the Lewis guns.

And from the farther side of the arena the French troops opened fire, their rifles blazing death, their Maxims spraying steady streams of bullets at the massed forms on the benches.

Suddenly there came a fearful detonation, accompanied by a blinding flare of flame. From somewhere on the French side a *bombe de main* – a hand grenade – was thrown, and like a bolt of lightning it burst against the stone wall shoring up the terraced seats about the colosseum.

The result was cataclysmic. The Roman architects who designed the place had built for permanency, but close upon two thousand years had passed since they had laid those stones, and centuries of pressing earth and trickling subsoil waters had crumbled the cement. When the Satanists turned back the earth they had not stopped to reinforce the masonry or shore up the raw edges of their cutting. Accordingly, the fierce explosion of the bursting bomb precipitated broken stone and sand and rubble into the ancient hippodrome, and instantly a landslide followed. Like sand that trickles in an open pit the broken stone and earth rushed down, engulfing the arena.

"Back – go back!" Ingraham cried, and we raced to safety with the earth falling from beneath our very feet.

It was over in a moment. Only a thin, expiring wisp of smoke emerging through a cleft in the slowly settling earth told where the palm-trees had been blazing furiously a few minutes before. Beneath a hundred thousand tons of sand and crumbling clay and broken stone was buried once again the ancient Roman ruin, and with it every one of those who traveled round the world to see a mortal woman wedded to the Devil.

"By gosh, I think that little Frog was right when he said '*fini*'," Ingraham exclaimed as he lined his Houssas up.

"*Hamdullah*, trouble comes, O Hiji!" Sergeant Bendigo announced. "Leopard fellers heard our shooting and come to see about it, Allah curse their noseless fathers!"

"By Jove, you're right!" Ingraham cried. "Form square – machine-guns to the front. At two hundred yards – fire!" The volley blazed and crackled from the line of leveled rifles and the shrewish chatter of the Lewis guns mingled with the wild, inhuman screams of the attackers.

On they came, their naked, ebon bodies one shade darker than the moonless tropic night, their belts and caps of leopard skin showing golden in the gloom. Man after man went down before the hail of lead, but on they came closer, closer, closer!

Now something whistled through the air with a wicked, whirring sound, and the man beside me stumbled back, a five-foot killing spear protruding from his breast. "All things are with Allah, the Merciful, the Compassionate!" he choked, and the blood from his punctured lung made a horrid gurgling noise, like water running down a partly occluded drain.

Now they were upon us, and we could see the cam-wood stains upon their faces and the markings on their wicker shields and the gleaming strings of human toe and finger bones which hung around their necks. We were outnumbered ten to one, and though the Houssas held their line with perfect discipline, we knew that it was but a matter of a quarter-hour at most before the last of us went down beneath the avalanche of pressing bodies and stabbing spears.

"*Basonette au cannon – Chargez!*" the order rang out sharply on our left, followed by the shrilling of a whistle from the right, and a half a hundred blue-clothed Senegalese *gendarmes* hurled themselves upon the left flank of our enemies, while as many more crashed upon the foemen from the right, bayonets flashing in the gun-fire, black faces mad with killing-lust and shining with the sweat of fierce exertion.

Now there was a different timbre in the Human Leopards' cries. Turned from hunters into quarry, like their bestial prototypes they stood at bay; but the lean, implacable Senegalese were at their backs, their eighteen-inch bayonets stabbing mercilessly, and Ingraham's Houssas barred their path in front.

At last a Leopard Man threw down his spear, and in a moment all were empty-handed. "*Faire halte!*" Renouard commanded, jamming his pistol back into its holster and shouldering his way between the ranks of cringing captives.

"*Monsieur le Capitaine*," he saluted Ingraham with due formality, "I greatly deprecate the circumstances which have forced us to invade your territory, and herewith tender our apologies, but–"

"Apology's accepted, sweet old soul!" the Englishman cut in, clapping an arm about the Frenchman's shoulders and shaking him affectionately. "But I'd like to have your counsel in an important matter."

"*Mais certainement*," Renouard returned politely. "The matter for discussion is–" he paused expectantly.

"Do we hang or shoot these blighters?" Ingraham rejoined, nodding toward the group of prisoners.

## 25. THE SUMMING UP

Renouard and Ingraham stayed behind to gather up loose ends – the "loose ends" being such members of the Leopard Men as had escaped the wholesale execution – for they were determined to exterminate the frightful cult. Grandin and I, accompanied by a dozen Senegalese *gendarmes*, took Alice overland to Dakar, and Renouard dispatched a messenger before us to advise the hospital that we would need a private room for several days.

Since the night de Grandin rescued her the girl had lain in a half-stupor, and when she showed signs of returning consciousness the little Frenchman promptly gave her opiates. "It is better that she wake when all is finished and regard the whole occurrence as a naughty dream," he told me.

"But how the deuce did they graft those devilish horns on her?" I wondered. "There is no doubt about it; the things are growing, but–"

"All in good time," he soothed. "When we arrive at Dakar we shall see, my friend."

We did. The morning after our arrival we took her to the operating room, and while she lay in anesthesia, de Grandin deftly laid the temporal skin aside, making a perfect star-shaped incision.

"Name of a little blue man, behold my friend!" he ordered, bending across the operating table and pointing at the open wound with his scalpel tip. "They were clever, those ones, *n'est-ce-pas?*"

The lower ends of the small horns had been skilfully riveted to thin disks of gold and these had been inserted underneath the skin, which had then been sewn in place, so that the golden disks, held firmly between skin and tissue, had acted as anchors for the horns, which thus appeared to grow upon the young girl's head.

"Clever?" I echoed. "It's diabolical."

"*Eh bien*, they are frequently the same, my friend."

He sewed the slit skin daintily with an invisible subcutaneous stitch, matching the cut edges so perfectly that only the thinnest hair-line of red showed where he worked.

"*Voila*," he announced. "This fellow Jules de Grandin puzzles me, my friend. When he acts the physician I am sure he is a better doctor than policeman, but when he is pursuing evil-doers I think he is better *gendarme* than physician. The devil take the fellow; I shall never make him out!"

The little freighter wallowed in the rising swells, her twin propellers churning the blue water into buttermilk. Far astern the coast of Africa lay like the faintest wisp of smoke against the sky. Ahead lay France. De

Grandin lit another cigarette and turned his quick, bird-like look from Renouard to me, then to the deck chairs where Davisson and Alice lay side by side, their fingers clasped, the light that never was on land or sea within their eyes.

"*Non*, my friends," he told us, "it is most simple when you understand it. How could the evil fellow leave his cell at the *poste de police*, invade Friend Trowbridge's house and all but murder *Mademoiselle*? How could he be lodged all safely in his cell, yet be abroad to kill poor Hornsby and all but kill the good Costello? How could he die in the electric chair, and lie all dead within his coffin, yet send his wolves to kidnap *Mademoiselle* Alice? You ask me?

"*Ah-ha*, the answer is he did not!

"What do you think from that, *hein*?"

"Oh, for heaven's sake, stop talking rot and tell us how it was – if you really know," I shot back crossly.

He grinned delightedly. "Perfectly, my friend. *Ecoutez-moi, s'il vous plait*. When these so trying questions first began to puzzle me I drew my bow at venture. 'If *la Sureté* can not tell me of him I am shipwrecked – no, how do you call him? Sunk?' – I tell me. But I have great faith. A man so wicked as Bazarov, and a European as well, has surely run afoul of the law in France, I think, and if he has done so the *Sureté* most certainly has his dossier. And so I get his photograph and fingerprints from the governor of the prison and forward them to Paris. My answer waited for me at police headquarters at Dakar. It is this:

"Some five and forty years ago there lived in Mohilef a family named Bazarov. They had twin sons, Grigor and Vladimir. They were Roman Catholics.

"To be a Roman Catholic in Imperial Russia was much like being a Negro in the least enlightened of your Southern states today, my friends. Their political disabilities were burdensome, even in that land of dreadful despotism, and they walked in daily fear of molestation by the police, as well, since by the very fact of their adherence to the Church of Rome they were more than suspected of sympathy with Poland's aspirations for independence. The Poles, you will recall, are predominantly Roman Catholic in religion.

"Very well. The brothers Bazarov grew up, and in accordance with their parents' fondest wish, were sent to Italy to study for the church. In time they came back to their native land, duly ordained as fathers in the Roman Church, and sent to minister to their co-religionists in Russia. The good God knows there was a need of fathers in that land of orphans.

"Now in Russia they had a law which made the person having knowledge – even indirect – of conspiracy to change the form of government, with or without violence, punishable by penal sentence for six years if he failed to transmit information to the police. A harmless literary club was formed in Mohilef and the brothers Bazarov attended several meetings, as a number of the members were of the Roman faith.

"When the police learned of this club, they pounced upon the members and though there was not evidence enough to convict a weasel of chicken-killing, the poor wretches were found guilty, just the same, and sentenced to Siberia. The two young priests were caught in the police net, too, and charged with treasonably withholding information – because it was assumed they must have heard some treasonable news when they sat to hear confessions! *Enfin*, they were confined within the fortress-prison of St. Peter and St. Paul.

"They were immured in dungeons far below the level of the river, dungeons into which the water poured in time of inundation, so that the rats crawled on their shoulders to save themselves from drowning. What horrid tortures they were subject to within that earthly hell we can not surely say; but this we know: when they emerged from four years' suffering inside those prison walls, they came forth old and wrinkled men; moreover, they, who had received the rites of holy ordination, were atheists, haters of God and all his works, and sworn to sow the seed of atheism wherever they might go.

"We find them, then, as members of a group of anarchists in Paris, and there they were arrested, and much of their sad story written in the archives of the *Sureté*.

"Another thing: as not infrequently happens among Russians, these brethren were possessed of an uncanny power over animals. Wild, savage dogs would fawn on them, the very lions and tigers in the zoo would follow them as far as the limits of their cages would permit, and seemed to greet them with all signs of friendship."

"You comprehend?"

"Why – you mean that while Grigor was under arrest his brother Vladimir impersonated him and broke into my house, then went out gunning for Costello–" I began, but he interrupted with a laugh.

"Oh, Trowbridge, great philosopher, how readily you see the light when someone sets the lamp aglow!" he cried. "Yes, you are right. It was no supernatural ability which enabled him to leave his prison cell at will – even to make a mock of Death's imprisonment. Grigor was locked in prison – executed – but Vladimir, his twin and double, remained at large to carry on their work. But now he, too, is dead. I killed him when we rescued *Mademoiselle* Alice."

"One other thing, my Jules," Renouard demanded. "When they prepared to wed *Mademoiselle* to Satan, they made her walk all barefoot upon those burning stones. Was not that magic of a sort?"

De Grandin tweaked the needle-points of his mustache. "A

juggler's trick," he answered. "That fire-walking, he is widely practiced in some places, and always most successfully. The stones they use are porous as a sponge. They heat to incandescence quickly, but just as quickly they give off their heat. When they were laid upon the moistened sand these stones were cool enough to hold within your ungloved hand in thirty seconds. Some time was spent in mummery before they bade *Mademoiselle* to walk on them. By the time she stepped upon them they were cold as any money-lender's heart."

The ship's bell beat out eight quick strokes. De Grandin dropped down from his seat upon the rail and tweaked the waxed tips of his mustache until they stood out like twin needles each side his small and thin-flipped mouth. "Come, if you please," he ordered us.

"Where?" asked Alice.

"To the chart room, of course. The land has disappeared" – he waved his hand toward the horizon where rolling blue water met a calm blue sky – "and we are now upon the high sea."

"Well?" demanded John.

"Well? Name of a little green pig with most deplorably bad manners! I shall say it is well. Do not you know that masters of ships on the high seas are empowered by the law to solemnize the rite of marriage?"

Something of the old Alice we had known in other days looked from the tired and care-worn face above the collar of her traveling-coat as she replied: "I'm game;" then, eyes dropped demurely, and a slight flush in her cheeks, she added softly: "if John still wants me."

"Dearly beloved, we are gathered together here in the sight of God, and in the face of this company, to join together this man and this woman in holy matrimony," read the captain from the *Book of Common Prayer*. "If any man can show just cause why they may not lawfully be joined together, let him now speak, or else forever after hold his peace."

"Yes, *pardieu*, let him speak – and meet his death at Jules de Grandin's hands!" the little Frenchman murmured, thrusting one hand beneath his jacket where his automatic pistol rested in its shoulder holster.

"And now, with due solemnity, let us consign this *sacre* thing unto the ocean, and may the sea never give up its dead!" de Grandin announced when John and Alice Davisson, Renouard and I came from the captain's sanctum, the tang of champagne still upon our lips. He raised his hand and a silvery object glittered in the last rays of the setting sun, flashed briefly through the air, then sank without a trace beneath the blue sea water. It was the marriage girdle of the Yezidees.

"Oh," Alice cried, "you've thrown away 'the luck of the Humes'!"

"Precisely so, *cherie*," he answered with a smile. "There are no longer any Humes, only Davissons. *Le bon Dieu* grant there may be many of them."

\* \* \* \*

We have just returned from the christening of Alice's twin boys, Renouard de Grandin and Trowbridge Ingraham Davisson. The little villains howled right lustily when Doctor Bentley put the water on their heads, and:

"*Grand Dieu des porcs*, the Evil One dies hard in those small sinners!" said Jules de Grandin.

Ingraham, engrossed with ministerial duties in West Africa, was unable to be present, but the silver mugs he sent the youngsters are big enough to hold their milk for years to come.

As I write this, Renouard, de Grandin and Costello are very drunk in my consulting-room. I can hear Costello and Renouard laugh with that high-pitched cachinnation which only those far gone in liquor use at some droll anecdote which Jules de Grandin tells.

I think that I shall join them. Surely, there is one more drink left in the bottle.

# THE HOUSE OF GOLDEN MASKS

"An' so, Dr. de Grandin, sor," Detective Sergeant Costello concluded with a pitying sidelong glance his companion, "if there's anything ye can do for pore lad, 'tis meself that'll be grateful to ye for doin' it. Faith, if sumpin like this had happened to me whilst I was a-courtin' Maggie, I'd a' been a dead corpse from worry in less time than this pore felley's been sufferin'.

"Th' chief won't raise his hand in th' matter wid th' coroner's verdict starin' us in th' face, an' much as I'd like to do sumpin for th' boy, me hands is tied tighter'n th' neck of a sack. But with you, now, 'tis a different matter entirely. Meself, I'm inclined to agree with th' chief an' think th' pore gur-rl's dead as a herring, but if there's sumpin in th' case th' rest of can't see, sure, 'tis Dr. Jools de Grandin can spot it quicker than a hungry tom-cat smells a rat!"

Jules de Grandin turned his quick, bird-like glance from the big, red-headed Irishman to the slender white-faced young man seated beside him. "What makes you assume your beloved survives, *Monsieur?*" he asked. "If the jury of the coroner returned a verdict of suicide–"

"But, I tell you, sir, the jury didn't know what they were talking about!"

Young Everett Wilberding rose from his chair faced the little Frenchman, his knuckles showing white with the intensity of his grip on the table edge. "My Ewell *didn't* commit suicide. She didn't kill herself, neither did Mazie. You *must* believe that, sir!"

Resuming his seat, he fought back to comparative calm as he laced his fingers together nervously. "Last Thursday night Ewell and I were going to a dance out at the country club. My friend, Bill Stimpson, was to take Marie, Ewell's twin sister. The girls had been out visiting an aunt and uncle at Reynoldstown, and were to meet us at Monmouth junction, then drive out to the club in Ewell's flivver.

"The girls took their party clothes out to Reynoldstown with them, and were to dress before leaving to meet us. They were due at the junction at 9 o'clock, but Ewell was hardly ever on time, so I thought nothing of it when they failed to show up at half-past. But when 10 o'clock came, with no sign of the girls, we began to think they must have had a blow-out or engine trouble. At half-past 10 I went to the drug store and 'phoned the girls' uncle at Reynoldstown, only to be told they had left at a quarter past 8 – in plenty of time to reach the junction by 9, even if they had bad going. When I heard that I began to worry sure enough. By 11 o'clock I was fit to be tied.

"Bill was getting worried, too, but thought that one of 'em might have been taken ill and that they'd rushed right to Harrisonville without coming through the junction, so we 'phoned their house here. Their folks didn't know any more than we did.

"We caught the next bus to Harrisonville, and went right up to the Eatons'. When nothing was heard of the girls by 4 the next morning, Mr. Eaton notified the police."

"U'm?" de Grandin nodded slowly. "Proceed, if you please, young *Monsieur*."

"The searching parties didn't find a trace of the girls till next day about noon," young Wilberding answered; "then a State Trooper came on Ewell's Ford smashed almost out of shape against a tree half a mile or more from the river, but no sign of blood anywhere around. A little later a couple of hunters found Ewell's party dress, stockings and slippers on the rocks above Shaminee Falls. Mazie–"

"They found th' pore child's body up agin th' grilles leadin' to th' turbine intakes o' Pierce's Mills next day, sor," Costello put in softly.

"Yes, they did," Wilberding agreed, "and Mazie was wearing her dance frock – what was left of it. Why didn't Ewell jump in the falls with hers on, too, if Mazie did? But *Mazie didn't!*"

Sergeant Costello shook his head sadly. "Th' coroner's jury–" he began, as though reasoning with a stubborn child, but the boy interrupted angrily:

"Oh, damn the coroner's jury! See here, sir" – he turned to de Grandin as if for confirmation – "you're a physician and know all about such things. What d'ye say to this? Mazie's body was washed through the rapids above Shaminee Falls and was terribly mauled against the rocks as it came down, so badly disfigured that only the remnants of her clothes made identification possible. No one could say definitely whether she'd been wounded before she went into the water or not; but *she wasn't drowned!*"

"Eh, what is it you say?" de Grandin straightened in his chair, his level, unwinking stare boring into the young man's troubled eyes. "Continue, if you please, *Monsieur*; I am interested."

"I mean just what I say," the other returned. "They didn't find a half-teacupful of water in her lungs at the autopsy; besides, this is March, and the water's almost ice-cold – yet they found her *floating* next morning; if–"

"*Barbe dun chauve canard*, yes!" de Grandin exclaimed. "*Tu parles, mon garçon*! In temperature such as this it would be days – weeks, perhaps – before putrefaction had advanced enough to form sufficient gas to force the body to the surface. But of course, it was the air in her lungs which buoyed her up. *Morbleu*, I think you have right, my friend; undoubtlessly the poor one was dead before she touched the water!"

"Aw, Doc, ye don't mean to say *you're* fallin' for that theory?" Costello protested. "It's true she mightn't a' been drowned, but th' coroner said death was due to shock induced by–"

De Grandin waved him aside impatiently, keeping his gaze fixed intently on Everett. "Do you know any reason she might have had for self-destruction, *mon vieux*?" he demanded.

"No, sir – none whatever. She and Bill were secretly married at Hacketstown last Christmas Eve. They'd been keeping it dark till Bill got his promotion – it came through last week, and they were going to tell the world last Sunday. You see, they couldn't have concealed it much longer."

"Ah?" de Grandin's narrow brows elevated slightly. "And they were happy together?"

'Yes, sir! You never saw a spoonier couple in your life. Can you imagine–"

"*Tiens*, my friend," the Frenchman interrupted with one of his quick, elfish grins, "you would be surprised at that which I can imagine. Howevever, let us consider facts, not imaginings." Rising, he began pacing the floor, ticking off his data on his fingers as he marched. "Let us make a *précis*: Here we have two young women, one in love, though married – the other in love and affianced. They fail to keep an appointment; it is not till the day following that their car is discovered, and it is found in such a position as to indicate a wreck, yet nowhere near it is any sign of injury to its passengers. *Alors*, what do we find? The frock of one of the young ladies, neatly folded beside her shoes and stockings upon a rock near the Shaminee Falls. In the river, some miles below, next day is found the floating corpse of the other girl – and the circumstances point conclusively that she did not drown. What now? The mishap to the car occurred a half-mile from the river, yet the young men were able to walk to the stream where one of them cast herself in fully clothed; the other is supposed to have disrobed before immersing herself.

"*Non, non*, my friends, the facts, they do not make sense. Women kill themselves for good reasons, for bad reasons, and for no reasons at all, but they do it characteristically. Me, I have seen ropes wherewith despondent females have strangled themselves, and they have wrapped silken scarves about the rough hemp that it might not bruise their tender necks. *Tiens*, would a delicately nurtured girl strip herself to the rude March winds before plunging into the water? I think not."

"So do I," rumbled Costello's heavy voice in agreement. "Th' way you put it, Dr. de Grandin, sor, makes th' case crazier than ever. Faith, there's no sense to it from beginnin' to end. I think we'd better be callin' it a day an' acceptin' th' coroner's decision."

"*Zut!*" de Grandin returned with a smile, "Are you then so poor a poker player, *mon sergent?* Have you not learned the game is never over until the play is done? Me, I shall give this matter my personal attention. I am interested, I am fascinated, I am intrigued.

"To your home, Monsieur Wilberding," he ordered. "When I have some word for you, you will hear from me. Meantime do not despair."

"Trowbridge, *mon vieux*," de Grandin greeted next morning when I joined him in the dining-room, "I am perplexed; but yes, I am greatly puzzled; I am mystified. Something has occurred since last night which may put a different face upon all. Consider, if you please: half an hour ago I received a telephone call from the good Costello. He tells me three more young women have disappeared, in a manner to similar that of *Mon*sieur Wilberding's sweetheart as to make it more than mere coincident. At the residence of one *Monsieur* Mason, who resides in West Fells, there was held a meeting of the sorority to which his daughter belongs. Many young women attended. Three, *Mesdemoiselles* Weaver, Damroche and Hornbury, drove out in the car of *Mademoiselle* Weaver. They left the Mason house sometime after midnight. At 6 o'clock this morning they had not returned home. Their alarmed parents notified the police, and" – he paused in his restless pacing, halting directly before me as he continued – "a state dragoon discovered the motor in which they rode lying on its side, mired in the swamps beside the Albemarle Road, but of the young women no trace could be found. Figure to yourself, my friend. What do you make of it?"

"Why–" I began, but the shrill stutter of the office 'phone cut my reply in two.

"Allo?" de Grandin called into the transmitter. "Yes, Sergeant, it is I – *grand Diable!* Another? You do not tell me so!"

To me he almost shouted as he slammed the receiver back into its hook: "Do you hear, my friend? It is another! Sarah Thompford, an employee of Braunstein *frères'* department store, left her work at half-past 5 last evening, and has been seen no more. But her hat and cloak were found upon the piers at the waterfront ten little minutes ago. *Nom d'un chou-fleur*, I am vexed! These disappearances are becoming epidemic. Either the young women of this city have developed a sudden mania for doing away with themselves, or some evil person attempts to make a monkey of Jules de Grandin. In either case, my friend, I am aroused. *Mordieu*, we shall see who shall laugh in whose face before this business of the fool is concluded!"

"What are you going to do?" I asked, striving to keep a straight face.

"Do?" he echoed. "Do? *Parbleu*, I shall investigate, I shall examine every clue, I shall leave no stone unturned, but" – he sobered into sudden practicality as Nora McGinnis, my household factotum, entered the dining-room with a tray of golden-brown waffles – "first I shall eat breakfast. One can accomplish little on an empty stomach."

A widespread, though fortunately mild, epidemic of influenza kept me busy in office and on my rounds all day. Rainy, fog-bound darkness was approaching as I turned toward home and dinner with a profound sigh of thankfulness that the day's work was done, only to encounter fresh disappointment.

"Trowbridge, Trowbridge, *mon vieux*," an excited voice hailed as I was waiting for the crosstown traffic lights to change and let me pursue my homeward way, "draw to the curb; come with me – I have important matters to communicate!" Swathed from knees to neck in a waterproof leather jacket, his Homburg hat pulled rakishly down over his right eye and a cigarette glowing between his lips, Jules de Grandin stood at the curb, his little blue eyes dancing with excited elation.

"Name of a little blue man!" he swore delightedly as I parked my motor and joined him on the sidewalk; "it is a fortunate chance, this meeting; I was about to telephone the office in hopes you had returned. Attend me, my friend, I have twisted my hand in the tail of something of importance!"

Seizing my elbow with a proprietary grip, he guided me toward the illuminated entrance of a café noted for the excellence of its food and its contempt of the XVIIIth Amendment, chuckling with suppressed delight at every step.

"The young *Monsieur* Wilberding was undoubtlessly right in his surmises," he confided as we found places at one of the small tables and he gave an order to the waiter. "*Parbleu*, what he lacked in opportunity of observation he made up by the prescience of affection," he continued, "for there can be no doubt that *Mademoiselle* Mazie was the victim of murder. *Regardez-vous*: at the police laboratories, kindly placed at my disposal through the offices of the excellent Sergeant Costello, I examined the tattered remnants of the frock they took from the poor girl's body when they fished her from the river, and I did discover what the coroner, cocksure of his suicide theory, had completely overlooked – a small, so tiny stain. Hardly darker than the original pink of the fabric it was, but sufficient to rouse my suspicions. *Alors*, I proceeded to shred the chiffon and make the benzidine test. You know it? No?

"Very good. A few threads from the stained area of the dress I placed upon a piece of white filter paper; thereafter I compounded a ten per cent solution of benzidine in glacial acetic acid and mixed one part of this with ten parts of hydrogen peroxide. Next, with a pipette I proceeded to apply one little, so tiny drop of the solution to the threads of silk, and behold! a faint blue color manifested itself in the stained silken threads and spread out on the white filter paper. *Voilà*, that the stain of my suspicion had been caused by blood was no longer to be doubted!"

"But mightn't this bloodstain have been caused by an injury to Mazie's body as it washed over the falls?" I objected.

"*Ah bah*," he returned. "*You* ask that, Friend Trowbridge? *Pardieu*, I had looked for better sense in your head. Consider the facts: should you cut your finger, then immediately submerge it in a basin of water, would any trace of blood adhere to it? But no. Conversely, should you incise the skin and permit even one little drop of blood to gather at the wound and to dry there to any extent, the subsequent immersion of the finger in water would not suffice to remove the partly clotted blood altogether. Is it not so?

"*Très bon*. Had a sharp stone cut poor *Mademoiselle* Mazie, it would undoubtlessly have done so after she was dead, in which case there would have been no resultant hemorrhage; but even if a wound had been inflicted while she lived, bethink you of her position – in the rushing water, whirled round and round and over and over, any blood which flowed would instantly have been washed away, leaving no slightest stain on her dress. *Non*, my friend, there is but one explanation, and I have found it. Her gown was stained by blood before she was cast into the river. Recall: did not poor young *Monsieur* Wilberding inform us the car in which she rode was found a half-mile or more from the river? But certainly. Suppose, then, these girls were waylaid at or near the spot where their car was found, and one or both were done to death. Suppose, again, *Mademoiselle* Mazie's life-blood flowed from her wound and stained her dress while she was in transit toward the river. In that case her dress would have been so stained that even though the foul miscreants who slew her cast her poor, broken body into the water, there would remain stains for Jules de Grandin to find today. Yes, it is so.

"But wait, my friend, there is more to come. Me, I have been most busy this day. I have run up and down and hither and yon like Satan seeking for lost souls. Out on the Albemarle Road, where the unfortunate *Mademoiselle* Weaver's car was discovered this morning, I repaired when I had completed my researches in the city. Many feet had trampled the earth into the semblance of a pig-coop's floor before I arrived, but *grace a Dieu*, there still remained that which confirmed my worst suspicions.

"Finding nothing near the spot where the mired car lay, I examined the earth on the other side of the road. There I discovered that which made my hair to rise on end. *Pardieu*, my friend, there is the business of the Fiend himself being done here!

"Leading from the road were three distinct sets of foot-prints – girl's foot-prints, made by small, high-heeled shoes. Far apart they were, showing they had been made by running feet, and all stopped abruptly at the same place.

"Back from the roadway, a you doubtless remember, stands a line of trees. It was at these the foot-tracks halted, in each instance ending in two little pointed depressions, set quite close together. They were the marks of girls' slippers, my friend, and appeared to have been made as the young women stood on tiptoe.

"'Now,' I ask me, 'why should three young women leave the motor in which they ride, run from the road, halt on their toes beneath these trees, and leave no footprints thereafter?'

"'It seems they must have been driven from the road like game in a European preserve at hunting-time, then seized by those lying in wait for them among the tree-boughs as they passed beneath,' I reply. 'And you are undoubtlessly correct,' I answer me.

"Nevertheless, to make my assurance sure, I examined all those trees and all the surrounding land with great injury to my dignity and clothing, but my search was not fruitless; for clinging to a tree-bough above one of the girls' toe-prints I did find this." From his pocket he produced a tiny skein of light-brown fiber and passed it across the table to me.

"U'm?" I commented as I examined his find. "What is it?'

"Burlap," he returned. "You look puzzled, my friend. So did I when first I found it, but subsequent discoveries explained it – explained it all too well. As I have said, there were no footprints to be found around the trees, save those made by the fleeing girls, but, after much examination on my knees, I found three strange trails leading toward the road, away from those trees. Most carefully, with my nose fairly buried in the earth, I did examine those so queer depressions in the moist ground. Too large for human feet they were, yet not deep enough for an animal large enough to make them. At last I was rewarded by finding a bit of cloth-weave pattern in one of them, and then I knew. They were made by men whose feet had been wrapped in many thicknesses of burlap, like the feet of choleric old gentlemen suffering from gout.

"*Nom d'un renard*, but it was clever, almost clever enough to fool Jules de Grandin, but not quite.

"Feet so wrapped make no sound; they leave little or no track, and what track they do leave is not easily recognized as of human origin by the average Western policeman; furthermore, they leave no scent which may be followed by hounds. However, the miscreants failed in one respect: they forgot Jules de Grandin has traveled the world over on the trail of wickedness, and knows the ways of the East no less than those of the West.

In India I have seen such trails left by robbers; today, in this so peaceful State of New Jersey, I recognized the spoor when I saw it. Friend Trowbridge, we are upon the path of villains, assassins, apaches who steal women for profit. Yes," he nodded solemnly, "it is undoubtlessly so."

"But how–" I began, when his suddenly upraised hand cut me short.

Seated in the next booth to that we occupied was a pair of young men who had dined with greater liberality than wisdom. As I started to speak they were joined by a third, scarcely more temperate, who began descanting on the sensational features of a current burlesque show.

"Aw, shut up, how d'ye get that way?" one of the youths demanded scornfully. "Boy, till you've been where Harry and I were last night you ain't been nowhere and you ain't seen nothin'. Say, d'ye ever see the *chonkina?*"

"*Dieu de Dieu!*" de Grandin murmured excitedly, even as the other young man replied:

"*Chonkina?* What d'ye mean, *chonkina?*"

"You'd be surprised," his friend assured him. "There's a place out in the country – mighty exclusive place, too – where they'll let you see something to write home about – if you're willing to pay the price.'

"I'm game," the other replied. "What say we go there tonight? If they can show me something I never saw before, I'll blow the crowd to the best dinner in town."

"You're on," his companion accepted with a laugh, but:

"Quick, Friend Trowbridge," de Grandin whispered, "do you go straightway to the desk and settle our bill. I follow."

In a moment we stood before the cashier's desk, and as I tendered the young woman a bill, the Frenchman suddenly reeled as though in the last stages of drunkenness and began staggering across the room toward the booth where the three sportively inclined youths sat. As he drew abreast of them he gave a drunken lurch and half fell across their table, regaining his balance with the greatest difficulty and pouring forth a flood of profuse apologies.

A few moments later he joined me on the street, all traces of intoxication vanished, but feverish excitement shining in his small blue eyes.

"*C'est glorieux!*" he assured me with a chuckle. "Those three empty-headed young rakes will lead us to our quarry, or I am more mistaken than I think. In my pretended drunkenness, I fell among them and took time to memorize their faces. Also, I heard them make a definite appointment for their trip tonight. Trowbridge, my friend, we shall be there. Do you return home with all speed, bring the pistols, the flashlight and the horn-handled knife which you will find in my dressing-case, and meet me at police headquarters at precisely a quarter of midnight. I should be glad to accompany you, but there is a very great much for me to accomplish between now and then, and I fear there will be little sleep for Jules de Grandin this night. *Allez*, my friend, we have no time to waste!"

De Grandin had evidently perfected his arrangements by the time I reached headquarters; for a police car was waiting, and we drove in silence, with dimmed lights, through the chill March rain to a lonely point not far from the country club's golf links, where, at a signal from the little Frenchman, we came to a halt.

"Now, Friend Trowbridge," he admonished, "we must trust to our own heels, for I have no desire to let our quarry know we approach. Softly, if you please, and say anything you have to say in the lowest of whispers."

Quietly as an Indian stalking a deer he led the way across the rolling turf of the links, pausing now and again to listen attentively, at length bringing up under a clump of mournful weeping willows bordering the Albemarle Road. "Here we rest till they arrive," he announced softly, seating himself on the comparatively dry ground beneath a tree and leaning his back against its trunk. "Name of a name, but I should enjoy a cigarette; but" – he raised a shoulder in a resigned shrug – "we must have the self-restraint, even as in the days when we faced the *sale bosch* in the trenches. Yes."

Time passed slowly while we maintained our silent vigil, and I was on the point of open rebellion when a warning ejaculation in my ear and the quick clasp of de Grandin's hand on my elbow told me something was toward.

Looking through the branches of our shelter, I beheld a long, black motor slipping noiselessly as a shadow down the road, saw it come to a momentary halt beside a copse of laurels some twenty yards away, saw three stealthy figures emerge from the bushes and parley a moment with the chauffeur, then enter the tonneau.

"Ha, they are cautious, these birds of evil," the Frenchman muttered as he leaped from the shadow of the willows and raised an imperative hand beckoningly.

It was with difficulty I repressed an exclamation of surprise and dismay as a dozen shadowy figures emerged, phantom-like, from the shrubbery bordering the highway.

"Are you there, *mon lieutenant*?" de Grandin called, and I was relieved as an answering hail responded and I realized we were surrounded by a cordon of State Troopers in command of a young but exceedingly business-like-looking lieutenant.

Motorcycles – two of them equipped with sidecars–were wheeled from their covert in the bushes, and in another moment we were proceeding swiftly and silently in the wake of the vanishing limousine, de Grandin and I occupying the none too commodious "bathtubs" attached to the troopers' cycles.

It was a long chase our quarry led us, and had our machines been less powerful and less expertly managed we should have been distanced more than once, but the automobile which can throw dust in the face of the racing-cycles on which New Jersey mounts its highway patrols has not been built, and we were within easy hail of our game as they drew up before the gateway of a high-walled, deserted-looking country estate.

"Now, my lieutenant," de Grandin asked, "you thoroughly understand the plans?"

"I think so, sir," the young officer returned as he gathered his force about him with a wave of his hand.

Briefly, as the Frenchman checked off our proposed campaign, the lieutenant outlined the work to his men. "Surround the place," he ordered, "and lie low. Don't let anyone see you, and don't challenge anyone going in, but – nobody comes out without permission. Get me?"

As the troopers assented, he asked, "All set?"

There was a rattle of locks as the constables swung their vicious little carbines up to "'spection arms", and each man felt the butt of the service revolver and the riot stick swinging at his belt.

"All right, take cover. If you get a signal from the house, rush it. If no signal comes, close in anyhow at the end of two hours. I've got a search warrant here" – he patted his blouse pocket – "and we won't stand any monkey business from the folks inside. De Grandin's going in to reconnoitre; he'll give the signal to charge with his flashlight, or by firing his pistol when he's ready, but–"

"But you will advance, even though my signal fails," de Grandin interrupted grimly.

"Right-o," the other agreed. "Two hours from now – 3 o'clock – is zero. Here, men, compare your watches with mine; we don't want to go into action in ragged formation."

Two husky young troopers bent their backs and boosted de Grandin and me to the rim of the eight-foot brick wall surrounding the grounds. In a moment we had dropped silently to the yard beyond and de Grandin sent back a whispered signal.

Flattening ourselves to the ground we proceeded on hands and knees toward the house, taking advantage of every shrub and bush dotting the grounds, stealing forward in little rushes, then pausing beneath some friendly evergreen to glance cautiously about, listening for any sign or sound of activity from the big, darkened house.

"I'm afraid you've brought us out on a fool's errand, old chap," I whispered. "If we find anything more heinous than bootlegging here I'll be surprised, but–"

"*S-s-sh*!" his hissing admonition silenced me. "To the right, my friend, look to the right and tell me what it is you see."

Obediently, I glanced away from the house, searching the deserted park for some sign of life. There, close to the ground, shone a faint glimmer of light. The glow was stationary, for we watched it for upward of ten minutes before the Frenchman ordered, "Let us investigate, Friend Trowbridge. It may betoken something we should know."

Swerving our course toward the dim beacon, we moved cautiously forward, and as we approached it I grew more and more puzzled. The illumination appeared to rise from the ground, and, as we drew near, it was intercepted for an instant by something which passed between it and us. Again and yet again the glow was obscured with methodical regularity. For a moment I thought it might be some signal system warning the inmates of the house of our approach, but as we crawled still nearer my heart began to beat more rapidly, for I realized the light shone from an old-fashioned oil lantern standing on the ground and the momentary interruptions were due to shovelfuls of earth being thrown up from a fairly deep excavation. Presently there was a pause in the digging operations and two objects appeared above the surface about three feet apart – the hands of a man in the act of stretching himself. Assuming he were of average height, the trench in which he stood would be some five feet deep, judging by the distance his hands protruded above its lip.

Circling warily about the workman and his work we were able to get a fairly clear view. The hole was some two feet wide by six feet long, and, as I had already estimated, something like five feet deep.

"'What sort of trench usually has those dimensions?" The question crashed through my mind like an unexpected bolt of thunder, and the answer sent tiny ripples of chills through my cheeks and up my arms.

De Grandin's thought had paralleled mine, for he whispered, "It seems, Friend Trowbridge, that they prepare sepulture for someone. For us, by example? *Cordieu*, if it be so, I can promise them we shall go to it like kings of old, with more than one of them to bear us company in the land of shadows!"

Our course brought the grave-digger into view a we crept about him, and a fiercer, more bloodthirsty scoundrel I had never before had the misfortune to encounter. Taller than the average man by several inches he was, with enormously wide shoulders and long, dangling arms like those of a gorilla. His face was almost black, though plainly not that of a Negro, and his cheeks and chin were adorned by a bristling black beard which glistened in the lantern light with some sort of greasy dressing. Upon his head was a turban of tightly twisted woolen cloth.

"U'm?" de Grandin murmured quizzically. "A Patan, by the looks of him, Friend Trowbridge, and I think no more of him for it. In upper India they have a saying, 'Trust a serpent or a tiger, but trust a Patan never', and the maxim is approved by centuries of unfortunate experience with gentlemen like the one we see yonder.

"Come, let us make haste for the house. It may be we shall arrive in time to cheat this almost-finished grave of its intended tenant."

Wriggling snake-like through the rain-drenched grounds, our progress rendered silent by the soft turf, we made a wide detour round the dark-faced gravedigger and approached the big, forbidding mansion through whose close-barred windows no ray of light appeared.

The place seemed in condition to defy a siege as we circled it warily, vainly seeking some means of ingress. At length, when we were on the point of owning defeat and rejoining the troopers, de Grandin came to a halt before an unbarred window letting into a cellar. Unbuttoning his leather topcoat, he produced a folded sheet of flypaper and applied the sticky stuff to the grimy windowpane, smoothed it fiat, then struck sharply with his elbow. The window shattered beneath the impact, but the adhesive paper held the pieces firm, and there was no tell-tale clatter of broken glass as the pane smashed. "One learns more tricks than one when he associates with *les apaches*," he explained with a grin as he withdrew the flypaper and glass together, laid them on the grass and inserted his hand through the opening, undoing the window-catch. A moment later we had dropped to the cellar and de Grandin was flashing his electric torch inquiringly about.

It was a sort of lumber room into which we had dropped. Bits of discarded furniture, an old rug or two and a pile of miscellaneous junk occupied the place. The stout door at the farther end was secured by an old-fashioned lock, and the first twist of de Grandin's skeleton key sprung the bolt.

Beyond lay a long, dusty corridor from which a number of doors opened, but from which no stairway ascended. "Um?" muttered the Frenchman. "There seems no way of telling where the stairs lie save by looking for them, Friend Trowbridge." Advancing at random, he inserted his key in the nearest lock and, after a moment's tentative twisting, was rewarded by the sound of a sharp click as the keeper shot back.

No ray of moonlight filtered through the window, for they were stopped with heavy wooden shutters. As we paused irresolute, wondering if we had walked into a cul-de-sac, a faint, whimpering cry attracted our attention. "*Un petit chat!*" de Grandin exclaimed softly. "A poor little pussy-cat; he has been locked in by mistake, no doubt, and – ha! *Dieu de Dieu de Dieu de Dieu, regardez, mon ami*! Do you, too, behold it?"

The beam of his questing flashlight swept through the darkness, searching for the feline, but it was no cat the ray flashed on. It was a girl.

She lay on a rough, bed-like contrivance with a net of heavily knotted, coarse rope stretched across its frame where the mattress should have been, and was drawn to fullest compass in the form of a St. Andrew's cross; for leathern thongs knotted to each finger and toe strained tautly, holding hands and feet immovably toward the posts which stood at the four corners of the bed of torment. The knots were cruelly drawn, and even in the momentary flash of the light we saw the thongs were of rawhide, tied and stretched wet, but now dry and pulling the tortured girl's toes and fingers with a fury like that of a rack. Already the flesh about her fingers and toe-nails was puffy and impurpled with engorged blood cut off by the vicious cinctures of the tightening strings.

The torment of the constantly shortening thongs and the cruel pressure of the rope-knots on which she lay were enough to drive the girl to madness, but an ultimate refinement had been added to her agony; for the bed on which she stretched was a full eight inches shorter than her height, so that her head hung over the end without support, and she was obliged to hold it up by continued flexion of the neck muscles or let it hang downward, either posture being unendurable for more than a fraction of a minute.

"O Lord," she moaned weakly between swollen lips which had been gashed and bitten till the blood showed on them in ruddy froth, "O dear Lord, take me – take me quickly – I can't stand this; I can't – *oh, ah, o-o-oh*!" The prayerful exclamation ended in a half-whispered sob and her anguished head fell limply back and swung pendulously from side to side as consciousness left her.

"*Ohé, la pauvre creature!*" De Grandin leaped forward, unsheathing his knife as he sprang. Thrusting the flashlight into my hand, he slashed the cords from her hands and feet, cutting through each group of five strings with a single slash of his razor-sharp knife, and the thongs hummed and sang like broken banjo strings as they came apart beneath his steel.

As de Grandin worked I took note of the swooning girl. She was slight, almost to the point of emaciation, her ribs and the processes of her wrists and ankles showing whitely against the flesh. For costume she wore a wisp of printed cotton twisted bandeau-wise about her bosom, a pair of soiled and torn white-cotton bloomers which terminated in tattered ruffles at her ankles and were held in place at the waist by a gayly dyed cotton scarf secured by a sort of four-in-hand knot in front. A close-wrapped bandanna kerchief swathed her head from brow to nape, covering hair and ears alike, and from the handkerchief's rim almost to the pink of her upper lip a gilded metal mask obscured her features, leaving only mouth, nose-tip and chin visible.

As de Grandin lifted her from the bed-frame and rested her lolling head against his shoulder, he tugged at the mask, but so firmly was it bound that it resisted his effort.

Again he pulled, more sharply this time, and, as he did so, we noticed a movement at the side of her head beneath the handkerchief-turban. Snatching the headgear, the Frenchman fumbled for the mask cords, then started back with a low cry of horror and dismay. The mask was not tied, but *wired to her flesh*, two punctures having been made in each ear, one in the lobe, the other in the pinna, and through the raw wounds fine golden wires had been thrust and twisted into loops, so that removal of the mask would necessitate clipping the wire or tearing the tender, doubly pierced ears.

"Oh, the villains, the assassins, the ninety-thousand-times-damned beasts!" de Grandin gritted through his teeth, desisting in his effort to take off the metallic mask. "If ever Satan walked the earth in human guise I think he lodges within this accursed kennel of hell-hounds, Friend Trowbridge, and, *cordieu*, though the monster have as many gullets as the fabled hydra, I shall slit them all for this night's business!"

What more he would have said I do not know, for the fainting girl rolled her head and moaned feebly as she lay in his arms, and he was instantly all solicitude. "Drink this, *ma pauvre*," he commanded, drawing a silver flask from his pocket and pressing it to her pale lips.

She swallowed a bit of the fiery brandy, choked and gasped a little, then lay back against his arm with a weak sigh.

Again he applied the restorative; then: "Who are you, *ma petite?*" he asked gently. "Speak bravely; we are friends."

She shuddered convulsively and whimpered weakly again; then, so faint we could scarcely catch the syllables, "Ewell Eaton," she whispered.

"*Cordieu*, I did know it," de Grandin exclaimed delightedly. "*Gloire a Dieu*, we have found you, *ma petite!*

"The door, Friend Trowbridge – do you stand guard at the portal lest we be surprised. Here" – he snatched a pistol from his pocket and thrust it into my hand – "hesitate not to use it, should occasion arise!"

I took station at the entrance of the torture chamber while de Grandin set about making the half-conscious girl as comfortable as possible. I could hear the murmur of their voices in soft conversation as he worked frantically at her swollen feet and hands, rubbing them with brandy from his flask and massaging her wrists and ankles in an effort to restore circulation, but what they said I could not understand.

I was on the point of leaving my post to join them, for the likelihood of our being interrupted seemed remote, when it happened. Without so much as a warning creak from without, the door smashed suddenly back on its hinges, flooring me as the kick of a mule might have done, and three men rushed pell-mell into the room. I saw de Grandin snatch frantically at his pistol, heard Ewell Eaton scream despairingly, and half-rose to my feet, weak and giddy with the devastating blow I had received, but determined to use my pistol to best advantage. One of the intruders turned savagely on me, brought the staff of a long, spear-like weapon he carried down upon my head, and caught me a smashing kick on the side of the head as I fell.

"Trowbridge, my friend, are you living – do you survive?" Jules de Grandin's anxious whisper cut through the darkness surrounding me.

I was lying on my back, wrists and ankles firmly bound, a bump like a goose-egg on my head where the spear-butt had hit me. Through the grimy window of our cellar prison a star or two winked mockingly; otherwise the place was dark as a cave. How long we had lain there I had no way of telling. For all I knew the troopers might have raided the place, arrested the inmates and gone, leaving us in our dungeon. A dozen questions blazed through my mind like lightning-flashes across a summer night as I strove to roll over and ease the pressure of the knots on my crossed wrists.

"Trowbridge, *mon vieux*, do you live, are you awake, can you hear?" the Frenchman's murmured query came through the darkness again.

"De Grandin – where are you?" I asked, raising my head, the better to locate his voice.

"*Parbleu*, here I lie, trussed like a capon ready for the spit!" he returned. "They are prodigal with their rope, those assassins. Nevertheless, I think we shall make apes of them all. Roll toward me if you can, my friend, and lie with your hands toward me. *Grace a Dieu*, neither age nor overeating has dulled my teeth. Come, make haste!"

There followed a slow, dragging sound, punctuated with muttered profanities in mingled French and English as he hitched himself laboriously across the rough cement floor in my direction.

In a few moments I felt the stiffly waxed hairs of his mustache against my wrists and the tightening of my bonds as his small, sharp teeth sank into the cords, severing strand after strand.

Sooner than I had hoped, my hands were free, and after a few seconds, during which I wrung my fingers to restore circulation, I unfastened the ropes binding my feet, then released de Grandin.

"*Morbleu*, at any rate we can move about, even if those *sacré* rogues deprived us of our weapons," the Frenchman muttered as he strode up and down our prison. "At least one thing is accomplished – *Mademoiselle* Ewell is relieved of her torture. Before they beat me unconscious I heard her told tomorrow she would be strangled, but as the Spaniards so sagely remark, tomorrow is another day, and I trust we shall have increased hell's population by that time.

"Have you a match, by any kind of chance?" he added, turning to me.

Searching my pockets, I found a packet of paper matches and passed them over. Striking one, he held it torchwise above his head, surveying our prison. It was a small, cement-floored room, its single window heavily barred and its only article of furniture a large, sheet-iron-sheathed furnace, evidently the building's auxiliary heating-plant. The door was of stout pine planks, nailed and doweled together so strongly as to defy anything less than a battering-ram, and secured with a modern burglar-proof lock. Plainly, there was no chance of escape that way.

'U'm?" murmured de Grandin, surveying the old hot-air furnace speculatively. "Um-m-m? It may be we shall find use for this, if my boyhood's agility has not failed me, Friend Trowbridge."

"Use for that furnace?" I asked incredulously.

"*Mais oui*, why not?" he returned. "Let us see."

He jerked the heater's cast-iron door open, thrusting a match inside and looking carefully up the wide, galvanized flues leading to the upper floors. "It is a chance," he announced, "but the good God knows we take an equal one waiting here. *Au revoir*, my friend, either I return to liberate us or we say good morning in heaven."

Next instant he had turned his back to the furnace, grasped the iron door-frame at each side, thrust his head and shoulders through the opening and begun worming himself upward toward the flue-mouth.

A faint scraping sounded inside the heater's interior, then silence broken only by the occasional soft thud of a bit of dislodged soot.

I paced the dungeon in a perfect fever of apprehension. Though de Grandin was slight as a girl, and almost as supple as an eel, I was certain I had seen the last of him, for he would surely be hopelessly caught in the great, dusty pipes, or, if not that, discovered by some of the villainous inmates of place when he attempted to force himself throng register. His plan of escape was suicide, nothing less.

*Click!* The strong, jimmy-proof lock snapped back. I braced myself for the reappearance of our jailers, but the Frenchman's delighted chuckle reassured me.

"*Mordieu*, it was not even so difficult as I had feared," he announced. "The pipes were large enough to permit my passage without great trouble, and the registers – God be thanked! – were not screwed to the floor. I had but to lift the first I came to from its frame and emerge like a jack-in-the-box from his case. Yes. Come, let us ascend. There is rheumatism, and other unpleasant things, to be contracted in this cursed cellar."

Stepping as softly a possible, we traversed a long, unlighted corridor, ascended two flights of winding stairs and came to an upper hallway letting into a large room furnished in a garish East Indian manner and decorated with a number of medieval sets of mail and a stand of antique arms.

The Frenchman looked about, seeking covert, but there was nothing behind which an underfed cat could hide, much less a man. Finally: "I have it!" he declared, "*Parbleu, c'est joli!*"

Striding across the room he examined the nearest suit of armor and turned to me with a chuckle. "Into it, *mon ami*," he commanded. "Quick!"

With de Grandin's help I donned the beavered helmet and adjusted the gorget, cuirass, brassards, cuisses and jambs, finding them a rather snug fit. In five minutes I was completely garbed, and the Frenchman, laughing softly and cursing delightedly, was clambering into another set of mail. When we stood erect against the wall no one who had not seen us put on the armor could have told us from the empty suits of mail which stood at regular intervals about the wall.

From the stand of arms de Grandin selected a keen, long-bladed misericorde, and gazed upon it lovingly. Nor had he armed himself a moment too soon, for even as he straightened back against the wall and lowered the visor of his helmet there came the scuffle of feet from the corridor outside and a bearded, muscular man in Oriental garb dragged a half-fainting girl into the room. She was scantily clad in a Hindu version of a Parisian night club costume.

"By Vishnu, you shall!" the man snarled, grasping the girl's slender throat between his blunt fingers and squeezing until she gasped for breath. "Dance you must and dance you shall – as the Master has ordered – or I choke the breath from your nostrils! Shame? What have *you* to do with shame, O creature? Daughter of a thousand iniquities, tomorrow there shall be two stretched upon the 'bed of roses' in the cellar!"

"*Eh bien*, my friend, you may be right," de Grandin remarked, "but I damn think you shall not be present to see it."

The fellow toppled over without so much a a groan as the Frenchman, with the precise skill of a practised surgeon, drove his dagger home where skull and spine met.

"Silence, little orange-pip!" the Frenchman ordered as the girl opened her lips to scream. "Go below to your appointed place and do as you are bidden. The time comes quickly when you shall be liberated and we shall drag such of these sow-suckled sons of pig as remain alive to prison. Quick, none must suspect that help approaches!"

The girl ran quickly from the room, her soft, bare feet making no sound on the thick carpets of the hall, and de Grandin walked slowly to the door. In a moment he returned, lugging a suit of armor in his arms. Standing it in the place against the wall he had vacated, he repeated the trip, filling my space with a second empty suit, then motioning me to follow.

"Those sets of mail I did bring were from the balcony at the stairhead," he explained softly. "In their places we shall stand and see what passes below. Perhaps it is that we shall have occasion to take parts in the play before all is done."

Stiff and still as the lifeless ornaments we impersonated, we stood at attention at the stairway's top. Below us lay the main drawing-room of the house, a sort of low stage or dais erected at its farther end, a crescent formation of folding-chairs, each occupied by a man in evening clothes, standing in the main body of the room.

"Ah, it seems all is ready for the play," the Frenchman murmured softly through the visor-bars of his helmet. "Did you overhear the tale the little *Mademoiselle* Ewell told me in the torture chamber, my friend?"

"No."

"*Mordieu*, it was a story to make a man's hair erect Itself! This is a house of evil, the abode of *esclavage*, no less, Friend Trowbridge. Here stolen girls are brought and broken for a life of degradation, even as wild animals from the jungle are trained for a career in the arena. The master of this odious cesspool is a Hindu, as are his ten retainers, and well they know their beastly trade, for he was a dealer in women in India before the British Raj put him in prison, and his underlings have all been *corah-bundars* – punishment-servants – in Indian harems before he hired them for this service. Parbl*eu*, from what we saw of the poor one in the cellars, I should say their technique has improved since they left their native land!

"The headquarters of this organization is in Spain – I have heard of it before – but there are branches in almost every country. These evil ones work on commission, and when the girls they steal have been sufficiently broken in spirit they are delivered, like so many cattle, and their price paid by dive-keepers in South America, Africa or China – wherever women command high prices and no questions are asked.

"Hitherto the slavers have taken their victims where they found them – poor shop-girls, friendless waifs, or those already on the road to living death. This is a new scheme. Only well-favored girls of good breeding are stolen and brought here for breaking, and every luckless victim is cruelly beaten, stripped and reclothed in the degrading uniform of the place within half an hour of her arrival.

"*Mordieu*, but their tactics are clever! All faces obscured by masks which can not be removed, all hair covered by exactly similar turbans, all clothing exactly alike – twin sisters might be here together, yet never recognize each other, for the poor ones are forbidden to address so much as a word to each other – *Mademoiselle* Ewell was stretched on the bed of torture for no greater fault than breaking this rule."

"But this is horrible!" I interrupted. "This is unbelievable–"

"Who says it?" he demanded fiercely. "Have we not seen with our own eyes? Have we not *Mademoiselle* Ewell's story for testimony? Do I not know how her sister, poor *Mademoiselle* Mazie, came in the river? Assuredly: attend me: the fiends who took her prisoner quickly discovered the poor child's condition, and they thereupon deliberately beat out her brains and cast her murdered body into the water, thinking the river would wash away the evidence of their crime.

"Did not that execrable slave-master whom I slew command the other girl to dance – what did it mean?" He paused a moment, then continued in a sibilant whisper:'

"This, *pardieu*! Even as we send the young conscripts to Algeria to toughen them for military service, so these poor ones are given their baptism into a life of infamy by being forced to dance before half-drunken brutes to the music of the whip's crack. *Nom d'une pipe*, I damn think we shall see some dancing of the sort they little suspect before we are done – no more, the master comes!"

As de Grandin broke off, I noticed a sudden focusing of attention by the company below.

Stepping daintily as a tango dancer, a man emerged through the arch behind the dais at the drawing-room's farther end. He was in full Indian court dress, a purple satin tunic, high at the neck and reaching half-way to his knees, fastened at the front with a row of sapphire buttons and heavily fringed with silver at the bottom; trousers of white satin, baggy at the knee, skin-tight at the ankle, slippers of red Morocco on his feet. An enormous turban of peach-bloom silk, studded with brilliants and surmounted by a vivid green aigrette was on his head, while round his neck dangled a triple row of pearls, its lowest loop hanging almost to the bright yellow sash which bound his waist as tightly as a corset. One long, brown hand toyed negligently with the necklace, while the other stroked his black, sweeping mustache caressingly.

"Gentlemen," he announced in a languid Oxonian drawl, "if you are ready, we shall proceed to make whoopee, as you so quaintly express it in your vernacular." He turned and beckoned through the archway, and as the light struck his profile I recognized him a the leader of the party which had surprised us in the torture chamber.

De Grandin identified him at the same time, for I heard him muttering through the bars of his visor. "Ha, toad, viper, worm! Strut while you may; come soon the time when Jules de Grandin shall show you the posture you will not change in a hurry!"

Through the archway stepped a tall, angular woman, her face masked by a black cloth domino, a small round *samisen*, or Japanese banjo, in her hand. Saluting the company with a profound obeisance, she dropped to her knees and picked a short, jerky note or two on her crude instrument.

The master of ceremonies clapped his hands sharply, and four girls came running out on the stage. They wore brilliant kimonos, red and blue and white, beautifully embroidered with birds and flowers, and on their feet were white-cotton *tabi* or foot-mittens with a separate "thumb" to accommodate the great toe, and *zori*, or light straw sandals. Golden masks covered the upper part of their faces, and their hair was hidden by voluminous glossy-black wigs arranged in elaborate Japanese coiffure and thickly studded with ornamental hairpins. On their brightly rouged lips were fixed, unnatural smiles.

Running to the very edge of the platform, with exaggeratedly short steps, they slipped their sandals off and dropped to their knees, lowering their foreheads to the floor in greeting to the guests; then, rising, drew up in rank before the musician, tittering with a loud, forced affectation of coy gaiety and hiding their face behind the flowing sleeves of their kimonos, as though in mock-modesty.

Again the master clapped his hands, the musician began a titillating tune on her banjo, and the dance was on. More like a series of postures than a dance it was, ritualistically slow and accompanied by much waving of hands and fluttering of fans.

The master of ceremonies began crooning a low, sing-song tune in time with the *plink-plink* of the banjo. "*Chonkina-chonkina*," he chanted; then with a slapping clap of his hands:

"*Hoi!*"

Dance and music came to a frozen top. The four girls held the posture they had when the call came, assuming the strained, unreal appearance of a motion picture when the film catches in the projecting reel.

For a moment there was a breathless silence, then a delighted roar from the audience; for the fourth girl, caught with one foot and hand upraised, could not maintain the pose. Vainly she strove to remain stone-still, but despite her efforts her lifted foot descended ever so slightly.

A guttural command from the show-master, and she paid the forfeit, unfastening her girdle and dropping it to the floor.

A wave of red mantled her throat and face to the very rim of her golden mask as she submitted, but the forced, unnatural smile never left her painted lips as the music and dance began afresh at the master's signal.

"*Hoi*!" Again the strident call, again the frozen dance, again a girl lost and discarded a garment.

On and on the bestial performance went, interminably, it seemed to me, but actually only a few minutes were required for the poor, bewildered girls, half fainting with shame and fear of torture, to lose call after call until at last they danced only in their cotton *tabi*, and even these were discarded before the audience would cry enough and the master release them from their ordeal.

Gathering up their fallen clothes, sobbing through lips which still fought valiantly to retain their constrained smiles, the poor creatures advanced once more to the platform's edge, once more knelt and touched their brows to the floor, then ran from the stage, only the fear of punishment holding their little baked feet to the short, sliding steps of their artificial run rather than a mad dash for sanctuary from the burning gaze and obscene calls of the onlookers.

"*Dieu de Dieu*," de Grandin fumed, "will not the troopers ever come? Must more of this shameless business go on?"

A moment later the showman was speaking again: "Let us now give undivided attention to the next number of our program," he was announcing suavely.

Something white hurtled through the archway behind him, and a girl clothed only in strings of glittering rhinestones about throat, wrists, waist and ankles was fairly flung out upon the stage, where she cowered in a perfect palsy of terror. Her hands were fettered behind her by a six-inch chain attached to heavy golden bracelets, and an odd contrivance, something like a bit, was fastened between her lips by a harness fitted over her head, making articulate outcry impossible. Behind her, strutting with all the majesty of a turkey-cock, came a man in the costume of a South American *vaquero* – loose baggy trousers, wide, nail-studded belt, patent leather boots and broad-brimmed, low-crowned hat of black felt. In his hand was a coiled whip of woven leather thongs – the bull-whip of the Argentine *pampas*.

"Good and the devil!" swore de Grandin, his teeth fairly chattering in rage. "I know it; it is the whipping dance – he will beat her to insensibility – I have seen such shows in Buenos Aires, Friend Trowbridge, but may Satan toast me in his fires if I witness it again. Come, my friend, it is time we taught these swine a lesson. Do you stand firm and beat back any who attempt to pass. Me, I go into action!"

Like some ponderous engine of olden times he strode forward, the joints of his armor creaking with unwonted use.

For a moment guests and servants were demoralized by the apparition descending the stairs, for it was as if a chair or sofa had suddenly come to life and taken the field against them.

"Here, wash all thish, wash all thish?" demanded a maudlin young man with drunken truculence as he swaggered forward to bar the Frenchman's way, reaching for his hip pocket as he spoke.

De Grandin drew back his left arm, doubled his iron-clad fingers into a ball and dashed his mailed fist into the fellow's face.

The drunken rake went down with a scream, spewing blood and teeth from his crushed mouth.

"*Awai, a bhut!*" cried one of the servants in terror, and another took up the cry: "*A bhut! A bhut!*"

Two of the men seized long-shafted halberds from an ornamental stand of arms and advanced on the little Frenchman, one on each side.

*Clang!* The iron points of their weapon rang against his visor-bars, but the fine-tempered, handwrought steel that had withstood thrust of lance and glaive and flying cloth-yard arrow when Henry of England led his hosts to victory at Agincourt held firm, and de Grandin hardly wavered in his stride.

Then, with halberd and knife and wicked, razor-edged scimitar, they were on him like a pack of hounds seeking to drag down a stag.

De Grandin strode forward, striking left and right with mailed fists, crushing a nose here, battering a mouth there, or smashing jaw-bones with the iron-shod knuckles of his flailing hands.

My breath came fast and faster as I watched the struggle, but suddenly I gave a shout of warning. Two of the Hindus had snatched a silken curtain from a doorway and rushed de Grandin from behind. In an instant the fluttering drapery fell over his head, shutting out sight and cumbering his arms in its clinging folds. In another moment he lay on his back, half a dozen screaming Indians pinioning his arms and legs.

I rushed forward to his rescue, but my movement was a moment too late. From the front door and the back there came a sudden, mighty clamor. The thud of gun-butts and riot sticks on the panels and hoarse commands to open in the law's name announced the troopers had arrived at last.

*Crash!* The front door splintered inward and four determined men in the livery of the State Constabulary rushed into the hall.

A moment the Hindus stood at bay; then, with waving swords and brandishing pikes they charged the officers.

They were ten to four, but odds were not with numbers, for even as they sprang to the attack there sounded the murderous *r-r-r-rat-tat-tat* of an automatic rifle, and the rank of yelling savages wavered like growing wheat before a gust of summer wind, then went down screaming, while the acrid, bitter fumes of smokeless powder stung our nostrils.

"*Nom d'un porc, mon lieutenant,* you came not a moment too soon to complete a perfect night's work," de Grandin complimented as we prepared to set out for home. "Ten tiny seconds more and you should have found nothing but the deceased corpse of Jules de Grandin to rescue, I fear."

From the secret closets of the house the girls' clothing had been rescued, wire-clippers in willing hands had cut away the degrading golden masks from the captives' faces, and Ewell Eaton, the three sorority sisters and the poor little shop-girl whose disappearances had caused such consternation to their families were ready to ride back to Harrisonville, two in the troopers' side-cars, the rest in hastily improvised saddles behind the constables on their motorcycles.

"We did make monkeys out of 'em, at that," the young officer grinned. "It was worth the price of admission to see those guys in their dress suits trying to bluff us off, then whining like spanked kids when I told 'em it would be six months in the work-house for theirs. Gosh, won't the papers make hash of *their* reputations before this business is over?"

"Undoubtlessly," de Grandin assented. "It is to be deplored that we may not lawfully make hash of their so foul bodies, as well. Me, I should enormously enjoy dissecting them without previous anesthesia. However, in the meantime—"

He drew the young officer aside with a confidential hand upon his elbow, and a brief, whispered colloquy followed. Two minutes later he rejoined me, a satisfied twinkle in his eye, the scent of raw, new whisky on his breath.

"*Barbe d'un chameau*, he is a most discerning young man, that one," he confided, as he wiped his lips with a lavender-bordered silk handkerchief.